"Don't you ever get tired of being so angry at me?"

Neil's question echoed in Maddie's head. His fingers tightened before he unwrapped them from her arm. But he didn't move, and her pride wouldn't let her be the one to put that much distance between them. Not when he was watching her so intently, as if trying to figure out if she spoke the truth. As if surprised he couldn't tell.

"Good to know where we stand," he finally said, his voice a low, sexy rumble.

"You ever want to know where you stand with me, all you have to do is ask."

"I always admired that about you," he said quietly. "How open you were. How honest."

She'd long ago stopped thinking that brooding, emotionally bereft men with tragic pasts and a dangerous edge were attractive.

She shot a quick look at Neil. Yep. She'd stopped thinking that. Definitely.

Hey, even someone direct and honest could lie to themselves once in a while.

Dear Reader,

I love reunion stories. I love going on the journey as two people learn to forgive the mistakes of the past, start to respect, appreciate and love each other in the present and work toward building a future together. Maybe that's why I decided to write Neil and Maddie's story. Or maybe it's because there's nothing better to me than when a couple gets a second chance at their happily-ever-after.

Or maybe it's just because I like a challenge!

Writing *Talk of the Town* certainly pushed me as a writer. Like all of my characters, Neil and Maddie are complex, flawed and striving to be the best people they can be. The both made mistakes in the past, big mistakes that they need to be forgiven for, but in the end love, acceptance and compromise conquers all. And that is my very favorite part about writing romance.

I'm so excited about In Shady Grove, my new series for Harlequin Superromance, and I'm thrilled you picked up the first book. Shady Grove, Pennsylvania, may be fictional, but it has a lot in common with my own hometown—it's small and friendly, a great place to raise kids, and there's always something fun going on. Don't forget to look for James Montesano's book coming out in August 2013.

Please visit my website, www.bethandrews.net, or drop m a line at beth@bethandrews.net. I'd love to hear from you.

Happy reading!

Beth Andrews

Talk of the Town

BETH ANDREWS

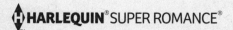

HARLEQUIN® SUPER ROMANCE®

Recycling programs
for this product may
not exist in your area.

ISBN-13: 978-0-373-71842-9

TALK OF THE TOWN

Printed in U.S.A.

www.Harlequin.com

ABOUT THE AUTHOR

Beth Andrews's latest series for Harlequin Superromance takes place in a fictional town based on her own hometown in Northwestern Pennsylvania. During the writing of *Talk of the Town,* Beth drank way too many iced coffees, listened to too many done-me-wrong love songs and visited five college campuses in two states and the District of Columbia with her eldest daughter. Beth is a Romance Writers of America RITA® Award Winner and can be found hugging her daughter every chance she gets. Learn more about Beth and her books by visiting her website, www.BethAndrews.net.

Books by Beth Andrews

HARLEQUIN SUPERROMANCE

*The Truth about the Sullivans

Other titles by this author available in ebook format.

For Anna Sugden.

Fellow hockey fan and fabulous friend.

CHAPTER ONE

THERE WAS NO place like home.

Or some sentimental, greeting-card bullshit like that.

Neil Pettit swung his duffel bag out of the back of his rental car and then slowly climbed the paved walkway toward the dark house. He supposed for some people going home was a big deal. A good deal. That it meant returning to a place of happy memories, home-cooked meals and comfort. A place where they belonged.

For others, it was nothing but a pain in the ass. He wished it wasn't. But instead of proving how far he'd come, whenever he returned to his hometown, all he remembered was what he'd come from.

Maybe his agent was right. Maybe he could do with a hefty dose of therapy.

He shifted his bag to his other hand and knocked on the front door. This house, with its fancy windows and various roof lines, its immaculate lawn and professional landscaping, was what he'd always dreamed of, what he'd worked so hard for. It was a testament to his work ethic, skills and talent.

He'd promised himself that when he was one of the top players in the NHL, his family would have the fanciest, biggest, most expensive house in Shady Grove. Mission accomplished.

So why did he still feel like that scrawny kid from the wrong side of town waiting on the stoop for someone to let him in? As if everything he'd always wanted for his family, for himself, was just out of reach.

Always out of his reach.

He rolled his head from side to side. Knocked again. A minute later, the porch light came on and the door opened to reveal Geraldine Pettit, her short, curly red hair disheveled, her mouth a thin line.

"Neil Pettit," she said, yanking the ties of her light blue robe together so tightly, Neil was surprised she didn't strangle a kidney. "Do you have any idea what time it is?"

He nodded once. "It's early."

He shifted before remembering that, not only did he have twelve inches and one hundred pounds on her, but he was also an adult now. Her disapproving look no longer had the power to affect him.

She turned that look up a few degrees. Set her hands on her nonexistent hips.

Sweat beaded on his upper lip. He couldn't stop himself from hunching his shoulders.

"Sorry if I woke you," he said before she fried him with another glare.

"Of course you woke me. It's not even six a.m. Your flight wasn't due to land until eight."

"I got an earlier flight." He scratched the side of his neck. "Should I wait out here for a few more hours?"

She harrumphed. "It'd serve you right if I told you to go on and do just that. Lucky for you," she said with the nobility of a queen, "I'm a forgiving soul."

A point her husband might dispute but one that was essentially true. "I appreciate it."

"As you should." But her expression softened and she finally stepped back enough to give him room to enter the airy foyer with its glossy woodwork and high ceiling. She shut the door. "It's good to see you."

Before he could evade, he was wrapped in a hard hug.

Still holding his bag, he awkwardly patted her upper back with his other hand. He wanted to push her away. Worse, so much worse, he wanted to pull her closer and just hold on.

"You saw me last week," he said as he stepped back. She and her husband, Carl, had come out to Seattle for game seven of the Stanley Cup playoffs not five days ago.

"You look much better now." She took his chin in her hand and turned his face this way, then that. Did another harrumph at the thin scar under his eye. "At least that new team doctor stitched you up nice and pretty. But I still can't believe the refs only gave that Russian bully two minutes in the penalty box. He should've been ejected from the game."

"It's all part of hockey." Though he could have lived just fine without getting whacked in the face with a hockey stick. "We won that game. That's all that matters."

"I suppose. But took great satisfaction in that goal you scored when you returned to the ice."

"How's a man supposed to sleep around here with you two yakking?" a male voice grumbled.

Neil glanced up then quickly looked down at the floor. But the memory of Carl Pettit—and his hairy legs and round stomach—stomping down the stairs in nothing but a pair of black-and-white checked boxers was permanently etched in his brain.

Neil really would need therapy after this visit.

"You were sleeping just fine when I tried to tell you someone was at the door," Gerry said. "Why, it could've been a burglar come to rob us blind."

"What kind of burglar knocks?" Carl asked.

"A polite one. Well? Aren't you going to say hello to your son?"

"You're my son when you piss her off," Carl told Neil

with a wink as he offered his hand. They shook, and Carl gave Neil an affectionate slap on the shoulder. "When you scored that winning goal in overtime in game three of the series, you were her son."

"I should've called," Neil said, shoving aside the weird sense of pride and longing Carl's words had invoked. "Told you I was getting in early."

But he wasn't used to sharing his schedule or discussing his decisions with others. Had always had a hard time remembering to let his adoptive parents know where he was going or what he was doing after spending the first ten years of his life not accountable to anyone.

"Yes," Gerry agreed, "you should have. But since you didn't—and since we're all up now—your father can make some coffee while I get breakfast."

"That's not nec—"

But she was already heading toward the kitchen.

"You know your mother," Carl said with another slap to Neil's shoulder, this one with enough behind it to have Neil taking a step forward to keep his balance. Though he was closing in on seventy, Carl was built like a bear and had the strength of a pro defenseman. "Always has to be doing something. Besides, it's not like she gets a chance to fuss over you very often."

Coming from anyone else, Neil would have thought he'd just been chastised. But Carl was as subtle as a knee to the groin. If he thought Neil should feel guilty about not coming back to Shady Grove very often, he'd come out and say so.

Or, more likely, demand that Neil get his sorry ass home.

Still, he considered trying to get out of the whole family reunion breakfast thing, but arguing with either Geraldine or Carl was a losing proposition. Getting your way when they were on the same side of an issue? Not going to happen.

And Neil didn't fight battles he couldn't win.

"Coffee sounds good," he said, though a few hours of sleep sounded better.

While Carl went back upstairs to get dressed—thank you, God—Neil put his bag in the guest suite at the end of the hall. Hanging on to a few of the limited moments he'd have to himself until he got back to Seattle, he changed into a fresh shirt then went into the bathroom and splashed water on his face. By the time he walked back toward the kitchen, the scents of brewing coffee, frying bacon and something sweet and yeasty filled the air.

He would have been happy with cold cereal and toast, but Gerry was the epitome of Go Big or Go Home. She'd shown Neil the joy of taking on a challenge if only to prove you were a match for it. From Carl he'd learned that hard work had its own rewards and quitting wasn't an option.

They'd taken in him and his younger sister, Fay, taught them what a normal, functional family was like and gave them both the tools they needed to become productive, successful adults.

Without them, he never would have been able to go from small-town kid with few prospects and no hope to one of the NHL's highest-paid players.

He owed them. Big-time. And he'd never forget it.

Neil slowed as he approached the room, stood just outside the doorway taking in the scene. Gerry bustled from the stainless-steel refrigerator to the six-burner stove to the granite-topped island and back again while Carl sat at the table, the morning paper spread out in front of him. Their voices were both pitched low but, as always, Gerry's words were quick and snappy while Carl's responses were more languorous.

Yin and yang, Neil thought. If he believed in soul mates, he'd say they completed each other. But he'd stick with thinking that they complemented each other, kept the other balanced. Out of all they'd done for him, all they'd taught and given him, he most appreciated how they'd raised him and Fay in a calm, positive atmosphere. They'd shown what a healthy relationship looked like, that one was possible.

Even if he didn't believe one was possible for himself.

Hearing footsteps on the stairs, he turned. Fay approached him slowly, as if unsure if he was real or not. Unsure of her welcome from him. As always, she was wary and nervous and easily injured.

As always, he'd be her strength, her protector.

"Neil. You're here."

Her words were soft and grateful, and so needy, it was like an elbow to the gut. Seeing her gave him that same hard tug of responsibility, the same punch of love he'd felt from the time he'd been old enough to realize it was up to him to take care of her.

Even if every once in a while he secretly, selfishly, wished she was strong enough to take care of herself.

He nodded, his throat tight with emotion. "I'm here."

She held out her hand and he gripped her fingers. Her eyes, a lighter shade of blue than his own, were huge in her narrow face, her complexion pale, her hair a wild tangle of shoulder-length strawberry-blond curls. The years melted away. Gone was the grown woman Fay had become—a mother with two sons of her own. In Neil's mind she was four years old again, gripping his hand like a lifeline, looking up to him as if he was her savior.

He'd been six.

The weight of her reliance on him, of his own sense of responsibility, pushed down on his shoulders, made it hard to take a full breath.

Funny how coming home made him feel like a fish out of water—floundering and gasping for air.

"Coffee's done," Gerry called.

With a final squeeze, Fay let go of Neil and walked ahead of him into the kitchen. "Good morning," she told Carl, touching his shoulder. She gave Gerry a quick hug. "What can I do to help?"

"You can sit down," Gerry said, whipping something in a bowl so quickly, her hands were a blur. "Save your energy to deal with those two boys when they get up."

Fay picked up a pair of tongs and began transferring slices of crisp, cooked bacon onto a paper-towel-covered plate. "Luckily, they never wake before seven."

Gerry set down the bowl and shooed Fay aside. "Still, I've got this under control. Sit down, have a cup of coffee with your brother."

"I can get it," Neil said, stepping into the middle of the room only to realize he had no idea where they kept the coffee cups. He'd bought this house for them eight years ago when he'd signed his first big contract, but hadn't spent more than a day or two at a time here.

But it didn't matter because Fay was already getting cups down from the upper cabinet to the left of the sink. Neil sat across from Carl while Fay poured coffee, sliding the carton of half-and-half toward Carl, handing Geraldine a pot holder without having to be asked.

The three of them were close. Affectionate. Comfortable together and with their respective roles: father, mother, daughter.

Neil was comfortable in his role as temporary houseguest.

He sipped his coffee. This must be what their mornings were like now that Fay and her two young sons had moved back home. Breakfasts together. Small talk about their plans for the day. A shared smile or soft laugh.

It wasn't for him, wasn't anything he'd ever wanted. But he was glad his sister had it. Glad Carl and Geraldine had come to Fay's rescue. Even if part of him resented he'd been unable to do so. At least in person.

Fay was too thin, he thought, narrowing his gaze. Her pajama pants were baggy, the matching T-shirt hanging on her. She'd always been slight. Delicate. But now her slim frame bordered on gaunt, her cheekbones sunken, her collarbones standing out in sharp relief.

He'd take her out to lunch later, he decided with another sip of coffee. Make sure she was eating enough and not just playing with her food or spending all her time lying in bed with the curtains drawn.

The way Annie Douglas, their mother—their real mother—had every time she'd found out about another of her husband's affairs.

"You look tired," he said when Fay poured more coffee into his cup. Tired. Defeated. And so much like Annie with her wild hair and sad eyes, it was all he could do not to shake her. To demand she stop acting like the woman who'd washed down a handful of sleeping pills with a bottle of vodka, leaving her children to find her cold, dead body when they got home from school. "Why don't you go back to bed? We can catch up later."

And it'd give Neil a chance to question Geraldine and Carl about what really happened between Fay and that bastard she'd married.

"No woman likes to be told she looks anything less than her best," Gerry said. "Have I taught you nothing?"

"Just because we teach," Carl said, sounding like some Zen master, "doesn't mean anyone learns."

"More fortune-cookie wisdom?" Geraldine asked, pouring scrambled eggs into a pan.

"Today's horoscope." Carl looked over the paper at Fay. "But Neil's right. You look exhausted." He inclined his head toward the door. "Go on. Take a nice long nap. Gerry and I will wrangle the boys when they wake up."

Fay, her eyes downcast, traced her fingertip around the edge of her cup. "I suppose I could shut my eyes for a few more minutes…." She lifted her gaze to Neil. "You really don't mind?"

He wanted to tell her not to ask his permission, to decide for herself what she wanted, what she needed. To demand she make her own way instead of following someone else's lead.

"I'm going to head over to Bradford House later this morning," he told her. He was having the run-down Victorian-era house renovated. "Why don't you meet me there? Bring the boys then we'll get some lunch after."

She frowned. Nibbled on her pinkie nail, a habit she'd had since she was three. "What about Bree? Aren't you going to see her today?"

Breanne, his eleven-year-old daughter, didn't even know he was in town yet. He'd put off calling her, telling himself he wanted to make sure his plans were firm before letting her know he'd be around for a few days. But even he wasn't that good at lying to himself. Not when he had so many conflicting feelings toward his daughter. Affection and resentment tangled up inside of him, making a toxic brew, one he hated, one he tried like hell to hide, but couldn't deny.

And he was afraid she knew it. That she saw right through him. Just like her mother always had.

"I'll have Bree spend the night here," he said.

"Well," Fay hedged, "if you're sure…"

"He's sure," Gerry said, wrapping her arm around Fay's shoulders and guiding her toward the door. "We'll save you some breakfast," she promised, giving Fay a nudge into the hall. A moment later, she turned back to Neil and Carl and lowered her voice. "She wouldn't be so tired if she didn't spend every night crying over that SOB."

"She'll get through it," Carl said. "She needs time."

Gerry went back to the stove. "What she needs is a good divorce attorney."

"It's come to that?" Neil asked, knowing only that Fay and Shane Lindemuth, her husband of five years, were having problems, and she and the boys had moved back home two weeks ago.

"If you call him running around on her a problem, then yes," Gerry said, turning off the heat under the eggs.

"He cheated on her?" How Neil managed to sound so damned calm when he wanted to go across town to the little house he'd bought his sister as a wedding present and rip his brother-in-law's throat out, he had no idea.

Carl frowned at his wife. "We don't know that he's cheated. Could be he's just having a tough time adjusting to civilian life."

Shane had recently been discharged from the Marine Corps after serving in Afghanistan for almost a year.

It didn't matter to Neil why Shane was being an ass. Neil wasn't there to play marriage counselor. He had responsibilities, ones he took seriously. People who relied on him.

He'd help Fay get back on her feet. Let Gerry fuss over him. Hang out with Carl at the old man's favorite coffee shop. He'd spend time with his daughter.

He'd do what had to be done. Then he'd get the hell out of there.

THE SLIGHT WEIGHT of her hammer resting on her right shoulder, Maddie Montesano opened and closed her fingers around the handle like a ballplayer up to bat. Aiming where it'd do the most damage, she swung, connecting solidly with her brother James's fat head.

Bits of plaster and splinters of the thin, wooden lath behind it flew, stung her bare arms. Clung to her clothes. Dust exploded only to hang momentarily in the thick, still air before drifting to the drop cloth covering the ugly, faded maroon carpet. She wrenched the hooked end of the hammer from the wall where she'd sketched a decent likeness of her eldest brother—complete with devil horns and a pointier, more sinister version of his stupid goatee.

Swear to God, one of these nights she was going to sneak into his house and shave that scraggly thing right off his face.

One thing was for sure, James no longer looked so smug. It was hard to pull off a good I-am-smarter-and-more-capable-than-you-because-I-am-older-and-carry-around-an-extra-appendage-in-my-pants look when there was a hole where your mouth and nose had been.

Her hands sweating in her work gloves, she adjusted her grip and swung again, this time taking out his beady eyes. Twenty minutes later, her arms ached, her back and shoulders were tight with pain and a layer of dust covered her safety goggles. But she kept right on swinging, matching her movements to Three Dog Night's "Shambala" blaring through the speakers of her iPod.

By the end of the song, her hands were cramping, her breathing was ragged inside her respirator mask and only small pieces of lath remained of the parlor's northern wall.

Best of all, she no longer had the urge to drive over to her brother's work site and slash his tires for messing up her schedule and being a condescending jerk.

When you had a hammer, who needed therapy?

Stretching onto her toes, Maddie tore out a loose piece of lath then froze, the back of her neck prickling with the sensation of being watched.

Before she could turn, the prickle turned into an out-and-out warning. One telling her the person behind her was dangerous and she needed to march herself right out the front door. To put as much distance between them as possible. Worse, it told her exactly who stood there.

When it came to Neil Pettit, she'd always had a very good sense of when he was around. Like there was some sort of homing device imbedded inside of her. *There he is! The man of your adolescent dreams!*

It was annoying as hell.

And after all these years, still as powerful as it'd been when she'd been young and stupid with love for him.

Keeping her back to him, she set the hammer down before crossing to the iPod to shut it off. Only because she was in no hurry to give him any of her time, her attention. Not because she was afraid to face him. Certainly not because she thought, even for a partial second, that seeing him and looking into his eyes would cause her the slightest twinge of pain.

She'd gotten over Neil a long time ago.

Maddie blew out a heavy breath, the sound loud and Darth Vader-ish to her ears. She'd pray her instincts were way off base, but while she didn't mind asking God for the occasional favor, she knew better than to count on something as nebulous as prayers or wishes or positive thinking.

No, the only thing she could count on was what she saw with her own eyes. What she could control herself.

She tossed her goggles onto the mantel of the marble fireplace and pulled down the respirator mask so that it hung around her neck then turned. And had to lock her knees so she wouldn't whirl right back around again.

Damn it, why did she always have to be right?

Neil leaned against the doorjamb, his broad shoulders filling the space, his ankles crossed as he lazily, deliberately, slid his gaze from the top of her head to the toes of her work boots.

She fidgeted, realized what she was doing and stiffened her spine. So what if his toned athlete's body, sharply planed face and blue eyes caused hormones she'd begun to fear were dead to spring miraculously to life with a rousing cheer?

Seeing as how she hadn't physically responded to a real live man in ages, he definitely deserved a good rah-rah. Maybe even a backflip or two. But she'd eat rusty nails for breakfast before she gave him the satisfaction of knowing he still affected her.

God, there should be some sort of law, a sacred decree that when a woman saw her ex, she looked completely hot. Sexy, don't-you-wish-you-hadn't-tossed-me-aside hot.

Not sweaty, I've-spent-the-afternoon-whaling-away-at-walls-and-am-a-total-mess hot.

And it didn't matter that she'd seen Neil plenty of times since their breakup. Or that he was a lying bastard who couldn't be trusted to give an honest report of the weather outside.

He should regret, at least a little bit, walking away from her. He should suffer and want to turn back time so he could undo his mistake. He should want her.

If only so Maddie could laugh in his face.

"Hey, babe," he said. "Looking good."

His voice was deep. Husky. Inviting. His greeting the same as it'd been in high school when he'd wait for her at her locker after school. He'd watch her approach, his intense gaze following her every movement. Oh, how her heart had raced as so many wonderful, conflicting emotions zipped through her. Happiness. Excitement. The first tug of sexual longing.

And fear. The realization that her feelings for him were too much. Too big. That they'd take over her life, cause her to be stupid, to forget who she was. That he'd break her heart.

Right again.

"It's the tool belt," she said, not bothering to keep the flatness from her voice. "No man can resist it."

He straightened and walked toward her, looking like some freaking model in his jeans—undoubtedly designer and expensive—and a V-neck, white T-shirt that clung to the hard planes of his chest. His hair, a sandy blond, was shorter than when she'd seen him last, which must have been a year…no, a year and a half ago.

Such a long time and yet, not long enough.

"It's not the tool belt," he murmured. He edged even closer, the toes of his sneakers bumping against her boots. "It's the whole package."

She rolled her eyes. "Please. I just threw up in my mouth."

His mouth twitched but no smile softened his features. Golden stubble covered his cheeks and chin, and this close, she noticed the faint lines bracketing his eyes, the dark circles under them. He looked tired. And that hint of vulnerability, that glimpse of the boy he used to be, the one she'd adored, made him seem approachable and real.

But then she saw the new scar high on his right cheek, the faded one on his chin, and he went back to being the untouchable, megastar professional hockey player he'd become.

"Something I can do for you?" she asked, wishing he'd

back the hell up already. "Or did you just stop by to practice your smarmy-creep act?"

"Smarmy? That hurts."

"I doubt that. In order for someone to be able to hurt you, you'd have to care about what that person thought of you."

Now he grinned, one of his slow, panty-melting smiles, and she found herself holding her breath, bracing against the full effect. Sweet God, it was even more potent, more devastating now than it'd been twelve years ago.

"You know how much your opinion means to me," he said.

Yeah. Nothing.

Just as she meant nothing to him.

Her throat constricted. From breathing in the dust floating in the air, she assured herself. There was no other possible explanation.

Finally, thankfully, he stepped back and glanced around. Giving her time to catch her breath, to get her bearings.

"Is Bree here?" he asked.

"Not unless she's finally managed to purchase Harry Potter's Cloak of Invisibility online," Maddie said, spreading her hands to indicate the large room. "Why?"

He sent her a bland look. "I'd like to see my daughter."

Okay, if he wanted to get technical, he could claim paternity. There was no ignoring the fact that Bree had his DNA and, to Maddie's endless annoyance, his eyes.

But in every way that counted, she was a Montesano. Maddie's daughter. The best thing that had ever happened to her.

And the only reason she could never regret being with Neil.

"So who's stopping you?" Maddie asked, hating that, even at five-nine, she had to tip her head back to maintain eye contact with him. "She's probably just getting up. I'm sure you can catch her before she heads to soccer practice."

He frowned. "She's at home?"

"I believe I made that clear."

"You left her home." This time, it wasn't a question. "Alone."

"I'm not sure how alone she is seeing as how Pops and my parents live across the street—"

"Isn't she a little…young to be home by herself?"

Pursing her lips, Maddie pretended to think that through. "Nope."

"If you can't find or afford a sitter—"

"Your financial planner deposits an obscenely large amount of money into my bank account each month. I'm pretty sure I can not only afford a sitter, but also a chauffeur, personal chef and full-time bodyguard. And still have cash left over." She kept her tone mild. Reasonable. Seriously, someone should give her a medal for this unexpected deep well of patience she'd discovered because honestly, the man was getting on her last nerve. How dare he show up unannounced and question her decisions like this? "Bree doesn't want or need a sitter. She's eleven—"

"I know how old she is, Maddie."

Yes. He did. But that didn't mean he knew their daughter. Her likes and dislikes. How, for all her quiet sweetness, Bree could be as stubborn as her mother. And her father.

"Old enough," she continued, "and responsible enough to get herself up in the morning, eat breakfast, do her chores and then walk to the park."

"I don't want her walking to the park by herself," he said, but despite his dark expression, the hard line of his mouth, his tone remained quiet and calm.

Shades of the past. He never raised his voice or showed his anger, showed any of what he was feeling. She used to think if she could get him to open up, to share with her whatever emotions and pain lay beneath that hard, stoic exterior, she could save him. Make him love her as much as she'd loved him.

No, he hadn't changed. But she had. No more fixer-upper men for her, only houses. They were less work.

"What are you doing?" she asked when he pulled his cell phone from his pocket. "You'd better not be calling some sitter service."

"I'm calling Geraldine." He held the phone to his ear. "She'll take Bree to practice."

"Put that away." She'd make a grab for it but the chances of her snatching a phone from one of the NHL's quickest, most agile athletes were zero to none. "Your mom is not going to come into town every morning to drive Bree two blocks down the road."

The house he'd bought for his parents—a monstrous McMansion of mixed architectural styles, like some hybrid house gone mad—was too big, had too many windows and zero warmth or charm. It was also on thirty prime acres of real estate ten miles outside of town.

"She won't mind," he insisted, but he ended the call before speaking with Gerry—who would only be more than happy to do anything he asked. "I'd feel better if Bree had a ride."

"Do you really think I'd let Bree do something if it wasn't safe?"

"No," he said, his quick answer doing little to appease her. "But I don't think you're seeing the big picture here. Everyone knows Bree is my daughter."

She snorted softly. Yeah, everyone but him. He only remembered when it suited him and didn't interfere with his lifestyle, his schedule, his goals. "What does that have to do with anything?"

He had the balls to look at her as if that was the dumbest question he'd ever heard. She wanted to kick him in the shin.

"Bree's a target," he explained slowly, as if she was one of his airheaded bimbos, the desperate, obvious women who hung around the ice rink in their short skirts and tight shirts hoping to get his attention. "Someone could kidnap her or use her to get to me."

Maddie's jaw dropped, and for a brief moment in time, she found herself speechless—an unusual occurrence, one her three older brothers would all surely be sorry they missed.

"Is that what this is about?" she finally managed to ask. "Your money?"

"It's about keeping Bree safe."

He seemed so sincere, so completely honest, she almost believed him.

But she'd learned the hard way that what Neil said and what he meant were often two very different things.

Noticing she still had her gloves on, she yanked them off and tossed them onto the floor instead of whipping them at his head. "I have news for you and that enormous ego you've dragged in here. Not everyone in Shady Grove knows, or cares, who you are. Bree has lived here her entire life and never had any problems."

He crossed his arms, his biceps stretching the sleeves of his shirt. Looked down on her, all big and solid and imposing, as if he could intimidate her. The man must have forgotten who he was dealing with. "I don't want her walking to the park by herself."

"Too bad." She jabbed a finger at his chest, stopping short of making contact and puncturing his lung. "Don't make the mistake of thinking you can dictate how I raise my daughter—"

Maddie's words died in her throat when his hand whipped out and grabbed her wrist. Damn him, he'd always been fast. "Bree's my daughter, too."

The feel of his fingers against her skin, so strong, so warm, was familiar yet new, too. Being close to him, inhaling the spicy scent of his cologne—some fragrance she didn't recognize—and seeing the ring of darker blue in his eyes made it all too easy to forget the past twelve years. Reminded her of a time when all she'd wanted was to have him hold her hand, to be next to him. Always.

How she would have done anything, been anyone, to stay with him.

"Seems to me, she's only your daughter when it suits your purposes." Which was Maddie's own fault. Her punishment. One she deserved, but their daughter didn't. "Because I distinctly remember when she was born—"

"Don't," he warned roughly.

But she was too far gone to stop the words, to stop from reminding him of what he'd said, how he'd acted. "You didn't call her your daughter then. All she was to you then, all she's ever been to you, is your greatest mistake."

CHAPTER TWO

NEIL'S FINGERS TIGHTENED on Maddie's wrist, but if she noticed, she gave no indication, just held his gaze, her words hanging in the air between them. Toxic. Accusatory.

True.

He let go of her, his stomach churning with shame and regret. "You always did go straight for the jugular."

"That's all you have to say?" Bending, she swiped up her gloves and slapped them against her palm. "You are some piece of work."

No, just unable to win this game of one-upmanship he and Maddie had going on. Nothing he said or did could ever make up for the mistakes he'd made all those years ago. He'd never be forgiven.

That was as clear as the dust in the tail of long, dark hair trailing down Maddie's back and the red marks on her face from the goggles and mask.

She hadn't changed much. Time and carrying his child had left only subtle marks; her face was narrower, her body—always curvy—was more lush.

She wasn't beautiful. Would never be in the same league as the models and actresses he dated with their narrow bodies and cool blond looks. Maddie's brows were heavy, her nose a tad too long, her mouth too wide. Her dark hair still reached the middle of her back. Her eyes, a rich chocolate-brown, were large and almond-shaped.

And looked right through him.

"What do you want from me, Maddie?" he asked.

"Nothing. I just don't think you have any right to come in here and make demands about how I raise Bree. You haven't even seen her in over six months—"

"I called. Every week."

"Well, aren't you Father of the Year?"

He wasn't, wasn't even close to being the father Bree needed. But he'd always done the best he could by her.

"I wanted her to fly out to Seattle a few months ago," he said. "And again last week when Carl and Gerry came out. You said she couldn't come."

Maddie averted her gaze, as if putting her gloves back on required considerable time and attention. "She was getting over a cold last week. And she had school in April."

"She could've brought her schoolwork with her."

Her movements jerky, her ponytail falling forward, Maddie picked up the hammer. "Look, this isn't up for discussion. Bree doesn't need a babysitter and she will continue to walk to soccer practice. Now, I have work to do so you'd better back up." She lightly swung the hammer, stopping an inch from his knee. "Wouldn't want to risk you getting hurt. Everyone knows how important your career is to you."

He didn't move. "I'd like Bree to spend the night with me at Gerry and Carl's tonight," he said, hating that he had to ask for permission to see his own kid, knowing it was his own fault he had to do so.

Maddie's expression clearly said she wanted to refuse him, but then she lifted a shoulder. "What time should I tell her you'll pick her up?"

"Three-thirty."

"Fine. I'll make sure she's ready."

Tucking the hammer under her arm, she put her mask back on, then her safety glasses. She brushed past him and started swinging at the wall to her right with a ferocity that had him moving to the other side of the room.

He grabbed the back of his neck, tried not to breathe in the dust and bits of plaster flying through the air. How had it gotten so messed up? All he'd wanted was to see his daughter. Spend a few days with her before he headed back to Seattle. Instead, Maddie had somehow turned it all around, once again throwing his past into his face. As if he had no say in what went on in his daughter's life. As if he had no right to be concerned about his daughter's welfare.

Hell, maybe he didn't.

But he was damned tired of being punished for the choices, the mistakes, he'd made as an eighteen-year-old kid. No matter what he did, no matter how hard he tried, it was never enough for Maddie. And, he suspected, for Bree as well.

His daughter was very much like her mother.

Maddie stopped swinging suddenly and whirled around. She said something, her words muffled by the mask. But he got the gist that she wanted him to go screw himself.

"I'm not even sure that's physically possible."

She slid the mask down again, took off her safety goggles. "I asked if there was something else."

"What's going on—really going on—between Shane and Fay?"

"As I'm not a part of their marriage, I couldn't *really* say."

"You're her best friend." Though he'd never understood the dynamics between hard-ass, prickly Maddie Montesano and his sweet, passive sister.

Didn't understand it, didn't particularly like that after all these years the friendship between them had survived, but no one knew Fay like Maddie did. Not even him.

"Just because we're friends doesn't mean we stay up late giggling, braiding each other's hair and sharing secrets."

"You used to."

She blushed, and he wondered if she, too, remembered it was at one of those sleepovers that his interest in Maddie began. His mouth twisted. Interest. More like an addiction. One he'd been terrified he'd never be free from.

It had started, as so many vices do, innocently enough. It'd been late and he'd still been up, the summer heat and his own constantly spinning mind keeping him awake. He'd gone to the kitchen for a glass of water and was heading back to bed when Maddie practically ran him over as she came out of the bathroom.

That was Maddie. Always rushing, always in a hurry to get where she wanted to be. He'd grabbed her upper arms to stop them both from toppling over and she'd laughed softly as she apologized.

Christ, but he'd always loved the sound of her laugh. Even back then it was low and husky and seemed to rub across his skin like a caress.

Their eyes had met and for a moment, one breathless, perfect moment, everything else in his mind—all his doubts and fears, so many fears—had faded. Because of her.

"That was a long time ago," Maddie said, her eyes giving away nothing, her laugh nowhere to be found. "Things change."

That they did. He'd wanted them to. Had needed them to.

"Fay hasn't confided in you?" he asked, finding it hard to believe that two women who were as close as Fay and Maddie didn't know every thought the other had.

"I'm not a priest. Maybe she wants to keep whatever's going on between her and Shane just that. Between them."

He studied her carefully. "What did you do?"

Her gaze flew to his, startled and, if he wasn't mistaken, guilty as hell. "What are you talking about?"

But her stiff tone didn't fool him. "You're acting defensive. Usually, you're just…offensive—"

"I'll show you offensive," she muttered, hefting the hammer higher.

"Your cheeks are pink, you can't meet my eyes for more than a few seconds and you're doing that thing with your hair," he added, gesturing to her free hand, which was twisting, twisting, twisting a strand at the nape of her neck. "You did something." A thought occurred to him, had him stepping closer to her, his fingers curled into his palms. "Tell me you didn't sleep with Shane."

Her head snapped back as if he'd popped her a good one on the nose. "You seriously want me to bash your head in, don't you?"

Her voice was low and controlled—unusual for Maddie, who was all emotion all the time—her chin tilted at a definite go-to-hell angle, her eyes blazing. But behind the anger and indignation, he saw the hurt. Pain he'd caused.

He hadn't thought he had the power to hurt her. As with most of his dealings with Maddie, he'd messed up. He never knew what to say or how to act. How to respond to her blatant animosity, so he did what was easiest for her and Bree and, yes, himself.

He avoided her.

It was a good plan. One that had worked well for him for the past twelve years. He needed to stick to it.

Taking his life into his own hands, he stepped even closer. Hell, maybe he deserved for her to take a shot at him. "Gerry mentioned some rumors about Shane cheating on Fay—"

"And your first thought to that was, 'Well, hey, I bet Maddie's screwing her best friend's husband'?"

Actually, he didn't let himself think of Maddie with other men. Ever. "That's not quite how it went."

"Oh, really?" She crossed her arms. "Why don't you enlighten me?"

He opened his mouth only to shut it again when he realized any explanation on his part would make things worse. "I apologize."

"Save it. I don't want or need your useless apology. And so this doesn't keep you up at night…no. I'm not, and never have, slept with Shane."

"Maddie, I—"

"Some of us still have integrity, morals and, oh, yeah, loyalty to those we love. But then," she continued softly, "you wouldn't know anything about any of those things, would you, Neil?"

MADDIE HAD TO give him credit. He didn't flinch. Other than the slight tightening of his jaw, he gave no reaction to her verbal slap.

Just as well. It had been a cheap shot. Deserved, but cheap all the same.

Good thing she didn't mind fighting dirty if the situation called for it or she might be forced to issue her own apology.

"I don't want to argue with you," he said—though he did pluck the hammer from her hand and set it on the sawhorse behind him. Out of her reach. "I want to know what's going on with my sister."

Nothing new there. Even when they'd been kids and she'd had a good mad going on, he'd remained calm and completely in control, making her feel immature and reckless for itching for a fight. And Fay had always been his first concern. His sense of responsibility toward his sister had been one of the things Maddie had admired about him. She'd foolishly thought he kept his true feelings carefully hidden in order to protect himself from getting hurt.

And then she'd realized that it didn't matter why he kept himself so closed off. Not when all she'd ever wanted was for him to open up—wholly, gladly and without reservation—to her.

"If you want to know what's going on with Fay," Maddie said, "I suggest you ask her."

"She was too tired when I got in this morning and she was still sleeping when I left the house to come here."

"Sleeping? At—" Maddie checked her watch "—eleven a.m.? What about the boys?"

"Gerry and Carl were watching them."

Of course they were.

"What?" Neil asked.

"I didn't say anything."

"No, but there's something on your mind."

She frowned. He shouldn't know that. She'd changed. She wasn't the same girl she'd been so there was no way he could still read her so easily.

Damn him.

"I don't think enabling Fay to wallow is in her best interest," Maddie said, sounding prim and, yes, a tad sanctimonious. So be it.

"We're not enabling her. We're helping her through a rough time." He leaned against the sawhorse. "I would've thought you'd be on board with that."

"I'm on board with Fay getting her life back but I don't think spending most of the day in bed is the way to accomplish that."

He straightened, the move somehow graceful despite the suddenness of the motion. "She spends all day in bed?"

Guilt, rarely acknowledged and not often accepted, crept up on Maddie. Made her feel as if she was giving away her friend's secrets. As if she was spitting on that loyalty she'd just—oh, so self-righteously—claimed to have.

"Not every day," she said slowly, her worry for Fay's well-being nudging her into the admission. She slid a screwdriver out of her tool belt, turned it in her hand. "Enough that we sort of had a…disagreement over it."

"You and Fay had a fight?"

"Please, you know Fay doesn't fight. She gets quiet. Withdrawn."

It seemed as if Maddie had spent most of her life trying to draw Fay and Neil out, hoping she'd say the right thing, do what was needed to get one or both of the Pettit siblings to open up.

She was starting to wonder why she bothered.

"So instead of letting Fay keep her thoughts to herself," Neil said equably, "you pushed."

Maddie shoved the screwdriver back into its pocket. "I suggested…nicely…that she should stop crying over someone who wasn't worth her time, energy or love and start living her life again." A lesson Maddie had learned thanks to the man in front of her. "She said she appreciated my concern and advice—in that sweet, polite tone of hers—but that she didn't want me worrying about her and her problems."

"Which is her way of telling you to mind your own business."

"You got it."

Maddie had backed off. Not that she had any intention of letting her closest friend go through the worst time of her life by herself, but she could understand Fay's need for space. For time to heal on her own, in her own way.

Even if Maddie didn't agree with how she went about that healing.

"I'm here now," Neil said. "I'll talk to her. Take care of it."

Fay didn't need him to take care of her. She needed to learn to stand on her own two feet, to make her own way without him.

Just as Maddie had.

Not her place to say anything, she decided. Or her problem. Besides, she knew how Neil worked. Sure, he'd come to Shady Grove, a minor aberration in and of itself, but he wouldn't stay more than a day or two. He'd throw some money at the problem, pat Fay on the head, spend whatever short amount of time he deemed acceptable with Bree and be on his way again.

Hard to believe there was a time, not so very long ago, when all Maddie wanted was to keep him close. She'd been completely convinced that they were meant to be together forever. That he loved her, as desperately as she'd loved him.

That she couldn't live without him.

Guess every once in a while even she could be mistaken. Because she hadn't collapsed into a quivering, sobbing mass of hysteria and emptiness when he'd walked out on her. Her heart may have been battered but it had continued to beat, her pride bruised but still intact. She'd discovered her strength, her independence and the importance of self-reliance.

He'd helped shape the woman she'd become.

Maybe, instead of being pissed at him, she should be thanking him.

MADDIE WAS SMIRKING at him.

He shouldn't find it so damned sexy.

When Neil found his gaze going, once again, to that damned tool belt hanging low on her curvy hips, he shut his eyes and inhaled deeply, ridding himself of any and all thoughts related to Maddie and sex. It was just his sleepless night and the exhaustion of the past few weeks catching up with him.

"You having some sort of spiritual experience over there?" Hearing that smart-ass tone of hers, the one that grated on his last nerve, he forced his eyes open. "Because if you are, could you have it in a church or something? I'm trying to work here."

He heard a car pull into the driveway. "I'm not in your way."

"I say you are, so therefore, you must be. My workplace. My rules."

"Doesn't everything have to be by your rules?"

He bit back a wince. Shit. Why had he said that? He wasn't trying to tick her off. Fighting with Maddie had always been a losing proposition. She was easily offended, twisted everything to suit her own purposes and kept at you with a relentlessness that wore down even the hardiest soul.

Luckily, she didn't get all prickly, just lifted one shoulder in a careless shrug. "Now you're catching on. Though you seem to be a little slow figuring out I'd like you to leave." She wrinkled her nose in an expression of fake concern. "Am I being too subtle? Would it help if I physically pushed you toward the door? I don't mind."

"Subtlety has never been one of your strengths."

She laughed, a surprised burst of sound so familiar, his gut tightened. "No," she said, still grinning. And he wondered what he'd have to do, what he'd have to say to get her to keep smiling at him. To stop hating him, just for another minute. "I guess it's not. I've always preferred the direct route to getting what I want."

True. It'd always been her way or no way. He'd been content to follow her lead. Until her way had threatened everything he'd worked so hard for.

The sound of the door opening reached them, followed by running footsteps. A moment later Elijah, his four-year-old nephew, raced into the room only to skid to a stop, his upper body still moving while his feet stayed planted, so that he almost toppled over.

His eyes wide, he stared at Neil, his pale blond hair sticking up at the back.

"Hey, bud," Neil said, looking over Elijah's head for Fay. "Where's your mom?"

Elijah shook his head then launched himself at Neil's legs, wrapping his skinny arms around Neil's knees.

"Uncle Neil!" he yelled, his voice reaching decibels Neil would have thought impossible for someone who topped off at forty pounds. "I didn't know you were here! Is that your Lightning car?"

Neil frowned. "Lightning car?"

Elijah nodded, bounced on his toes and did a little shake of his shoulders. All the while keeping ahold of Neil. Kid had an impressive grip.

He wasn't sure what to do with his arms, couldn't put them down with Elijah wrapped around him like a blond boa constrictor. Finally he settled on giving his nephew a pat on the head then crossed them.

"Your rental car is a Corvette?" Maddie asked, peering out the large window at the front of the house. "Really?"

The back of his neck heated. "I like how it drives."

She made a humming sound, just like he'd heard Gerry make many times. Must be one of those things they teach mothers, some sort of code for *you are such an idiot.* "Yes. And it's so practical."

"Can I ride in Lightning, Uncle Neil?" Elijah asked. "Can I? Please?"

Neil looked from him to Maddie. "Would it kill you to help me out?"

Her look clearly told him that while it might not kill her, it would pain her greatly. Still, she lifted a hand to someone outside—Fay most likely—then faced him. "He means Lightning McQueen." He must have looked as blank as his brain felt because she added, "It's a character from the *Cars* movie."

"And *Cars 2,*" Elijah piped up. "Can I ride in it?"

Take his nephew for a ride? The kid couldn't stay still for longer than thirty seconds and had talked nonstop for over an hour the last time Fay had flown out to Seattle. He didn't even always make it to the bathroom in time.

"I don't know if that's a good idea," Neil said, not caring if he sounded desperate and out of his element. He *was* desperate and out of his element.

"Why not?" Elijah asked, loosening his grip—all the better to lean back and send Neil a wide-eyed, imploring look.

Why not? Good question. Neil searched the room, as if something in there would supply inspiration.

"Oh, for the love of…" Maddie crossed over to them. "If you don't want to take him in the car, say no. But you'd better do it before he asks his mother. Fay hasn't quite grasped the concept of 'no,' or the power of 'because I said so.'"

"But I want to ride with you," Elijah whined.

"No," Neil said, sounding gruff and vehement to his own ears.

Elijah's eyes welled with tears. Shit. Neil opened his

mouth, ready to promise the kid he could drive the car if he wanted, but Maddie interrupted.

"Your booster seat won't fit in a car like Lightning." She crouched to look Elijah in the eye. "And what's the rule?"

Elijah sniffed, wiping his nose with the back of his hand and then wiping the back of his hand on Neil's jeans. Neil tipped his head back and sighed.

"I haf to be in a booster until I'm eight," Elijah said, as if that was a fate worse than death.

"Right. Or until you're big enough to use a grown-up seat belt." Tipping her head to the side, Maddie studied him. "You know…you do look a little taller than last week."

"I do?" he asked in awe.

"I think so, but there's only one way to be sure…." She took out her tape measure. "Okay, you know the drill."

Elijah let go of Neil and ran over to press his back against the doorjamb separating the large front room from the entryway. "I'm ready."

While Maddie measured the kid, Neil took the opportunity to wipe at the wet spot on his jeans and check out the window for Fay. Through the open back door of her minivan, he spotted her talking on the phone while trying to keep Mitchell, her eight-month-old son, from toppling out of the car.

"Yep," Maddie told Elijah. "It's official. You grew."

"How much?"

"An eighth of an inch." She straightened and offered him a high five. "Way to go."

Elijah slapped her palm. "Yes!" He turned to beam at Neil. "I grew, Uncle Neil."

"I heard." But now both the kid and Maddie were looking at him expectantly. He had no clue why.

"What Uncle Neil means," Maddie said, her hand on Elijah's shoulder, "is *good job.*"

"I'm going to tell Mom," Elijah said. "Can I take the tape measurer and show her how much?"

"Sure," she said, handing it to him, "but remember it snaps back quickly so don't pull it out too far. You hear me?"

"Uh-huh." Elijah nodded as he did a little happy dance, his attention clearly not on one thing she was saying. "Mom," he called, though Fay was still outside and couldn't hear him. "Mommy! Look what I did."

And he was off, his feet slipping on the floor in his haste.

"He grew," Neil muttered once he and Maddie were alone, Elijah's excited conversation with his mother a muffled explosion of words. "He had no control over it."

"He wants you to be excited for him," Maddie said. "Praise him."

"Like a dog?"

She stared at him. "Yes, Neil," she said, her tone all sorts of dry. "Like a dog. So, why don't you tell me why you—and now your sister—are here?"

"I'd like a tour."

"A tour?" Maddie repeated as if she'd never heard of the concept before. "This isn't Gettysburg."

"No," he said, crossing to stand before her. "It's a job site. One I'm paying for."

"Let's pretend you're not the one footing the bill. It'll make it easier for me to live with myself."

"Don't think of me as your boss—"

"No chance of that happening. Ever."

"Just think of me as the man who signs your paycheck."

She smiled thinly. "Now who's going straight for the jugular?"

"I'm simply interested in my investment."

A lie, but what was one more at this point in his life?

Short of Maddie blowing it to bits, he couldn't care less what she did to Bradford House. He glanced around. Two of the walls had been gutted down to their frames, the plaster on the other two was cracked, stained and, in a few areas, missing, exposing the narrow pieces of wood underneath. The brick above the fireplace was crumbling and fractured and the fireplace itself was sinking into the floor.

Maybe blowing this place up wasn't such a bad idea.

But no matter how bad of shape it was in, the Montesanos would turn it around. That's why he hired them. He'd bought Bradford House so it could be renovated into a bed-and-breakfast for Fay to run, but she'd never believe he'd put up the money simply as a business venture if he didn't show interest in the progress Maddie was making.

"Tell you what," Maddie said with so much false cheer, Neil was surprised she didn't shoot singing elves from her ass. "I'm in the middle of something right now. How about we schedule a little look-see for this weekend? Say, Sunday afternoon?"

"I'm flying out Saturday," Neil said.

"Guess what they say about rest and the wicked is true. I'd think you'd have a few days off, what with being a Stanley Cup champion and all."

Don't think he didn't notice that she said "Stanley Cup champion" the way most people said "demon-spawn-of-Satan."

But she was right. He didn't have much time to rest, hadn't slept more than four hours a night or had so much as a day off since winning the Cup—hockey's highest trophy—a week ago. There had been celebrations and the parade in Seattle, press junkets and interviews, charity and promotional photo shoots.

He was tired and hungry and he didn't need more shit from Maddie.

Too bad he couldn't quite figure out how much he actually deserved.

"I signed a deal to endorse a new sports drink," he said. "The commercial's shooting first thing Monday morning."

"So you're going to get paid an ungodly amount of money to swill some electrolyte-laden drink? Well, big congrats to you," she added, sounding as if she was wishing him a lovely trip to hell.

"I'm lucky," he said slowly, "that playing the sport I love grants me opportunities to take care of my family."

"Yes, you're quite the saint. Always thinking of your family."

He did think of his family, but it'd do no good trying to convince Maddie of that. She'd always wanted, expected, so much more from him than what he gave. Than what he was capable of giving.

She had high standards, higher than most mere mortals could attain. He'd gotten tired of trying to meet them, of trying to be the boy she'd so desperately wanted him to be.

Maybe it was time for her to try to live up to *his* standards.

"I'm sure you can spare me a few minutes now," he told her, using the same tone he employed when making any other business deal. The one that said he not only played hockey to win, but he also played every game to win.

He held her gaze, could practically feel her resentment, her animosity, emanating from her. Maddie hated being put into a corner and being told what to do. She hated even more not getting her own way.

Some things, it seemed, would never change.

"Look," she said, "I tried to be nice—"

"I must've missed that part of the conversation."

"I realize you're used to people falling all over themselves just to make you happy, but in case you haven't noticed, I'm a carpenter, not a tour guide. You want to look around? Knock yourself out. And I mean that literally."

She brushed past him, haughty and so goddamned self-righteous, he grabbed her arm. Held on when she stiffened. Tried not to think about how he used to have permission to touch her whenever he wanted. How she used to welcome his hands on her.

How he shouldn't want to pull her closer, press his nose to the side of her neck and see if she smelled the same. If she still fit perfectly in his arms.

Those thoughts, and his own traitorous body, had him tugging her closer. Ignoring her quick intake of breath, he leaned down.

"Tell me, Maddie," he murmured, his lips brushing the curve of her ear. She shivered. Triumph, some sense that he wasn't the only one lost in the past, wrapped up in memories and regrets, washed over him. Encouraged him to step even closer so that his thigh touched her hip, the round edge of her screwdriver digging into his leg. "Don't you ever get tired of being so pissed at me?"

She faced him slowly, her gaze dropping to his mouth for one long, painful moment before she raised her eyes. "Not even a little."

CHAPTER THREE

DON'T YOU EVER get tired of being so pissed at me?

Neil's question echoed in Maddie's head. She didn't struggle, didn't try to break free of his hold, though it felt as if his fingers were burning her skin, scarring her with his touch.

Branding her.

Damn it. As much as it grated to admit, he rattled her with his intense blue eyes and grim expression. God, the man was a millionaire several times over, was at the top of his sport and he still looked as if it wasn't enough. As if there was something inside that made it impossible for him to ever be truly happy.

Not her problem, she assured herself, her chest tight, as if she wasn't getting enough air. She'd done her time trying to coax smiles from him, the occasional laugh. He'd always been so serious. So focused on his goals. When she'd been a girl, she'd found that intensity appealing and oh, so attractive. And, yes, she could admit now, challenging.

She'd wanted to be the one to get through to him, the boy from the wrong side of the tracks who carried his resentment on his sleeve, who pushed himself to be better than anyone else.

Now she only wanted him to give her some space so she could breathe again.

His fingers tightened before he unwrapped them from her arm. But he didn't move and her pride wouldn't let her be the one to put distance between them. Not when he was watching her so intently, as if trying to figure out if she spoke the truth. As if surprised he couldn't tell.

But then, he'd never had to dig too deeply, had he? She'd always been more than eager to give him everything. Her thoughts and feelings. Her heart.

"Good to know where we stand," he finally said, his voice a low, sexy rumble.

"You ever want to know where you stand with me, all you have to do is ask." She linked her hands together to stop from rubbing her fingertips over the spot he'd held. "Direct, remember?"

He shoved his hands into his pockets, still not backing up an inch, the bastard. "Right."

Succinct as always. But really, what was there to say after that? She didn't like him, didn't forgive him. Wasn't sure she ever could.

Even if he asked her to.

Half-afraid they'd be there hours from now, staring each other down, neither one giving an inch, she stepped back. Then took another step. "You'll excuse me for not walking you to the door? You've always been very good at finding a way out on your own."

It was another cheap shot. One she regretted as soon as the words left her mouth. Biting her lower lip so she wouldn't take the words back, she crossed to the wall, stared at it blindly.

"I always admired that about you," he said quietly. "How open you were. How honest."

She shut her eyes against a pinch of guilt. God, rub salt in the wound, why didn't he? And where did he get off saying that anyway? He admired her? Of course he did. Didn't most people admire traits in others they themselves lacked? Lord knew Neil was nothing if not closed off and guarded.

She'd long ago stopped thinking that brooding, emotionally bereft men with tragic pasts and a dangerous edge
were attractive.

She shot a quick look over her shoulder at him. Yep.
She'd stopped thinking that. Definitely.

Hey, even someone direct and honest could lie to themselves once in a while.

The front door slammed and a moment later, Elijah ran
into the room. She wasn't sure the kid even knew how to
walk.

And his return meant the delay of Neil's departure.
Crap.

"I told her, Aunt Maddie," Elijah said, holding the tape
measure up like a trophy. "I told Mom I grew and I measured the steps on the porch, too."

"Great. Why don't you help me out? Measure those
sawhorses for me?"

"Sure. I can do that," he said, hurrying over to the first
sawhorse, as if afraid if he didn't get there right away, it'd
take off on him. "I can do that real good."

"I'm so sorry I'm late," Fay told Neil as she came into
the room. She hitched Mitchell higher on her hip. "Elijah was watching his favorite TV show and then Mitchell
needed changing—" hearing his name, the baby grinned,
showing his uncle his two lethal-looking top teeth "—and
then we had to stop for gas—"

"Where'd you get gas?" Maddie asked, the question too
casual and innocent to be either.

Fay turned toward her, as if shocked to find Maddie
there. Shocked and a bit put out by what was a damned
good question.

"Maddie," Fay said with one of her sweet, guileless
smiles. "Hello."

Slipping her hands into her back pockets, Maddie sent

her an answering grin that was more I-am-so-not-buying-your-innocent-act-so-don't-even-try-it. "Where'd you stop for gas?"

"What does that matter?" Neil asked, as always, completely clueless as to what was going on in his sister's life.

How could he be so blind? Even though he hadn't been around, all it took was one look at Fay to see there was something wrong. She was nothing but a walking, talking, baby-carrying hot mess.

And that was being kind.

Her light blue shorts were wrinkled and bagged at the waist, and her shirt—dear Lord, her shirt—was some sort of explosion of brightly colored flowers in oranges, greens and pinks. She'd pulled her hard-to-tame curls back into a ponytail—probably because she thought people wouldn't notice she hadn't washed her hair recently. Wrong. All the style did was accentuate her slightly sunken cheeks and sickly pallor. Despite sleeping in, she still sported dark circles under her eyes, which were puffy and red-rimmed.

She'd been crying. Again.

Maddie felt like crying herself but that might just be the shirt causing her eyes to water.

"I went to the Quick Mart," Fay told Maddie, her chin lifted. But her cheeks had some color thanks to a rising blush, and her shoulders slumped.

Maddie's mouth tightened. "Which. One."

As if sensing his mother's distress, Mitchell laid his head on her shoulder. She patted his back but didn't meet Maddie's eyes. "On Mechanic Street."

"Oh, honey," Maddie said, her heart breaking for her friend, her brain screaming that she wasn't doing Fay any favors by coddling her. "Why?"

Neil stepped between them, glanced from Maddie to Fay and back again. "Someone want to fill me in?"

Maddie held her best friend's gaze, noted the pleading in Fay's eyes. The questions.

Will you tell him? Will you take care of this? Take care of me?

She shouldn't. Fay needed to step up. Or better yet, toughen up. It was as if she had a welcome-mat tattoo on her forehead, one begging people to walk all over her.

But Maddie couldn't point any of that out. Even she wasn't that big of a bitch.

"The girl Shane's been screw—"

"Maddie," Fay gasped, her eyes wide as she lunged toward Elijah as if to tackle him and cover his ears. The kid didn't even notice, so engrossed was he in measuring the windowsill, his little face puckered in concentration. Realizing Maddie had stopped speaking, Fay straightened and switched Mitchell to her other hip. "We don't even know if those horrible rumors are true."

They might have a better idea if Fay grabbed Shane by the scruff of the neck and demanded to know if he was cheating on her with a nineteen-year-old with a penchant for cowboy boots, short shorts—at the same time, for the love of God—and other women's husbands.

Maddie looked at Fay in pure exasperation. If she didn't like Maddie's word choice, why didn't she tell Neil what was going on herself? Jeez. Try to do someone a favor and they jump on your back.

"Fine," she said. "I'll rephrase. The girl—"

"Girl?" Neil asked.

"Girl. As in, not-old-enough-to-drink, still-lives-with-her-parents, uses-the-word-*like*-in-every-sentence girl Shane has *allegedly* been…seeing, works at the Quick Mart on Mechanic Street."

He raised his eyebrows at Fay. "You confronted her?"

"Of course not," she said, as if he'd wondered if she'd

taken a baseball bat to the girl's pinhead. Which would have been about as likely. Fay didn't do confrontation. She excelled at avoidance. "I just…I wanted her to see us. I…" She swallowed visibly, her eyes welling with tears. She sniffed them back. "I thought if she saw me and the boys, we'd be more real to her. She'd realize that Shane has a family, one who loves him and needs him more than she does. And that she should leave him alone, stop chasing after him so that he'll come home. Back where he belongs."

"Honey," Maddie said, forcing her tone to be gentle, despite the urge to shout at her best friend. "Shane's a grown man. She's not forcing him to do anything he doesn't want to do. To be anywhere he doesn't want to be."

"He's confused. He was away for so long, he's not sure where he fits with us anymore. But he'll come back to us." Mitchell fussed and Fay dug into her huge bag, pulling out a packet of graham crackers before handing one to the baby, her simple gold wedding band flashing in the sunlight. "He'll come back," she repeated shakily. "He has to."

"No matter what happens," Neil told Fay, his tone grave, his expression fierce—but he reached out and touched his sister's arm with a gentle hand, "you'll get through it."

Fay didn't look convinced. Then again, it didn't seem to Maddie that Neil was trying to be convincing. He wasn't being placating or offering his sister comfort.

His words were a demand. One Maddie didn't doubt he thought would be heeded.

But getting over a broken heart was easier said than done. Especially for someone like Fay, who still believed true love conquered all and life was filled with fairy-tale endings.

Maddie stared at the floor and tried to control her ragged breathing, her racing heart. God, it was hard to believe she'd ever been like Fay—desperate to believe in the man she'd loved, the man she'd trusted.

Thankfully she'd gotten over her delusions right quick. Having the man of your dreams walk out on you while his baby grew in your belly did that.

Raising her head, she met Neil's gaze. Yeah, he'd done a number on her. But she'd survived him.

He'd left. And they'd both moved on. If it wasn't for Bree tying them together for the rest of their lives, they'd have no reason to see or speak to each other ever again.

But that didn't mean she had to like their connection. Didn't mean she had to put up with him for longer than absolutely necessary.

"Well, as much as I'd love to give you all that tour Neil requested," Maddie said, which was about as much as she'd love to pound nails using nothing but her fists, "I'm afraid I really do need to get back to work."

Neil stepped forward. "Maddie—"

"Of course," Fay said, wiping wet crumbs from Mitchell's chin before giving him another cracker. He shoved it into his already full mouth. "We don't want to interrupt you. Do we, Neil?"

"No." He ground out the word. "We wouldn't want to do anything to put Maddie out."

It didn't matter what Neil wanted, if he was happy or got his own way. She didn't owe him anything. Not even a few minutes of her time.

"Great," she said, smiling at Fay. "Give me a call tonight or tomorrow morning and we'll set something up."

Except she planned on being extremely busy and unable to accommodate any and all tours, informational sessions or conversations until after Neil left. No, she was not holding a grudge.

But she wasn't a saint, either.

She felt Neil's eyes on her as she turned and flipped the music on. Knew he still watched her as she went back to work, his gaze like a touch, insistent and real.

She wouldn't look back. Refused to give in to the itch between her shoulder blades, the one pushing her to turn, to meet his eyes one last time. There was no reason and very little sense in her giving him any more of her attention or thoughts. They each knew where they stood with the other. She had every right to her anger.

Anger he accepted without so much as flinching. As if it was his due. His penance. Sometimes she wished he wouldn't. There were times, few and far between, that she wished he'd push back at her. That he'd lay into her for once or, at the very least, defend himself.

Maybe then she'd finally stop feeling so damned guilty about her own mistakes.

SOME THINGS NEVER CHANGED, Neil thought two hours later as he chose a bottle of water and an exercise drink from the cooler of Jack's Place, a small grocery store on Main Street. The sun rose in the east, the sky was blue, grass was green.

And Jack Placer, the store's owner, watched him with a mixture of suspicion and active dislike most people reserved for rats, poisonous snakes and politicians.

It didn't matter that Neil—who had enough money to buy the store a few times over—was a known and generous supporter of several charities, and had just been fawned and fussed over by the waitress, the manager and at least half a dozen customers at lunch.

To Mr. Placer, he'd always be the snot-nosed kid with dirty hair and hand-me-down clothes who swiped a pack of gum or candy bar from the shelves. There was no pretense with the old guy. He clearly remembered Neil, his past and who and what he'd come from. And his success, money and fame hadn't changed Mr. Placer's opinion of him.

Christ, it was enough to make Neil want to reach across the checkout counter and hug the old bastard.

"Afternoon," he said, setting down his drinks.

Mr. Placer, a familiar scowl on his face, grunted and punched numbers into the electronic cash register. He looked as ancient, wrinkled and grumpy as he had when Neil hadn't towered over him by six inches. But the cash register was new, as was the deli offering fresh meats, cheeses and subs.

"Anything else?" Mr. Placer asked, his glare daring him to say yes.

"No, thanks."

"That's four-nineteen."

Neil took out his wallet. "On second thought, I think I'll get a few candy bars." He picked up a box of Kit Kat bars and set them on the counter. Then, for good measure, added boxes of taffy and M&M's. "That should do it."

Mr. Placer shifted his narrow gaze from the candy to Neil. "Should do what?"

Should make them even.

The amount he was spending more than made up for the few items he'd stolen then taken home to share with Fay.

Less than five minutes later, Neil was walking down the sidewalk, his gaze straight ahead, two bags of candy he didn't want in his hand, his drinks in the other. People watched him pass, a few called out greetings, more than one pointed. He nodded back, kept his stride easy. He might as well wear a sign—Hometown Boy Done Good.

He hit the unlock button on the key fob, tossed the bags onto the passenger seat then folded himself into the car. And whacked his head against the doorframe so hard, he saw stars.

Hissing out a breath between his teeth, he slammed the door shut then rubbed the sore spot. His knees hit the steering wheel and he couldn't quite get comfortable in the low-slung seat, not when it was so narrow, his shoulder blades hit the outer edges.

And it's so practical.

He cranked the engine hard enough to have it protesting. Exhaled and slowly peeled his fingers off the steering wheel. Damn it. It'd taken him years to get Maddie out of his head—he wasn't about to backslide now.

She'd always had the ability to look through him, see into his soul, his heart. To read his thoughts.

Wasn't he allowed to have his own thoughts? His own feelings? Why the hell had she always demanded he share everything, every piece of himself with her when he'd needed to keep a part of himself separate? He'd been so afraid of losing himself, of never achieving his goals if he didn't.

He pulled away from the curb. Tapped his fingers along to the Maroon 5 song playing on the radio. Not much had changed around here. Shady Grove was still small, quaint and friendly—Mr. Placer notwithstanding. Well-maintained buildings, most of them originally built at the end of the eighteenth century, none over three or four stories high, lined the street. Miranda's Books and Candles, with its fancy front window display, and Keely's Restaurant, where he'd taken Fay and the boys to lunch, were familiar sights, as was Smith-Worth Hardware and the Hargrove Building, which housed offices for accountants, doctors and even a beauty parlor.

He passed the movie theater where he'd had his first kiss, the fast-food place where he'd worked his first job. At the stoplight he glanced to the right. Same grocery store where, every Thursday evening, Gerry had bought their groceries. Behind it the Catholic church where she'd dragged Neil to mass every Sunday.

It was all the same, always the same, he thought, driving away from downtown. Same rolling hills, the lush, green trees hiding the dirt lease roads and oil derricks that dotted the woods. Same streets and buildings, schools and parks, stores and people.

It was like stepping back in time. Like he was seeing his old life, living it once again.

No wonder he never stayed in town more than a day or two.

He inched his way down Hanley Street, a narrow, winding road where houses were close together and kids still played in the road. Gravel crunched under his tires as he pulled into the back parking lot of Crawford Park.

Grabbing his bag from the trunk, he slung it over his shoulder and crossed the wooden footbridge to the ice rink. Inside, he headed down the short hallway, stopping at the manager's office on the left. The door was open so he rapped twice on the jamb.

Walt Benninger, leaning back in his chair, the phone to his ear, his considerable stomach hanging over his belt, grinned and held up a finger. Neil nodded and set down his bag while Walt finished his call.

"Neil Pettit," he said as he got to his feet—no small task given the fifty pounds he'd put on since Neil had last seen him. He came around the desk, offering his hand. "Good to see you."

"You, too."

Walt had aged. His hair—what was left of it—was gray, his face more lined and, if Neil wasn't mistaken, the man had shrunk by a good two inches.

Guess some things had changed.

Walt grabbed a set of keys from his desk. "Let's get you

set up," he said, motioning for Neil to precede him back into the hallway.

At the end of the hall, Walt unlocked the door to the storage locker. "I already opened up the locker room for you," he said as he flipped on the light. "Pucks are here—" he kicked a large plastic tub "—nets are already on the ice. When you're done, put everything back and lock up. If I'm not here, you can leave the key on my desk."

Neil took the key chain. "No problem. Thanks for opening the ice for me."

Walt grinned. "Hey, it's not every day we get a Stanley Cup champion skating in our rink. Congratulations. You did us all proud."

With a two-fingered salute, Walt was gone. Neil wrapped his fingers around the metal ring, the edge of a key digging into his palm. He hadn't set out to make anyone proud, just to make something of himself. He'd had something to prove.

There were days he wondered if he was still trying to prove it.

In the locker room, Neil changed into a pair of warm-ups and laced up his skates. He walked out to the rink, breathed in the scent of the ice, welcomed the cold slap of air against his cheeks. After setting the bucket of pucks aside and leaning his stick against the boards, he started skating, the swoosh of his blades the only sound.

He did laps to warm up, increasing his speed each go-round. But it wasn't enough. He could still see Fay, so pale the dark circles under her eyes stood out like bruises. So fragile and drawn and so much like Annie, it was as though he was reliving his worst nightmare.

Gritting his teeth, he pushed himself even more. His breathing grew labored, his thigh muscles burned. Sweat dripped down his face and stung his eyes. He kept going. Faster. Harder.

Fay wasn't Annie. More importantly, Neil wasn't a helpless kid. Not anymore. He had everything he needed to help his sister. Money. Connections. He'd do whatever it took to make sure she was okay.

I just don't think enabling Fay to wallow is in her best interest.

He took the corner fast, crossing his right skate over his left. The tips of his fingers skimmed the ice. Continued that pace until he'd successfully shoved Maddie's voice, opinions and the way she'd brushed aside his concerns about their daughter out of his head.

But his hands still tingled from touching her. Every inhalation brought her scent—something darker and sexier than when they'd been a couple. He'd found that fact both disappointing and way more appealing than it should have been.

Found himself wondering what else had changed about her. What had stayed the same. If she still sang along to all the songs on the radio and fought with her brothers over everything, anything and, at times, nothing at all. If she still played with her hair when it was down, twirling the long strands around her finger or flipping it off her face. If she still kissed with that mix of single-minded focus, heat and heart that had made him feel like king of the freaking world even while it scared the shit out of him.

He'd like to find out.

Movement on the bleachers caught his attention at the same time the truth of his last thought hit him. His blade slipped and he went down, not stopping until he crashed into the boards, his right shoulder hitting it with enough force to cause pain to shoot down his arm.

Shit. Even now she was trying to ruin his career.

He wiped the back of his hand across his forehead then

got to his feet to the sound of a slow clap, courtesy of the half-dozen boys gathered on the home team's bench.

"Smooth," one of them called out, which set the rest guffawing.

Neil slowly rotated his shoulder back then forth. A slight twinge. Nothing more. Not enough to sideline him.

He pushed off, ignoring his audience. You didn't make it in professional sports without being able to block out any and all distractions. He'd made a loop, was considering doing some shooting drills when one of the boys stepped out of the box.

"You're not supposed to be here," the kid called as Neil approached. "The ice is closed."

Neil swerved and kept right on skating.

His second trip around, the kid joined him. "Dude, didn't you hear me? I said the ice is closed."

"Then why are you on it?" Neil asked.

"My granddad runs the place."

Neil glanced at him, pegged him to be sixteen, maybe seventeen, and the obvious leader of the floppy-haired gang.

"You're Merilee's kid?" he asked, stopping.

"Yeah," the kid said slowly, his expression cocky and suspicious. "Who are you?"

Neil almost laughed. He couldn't go anywhere in Shady Grove without people stopping him, wanting to talk to him, shake his hand, get his picture taken with him. He removed his ball cap and ran his fingers through his sweat-dampened hair. "Neil Pettit."

The kid's eyes rounded but then he went back to acting as cool as the ice beneath their feet. "You look bigger on TV."

Seeing as how he still had two inches on the kid, Neil didn't take offense. "You don't have to be big to play in the

NHL," he said casually. "Just really good." He inclined his head toward the other kids. "You guys here for practice?"

"A pickup game."

Neil scanned the group of kids. Six. And his skating partner here made for uneven numbers. "You interested in adding another man to your roster?"

"You want to play with us?"

"If you've got room for one more guy."

"I guess we could fit you in. If, you know, you stay upright. And can keep up with us."

Yeah, this one here, definitely leader of the pack. He was quick on his feet and if his puck-handling skills equaled his skating, he was the man to beat.

So to speak.

And there was nothing Neil liked more than winning.

The boy was overly confident and cocky. Add in rampant hormones and an overwhelming influx of testosterone and he was practically begging to be taken down a peg or two. For his own sake.

He'd be doing him a favor, Neil assured himself. Never let it be said he didn't give back to the community.

He checked out the other boys, now all on the ice, and quickly summed up their skill level. From what he could tell, his skating partner here had the most talent on skates.

"How about this," Neil said easily. "You and I race four lengths of the rink. I win, I play and I get to captain one team."

"What about if I win?"

If this snot-nosed kid won, Neil would fill the Stanley Cup with water and drown himself in it. "Name it."

"Dude, get the car," one of his buddies called.

"That your 'Vette in the parking lot?" the kid asked.

"For the next few days."

"Good enough. If I win, I get it. For twenty-four hours."

Neil shrugged then held out his hand. "Deal."

They shook, the kid's grin wide and confident.

They lined up at the boards, one hand touching the wood, their body weight on the front of their skates. One of the boys counted down and they were off.

Neil let the kid set the pace for the first lap, one he easily matched. At the other side of the rink, they stopped with a spray of ice, touched the wall at the same time, then pushed off for lap two. By the time they touched the starting wall, the kid was breathing hard. For lap three, Neil put on a burst of speed, leaving the kid in his wake. He skated the fourth lap backward, did a quick half loop around the kid as he skated, then sailed on to victory.

"Good job," Neil said when the kid finally touched the wall to end the race.

The kid nodded, his hands on his knees, his shoulders rising and falling as he tried to catch his breath. "I took it…easy on…you." He raised his head and grinned. "You know, so you didn't…have a heart attack or something."

"I appreciate that," Neil said, wanting more than anything to challenge the kid to another race or a shoot-out, anything to prove that some smart-ass half his age couldn't best him. Not at his own game.

But he was afraid that was his inner demons talking, the ones reminding him that each year he played in the NHL could be his last. That there were always more kids coming into the league, players who were younger, faster, better puck handlers.

Players who could push him right out of a job if he let down his guard.

Luckily, he was always—*always*—on guard.

And right here, right now, he was on the ice doing what

he loved most in the world. Right here, right now, he was still one of the best players in the world.

He just wasn't sure what or who he'd be when he no longer was.

CHAPTER FOUR

BREANNE MONTESANO GLANCED at the microwave clock. Three forty-seven.

Her dad was late.

"Maybe he's not coming," she said, then bit her lower lip, tasting chocolate there from the cookie she'd eaten a few minutes ago. She licked the sweetness off and wondered if her wistful tone had sounded disappointed. Or hopeful.

Wondered what she actually felt.

Standing by the table, Pops, her great-grandpa, moved his knight on the chessboard. "He'll be here."

The timer on the oven buzzed and Pops slid on the red-checked pot holders she'd bought him for Christmas two years ago and removed the last tray of chocolate chip cookies from the oven. Bree inhaled deeply and held her breath, keeping the scent of warm, delicious, chewy cookies inside for as long as she could.

Well, for as long as she could before her lungs started burning and she had to exhale or risk dying. Or at least passing out on the kitchen floor.

Bet she wouldn't have to go with her dad then.

"I could call him," Bree said, checking the driveway once more—still empty. "Since he's already late, I could tell him I'll just stay here for a while longer." Or for the rest of the day. "That way I can help you clean the kitchen."

She hung out with Pops a few times each week during

the summer and they often baked in the afternoons. Her mom said they were nuts to bake on hot days, but the AC kept the house cool.

"I may be old and decrepit," Pops said in his booming voice, still heavy with an Italian accent even though he'd been in America since he was her mom's age, "but I think I can manage to wash a couple of bowls and cookie sheets. Especially if I take a nap halfway through." He waved a spatula at her. "Come now. It's your turn." He transferred a cookie to the cooling tray. "Unless you want to forfeit the match…"

She knew what he was doing. Baiting her. Daring her.

Grown-ups were so weird. They tell you to be yourself and not give in to peer pressure and then they go ahead and pressure you themselves as if they want you to give in.

Dragging her feet, Bree moved away from the large window. At the sound of a car, she hurried back but the sound faded as a truck disappeared down the road.

She sat down, slumping in her seat until Pops gave her a raised-eyebrow look—which made it seem as if he had two huge, fuzzy, gray caterpillars levitating on his forehead. With a sigh, she wiggled a bit and straightened, pulling her shoulders back. He winked then set a plate of still-warm cookies between them as he settled in his own chair across from her.

She studied the board, tried really hard to focus, to think ahead like Pops always told her. It wasn't enough to see what moves her opponent could make next—she needed to look ahead and try to figure out what options they had two, three, four moves down the line.

But it was hard to concentrate when all she could think about was that at any minute, her dad would be there.

Possibly.

Plus, those cookies smelled so good. She shifted. The

waistband of her sweatpants cut into her waist so she lifted her hips and tugged her pants up higher, knew without having to look the tight elastic had made a mark on her skin. She quickly pulled her shirt down to cover the rolls of her stomach.

Her hand hovered over one of her rooks but then she rubbed her fingertips across her palm, dropped her hand back to the table. Sneaked a look toward the window then toward the door. Nothing. No one.

Lowering her head as if she was deep in thought over the chessboard, she glanced at that plate of cookies. They were tempting her. Taunting her. She swallowed. She wasn't hungry. Or at least, she shouldn't be hungry. She'd eaten a late lunch and two cookies.

Plus a couple of spoonfuls of dough when Pops hadn't been looking.

No. She shouldn't be hungry. But she was. She really was, even though Grandma Gerry said that sometimes when people think they're hungry, they're really thirsty and should drink a big glass of water.

But Bree didn't want a glass of water. She wanted a cookie.

Her eyes on the chessboard, she picked up a cookie and bit into it, her face heating when a tiny moan escaped. Luckily, Pops didn't seem to notice. He was on his feet once again, this time putting the dirty pans in the sink.

Well, it deserved a moan, she told herself as she polished off the cookie in another two bites. It was good— sweet and chewy with melting chocolate.

So good, she took another one. Then another, eating them quickly, her shoulders rounded, her back turned slightly so Pops wouldn't see.

And she felt better. Not so empty. Not so sad. But then she noticed the crumbs on her shirt, the chocolate smeared on her fingers, and she got queasy. Her eyes pricked with tears. Which was stupid. It was only a few cookies. It wasn't as if she killed someone. Besides, all of her friends could eat dozens of cookies without worrying about their pants being tight or someone looking at them funny, as if they shouldn't ever put anything in their mouths except celery sticks and plain lettuce.

"Breanne."

She jumped and whirled around, her fingers curled tightly in her lap.

Pops frowned at her. "Aren't you going to answer me?"

"Uh…sorry. I didn't hear you."

"I asked if you had your overnight bag packed."

Nodding, she moved a pawn only to immediately regret it.

"That wasn't a smart move, girlie," he said with a tsk. Then, instead of giving her a second chance or having a bit of mercy on her, he captured her bishop. Pops never let her win. She had to earn it. He sent her one of his long, searching looks over the top of his glasses. "And you're a smart girl."

Her lower lip quivered. She bit it. Hard. She *was* smart. Didn't everyone always say so? She was smart and nice and polite. And she had such a pretty face.

Which was what people said to fat girls.

She really, really wanted another cookie.

Breanne jumped up and stepped away from the table. "I guess maybe I do forfeit this game," she said, hating that she couldn't even think straight just because her dad was coming to get her.

But she never knew how to act around him. What he wanted from her.

Crossing her arms, she rolled her eyes. Except, deep down, she did know what he wanted. For her to disappear.

To get out of his life forever. To never have been born in the first place.

Too bad for him, none of those things were possible.

He'd have to settle for waiting until she turned eighteen so he wouldn't have to spend time with her anymore.

"Tell you what," Pops said, using the fake, cheerful tone he always used when he was trying to make her feel better about something. "How about I move the board to a safe spot? We can finish the next time you come over."

"Okay," she mumbled, feeling silly and sick from nerves and that last cookie. "I guess I'll go wait on the porch."

Pops looked as if he wanted to say something else, but just nodded and held out his arms.

She practically jumped into them, felt like a baby as she held on tight. She rested her head on Pops's shoulder—easy enough to do as she was almost his height.

She wasn't tall like her mom or skinny like Aunt Fay. She was short and round with thighs that rubbed together when she walked and a belly that jiggled when she ran.

She resembled Santa Claus more than anyone she was actually related to.

But for a moment, being hugged by Pops, it didn't matter that she was the slowest person on her soccer team or that she hadn't been able to fit into her jeans yesterday morning. When Pops gave you one of his hard, long hugs, you knew you were loved no matter what.

"We can finish our game tomorrow," she told him, her face pressed into his chest, her words muffled.

He gave her forehead a smacking kiss before letting her go. "Don't you worry about that. You just enjoy spending time with your father and grandparents."

She didn't want to enjoy her time with them. She wanted the night to be over with already and it hadn't even started yet.

Out on the porch, she sat on the top step with her back against the rail, her legs straight. Sliding her bag over to her, she unzipped it and pulled out her book, but when she realized she'd read the same page three times and couldn't remember anything about it, she slammed it shut. Usually she had no problem losing herself in a book no matter what was going on around her. Until today.

And it was all her dad's fault.

A bunch of kids she recognized from the school bus yelled and called to each other as they rode their bikes past Pops's house.

Bree could be riding bikes with her own friend right now. Cailley had invited her to hang out at her house this afternoon but she hadn't asked until after Bree had mentioned her dad was picking her up at three-thirty.

Bree picked at a paint chip on the rail with her thumbnail. All her classmates—and even some of her teachers—wanted to meet him. They were probably only nice to her because they thought she'd introduce them or get him to sign a stupid hockey puck or something. They all thought he was cool, just because he played a professional sport. They didn't know what he was really like.

Come to think of it, Bree realized with a frown as she brushed the paint chips off her pants, neither did she.

Oh, he called her once a week—every Sunday night at nine, even though her mom had told him like a million times it was too late for long phone conversations.

That's probably why he did it. Because he knew Bree wouldn't be able to talk long.

And he sent these expensive, totally lame presents on her birthday and holidays. When he was in town, he did the whole Dad Thing of pretending he wanted to spend time with her when all they ever did was hang out at Grandpa Carl and Grandma Gerry's house.

But it was better than when she used to fly out to Seattle. Her grandparents or Aunt Fay would go with her, saving her from being bored to death waiting for her dad to be done working. He never was. There were always games, practices and training, interviews and photo shoots for ads and commercials to be taped.

The worst times were when his last girlfriend had insisted Bree needed to spend more time with them. As if they were a real family or something.

She had the only family she needed right here in Shady Grove, thank you very much.

Gretchen was nice enough, and pretty as a movie star. But if she'd been hoping to get on Neil's good side by being nice to his kid, she shouldn't have wasted her time. They broke up after a whole three months of being together.

A fancy red sports car slowed on the road then signaled that it was turning into the driveway. Bree's heart pounded. He was here.

She yanked open the book and held it so close to her face, the words were blurred. From the corner of her eye, she watched him get out of the car. The girls in her class all thought he was superhot, which was gross. Besides, it wasn't as if he was Channing Tatum or something. He was just her dad.

"Hi," he said as he approached, watching her warily. He did that a lot. Watched her as though she was some wild animal and he wasn't sure if she was dangerous or not. Or how close he wanted to get. He stopped at the bottom of the steps and frowned. "You cut your hair."

She touched the top of her head then curled her fingers into her palm. One of the actresses on Bree's favorite TV show had short hair. It was all sleek and shiny with sharp edges that accentuated the actress's eyes and long neck. Too bad the same style on Bree, with her round face and stupid lumpy body, made her look like a boy. She wished she'd never gotten it cut.

She wished she had another cookie.

"I wanted something different," she said, proud she sounded like her mom. Strong and confident instead of how she usually felt, scared and alone and ashamed of who she was, of how she looked.

Her dad nodded slowly, looking as if he thought her hair was so disgusting, he could throw up at any minute. "It's…different, all right."

Tears stung Bree's eyes but she blinked them back. She wasn't a baby anymore. And she'd promised herself she'd no longer cry over things that didn't matter. Over people who didn't matter.

"You're late." She tried to glare at him, to hold on to his gaze but her face was hot and her stomach felt funny so she stared at the book once again.

"Am I?" He sounded confused, as if he couldn't tell time. Or maybe he thought she wouldn't mind waiting forever for him to show up, that time itself should stop because he'd had better things to do than be there when he'd said he would. "I got hung up at the ice rink."

She looked up to find him standing over her, blocking the sun. She waited for him to say he was sorry he'd kept her waiting but instead he watched her in that way that made her want to yell at him to stop. To apologize for not being the type of kid he wanted.

"You ready to go?" he asked.

Did she have a choice? She stood and he stepped onto a lower stair.

"I'm all sweaty," he said. "You probably don't want to get too close to me."

She didn't, she assured herself, even as her throat grew tight. She didn't want to be anywhere near him. She was antsy and mad and felt as though she couldn't breathe, like if she wasn't careful, she'd open her mouth and start screaming at him.

And she'd never stop.

"I'm going to tell Pops I'm leaving," she mumbled, and even though she'd already told her great-grandpa goodbye, she headed back inside.

She needed one more hug.

THE DOOR SLAMMED SHUT.

Neil rolled his head from side to side. He had no idea what he'd done or said, but some way, somehow, he'd messed up. Bree was pissed at him, had looked at him the same way Maddie had.

As if she'd wish he'd drop dead at her feet if only so she could kick his body a few times.

He watched the door but it didn't open. He shifted. Climbed onto the porch and looked through the door's window to see Bree hugging Big Leo, Maddie's grandfather.

Neil frowned. Maybe *hugging* wasn't the right word. More like she was strangling the old guy, holding on to Pops as if she didn't want to let go.

As if she didn't want to go with her father.

Before he realized what he was doing, Neil knocked twice on the door then pushed it open far enough to stick his head inside. Hoped like hell Big Leo—who, at five feet two inches, had earned his nickname when Maddie's brother was named after him—didn't just chop it off at the shoulders.

"Mr. Montesano," Neil said with a nod.

Big Leo squeezed Bree then stepped back. But he kept a hand on his great-granddaughter's shoulder. "Neil."

"You ready?" Neil asked Bree.

She glanced up at Pops, who gave her a reassuring grin. Her answering smile was small and just this side of brave.

"Go on, now," Big Leo said softly, giving her a little nudge toward Neil.

One that barely moved her. What'd she do, nail her flip-flops to the floor? And why the hell did his daughter have to be nudged anyway? Used to be, Bree would race over to him the moment she saw him, her face lit with pure joy and a reverence that'd made him nervous.

Because he didn't deserve that sort of worship. Knew he couldn't live up to it.

Looked as if Bree finally figured those things out, too.

Bree sighed. Loudly. He got the picture. She didn't want to go with him, thought he was a loser. She didn't need to beat him over the head with it.

"I guess I'm ready." She sent her great-grandfather one more pleading look. "You'll pick me up in the morning, right?"

"First thing."

"I thought you'd spend the day at Carl and Gerry's," Neil said. His adoptive parents adored Bree.

"She has soccer practice," Big Leo said, as if Neil should already know that.

He was probably right.

Besides, Neil knew when he was in a battle he couldn't win. And refusing to participate in a fight was a hell of a lot better than losing one.

"We'll see you in the morning, then," he said, holding the door open.

Bree brushed past him without so much as a glance his way. He let the door shut behind him and caught up with her at the bottom of the porch steps.

He went ahead, opened her car door, glad he'd given

the boys at the rink the bags of candy, and waited for her to catch up. And waited. And waited.

If she walked any slower, she'd be moving back in time.

He hated that haircut. It was too short. He preferred it the way it'd been before, the dark strands long and loose to her shoulders. And what was with those clothes? Her pink sweatpants were snug, the bottoms dirty and frayed from dragging on the ground, her T-shirt huge, the hem reaching her midthigh.

He hoped like hell Maddie didn't let his daughter dress like that for school.

Bree stopped a foot away from him, looking so morose and resigned to her fate, he almost told her to forget the whole thing. That she could just stay with Big Leo.

But it was past time she learned she didn't always get what she wanted.

"We're going to your grandparents' house for dinner, maybe watch a movie," he told her, "not your execution by firing squad."

"I know," she said and, if he wasn't mistaken, there was a silent "duh" there at the end. She looked pretty damn regal, too, as she spoke. Shades of her mother again.

After she was in her seat and all buckled up for safety—which took her twice as long as it should have—her bag on her lap, he shut the door and went around to the driver's side. He backed out of the driveway. Glanced at her before heading down the street.

He sucked at this, didn't know how to deal with his daughter. What to do or say. Had no clue how to have a conversation with this child he'd helped create. He didn't understand her. Couldn't see even the slightest piece of himself in her, other than the color of her eyes. She was bright and sensitive. A straight-A student who always had her nose in a book while he'd barely made passing grades and couldn't remember the last time he read something that wasn't the newspaper or playbook.

"You have soccer practice tomorrow, huh?" he asked as he pulled up to a stop sign.

"Pops just told you that," she said.

Right. Neil cleared his throat. "How often does your team practice?"

She slouched in her seat. "Every day except Sundays."

"How'd today's practice go?"

"Fine."

"What position do you play?" He should probably already know that, but this was her first year playing soccer and he'd been busy winning the Stanley Cup and trying to get his sister's life in order.

"Left midfielder."

"That's a good position." He pulled ahead and signaled to take the on-ramp leading to the highway out of town. "Has your coach picked the starting lineup?" When she didn't answer he glanced over. "Bree?"

She shrugged.

"You don't know?" he asked. "Or he hasn't picked?"

She gave another one of those mournful sighs, as if completely put out by his interest in her, in what she was doing. "He says he'll let us know before our first game."

He waited, wanting her to fill in the silence. Wanting her to take a turn in this conversation, to ask him some questions or tell him a bit about herself and her life without him having to pull it out of her.

Wanting her to take some of the slack off of him.

No such luck.

"When's your first game?"

"Next Saturday," she mumbled. He felt, more than saw, her look at him. Watching him. Sensed her having some internal debate. "But we have a scrimmage this Saturday. You could come. If you want to."

His hands tightened on the steering wheel. "I would like to…." And he sounded as enthusiastic as if he was gearing up to have his eye poked out with a dull spoon. "Really. But I'm flying out Saturday morning."

"Oh."

"Maybe Grandpa Carl can record it, like he did that softball game last year."

"Maybe." There were no tears, no anger that he wouldn't be able to see her play.

He was busy, he assured himself. He had to get back to Seattle and start getting ready for next season. Winning the Cup was only the beginning. He wanted that rush again, that sense of fulfillment of having made one of his life-long goals a reality.

He had a job to do. One that provided her with the things he'd never had growing up. She'd never want for anything, would never have to wear someone else's clothes or go to bed hungry.

So why the hell did he still feel so guilty?

Bree stared out the window. He might not know much about preteen girls but he knew enough about females in general to know she didn't want to talk to him.

He turned on the radio. And kept his mouth shut for the rest of the drive.

CHAPTER FIVE

"You," MADDIE SPAT, her voice quivering with what she considered the perfect mix of righteous indignation and all-out fury, "are a dead man."

As entrances went, it was a good one. Dramatic and emphatic with just enough fury to get her point across. Definitely one of her better moments.

Or, at least, it would have been if the door she'd slapped open hadn't hit the doorstop with a dull thud and swung back at her. She leaped to the side to save herself from a broken nose.

Okay, maybe there had been a tad too much of that fury. Something to keep in mind the next time she had a good mad on.

But that wasn't the worst part. Oh, no. The absolute suckiest thing was that the object of her anger—anger she was extremely justified in having, by the way—didn't quake in fear, cry remorse or beg forgiveness. No. Her brother James raised his eyebrows, glanced from her to the door then pointed to the cell phone at his ear and went back to whatever inane conversation he was having.

At her mother's kitchen table, her brother Leo continued playing a handheld video game as if Maddie wasn't even there.

That was it? This complete…nonreaction was all she got? She growled and opened the door just so she could slam it shut again. Neither of them so much as blinked.

The men in her life were nothing if not uncooperative.

"You're lucky Mom's out in the garden. She finds out you came in here slamming doors and making idle threats," Leo said, his thumbs moving over the buttons in a blur, his attention still firmly on the toy's screen, "and you'll be the dead one."

"Please." Maddie sniffed. "I don't make idle threats. And unlike you, I'm an adult who is no longer afraid of my mommy." Which was such a blatant lie, she was surprised the floor didn't open up so she could fall into the burning fires of hell.

James ended his call and immediately began typing into his phone.

He and his handy-dandy BlackBerry kept Montesano Construction running smoothly. Her brother had a knack for organization and schedules she found both utterly fascinating and terrifying.

And if he kept ignoring her, she just might take his phone and shove it down the garbage disposal.

Maddie tapped the toe of her work boot against her mother's tile floor. She had things to do. Places to be and all that.

Another lie. Jeez, she was really racking them up this afternoon.

She sighed. Loudly. James turned his back to her and kept right on pressing buttons.

Crossing her arms, she glared at the back of his head, hoping to set his hair on fire with the force of her thoughts. Unfortunately, his dark strands—in desperate need of a trim—remained blaze-free. It was a sad, sad day when she couldn't even muster up a tendril of smoke.

Maddie dropped her arms and stormed over to the sink, filled a glass with water and drank it while staring out the window at her own house.

Just because she lived across the street from her parents didn't mean she wasn't her own person, she assured herself for what had to be the billionth time since she'd bought her house eight years ago. Nor did it mean she couldn't take care of herself and her daughter without help.

Even if she was grateful to have that help so close by.

"When a person is on the phone," James said, his tone so superior and lecturing she had no doubt he was talking to her, "it's considered rude to interrupt."

"I have to interrupt because you're always on your phone. Talking or texting or checking your schedule or the weather. Honestly, you are way too reliant on that thing. The first step in getting rid of an unhealthy addiction is to admit you have a problem."

"I sure wish I could quit *yew*," he told his phone in his best *Brokeback Mountain* drawl.

"You sleep with it, don't you?" Leo piped up from the table. "I bet you put it on the pillow next to you, tuck the sheets up around it. Maybe whisper sweet nothings to it while you drift off to sleep…"

"What happens between a grown man and his consenting smartphone is nobody else's business," James said.

Maddie's lips twitched but there was no way she'd let a smile slip out. Her older brothers were, and always had been, the bane of her existence. They were bossy, arrogant and a collective pain in her ass.

She'd disown all three if she wasn't so crazy about them.

"Now," James said, "what's this about me being a dead man?"

"Isn't it obvious?" Leo said. "She's pissed and somehow it's all your fault as you're lower than a slug, in cahoots with the devil himself—"

"Whoa, whoa." Maddie held her hand up. "I would

never, ever say *cahoots*. What are you?" she asked Leo. "Seventy?"

He grinned and leaned back in his chair, all dark good looks and charming grin. "Old enough to know twenty-eight is way past the appropriate age for temper tantrums."

She bristled so hard, the hair on her arms stood on end. On second thought, she could do without a brother. It wasn't as if she didn't have a couple to spare.

"Tantrum?" she repeated, knowing she sounded shrill and yes, damn it, like a two-year-old pitching a fit compared to Leo's teasing tone. But that's what her brothers did. They brought out the worst in her.

She slapped her palms onto the table and leaned forward. "I'll show you a tantrum, you son of a—"

"Let's leave Mom out of this, shall we? I get the point."

"Wish I could say the same," James said to Maddie. "What's got your panties all twisted now?"

She straightened. "You took my crew from me today."

"I needed them at the Simpson job. And they're not your crew. They're employees of Montesano Construction."

"And one of Montesano Construction's jobs is renovating Bradford House. Thanks to you, I'm now two days behind schedule."

"We all have our problems. Mine are numerous and include Peg Simpson changing her mind about the dining room floor—again—the painters being three days late and the distributors sending the wrong bathroom tiles. Leaving me stuck still working a job that should've been done two weeks ago." He crossed his arms. "I'm keeping them for the rest of the week."

She mimicked his stance. Tried not to think about how they resembled each other with their olive skin, dark hair and eyes. Or how much she adored him with his anal tendencies and calm demeanor.

"Don't expect me to feel sorry for you." Although, truth be told, she did. Peg Simpson was a nightmare in three-inch stilettos, bright pink lipstick and jeans tight enough to cause damage to her internal organs. "At least give me Heath back. Or Art."

"Dad needs Heath at the Morgans' and Art's working with Eddie on the Simpsons' kitchen cabinets. You can have Rob."

"Is Eddie here?" she asked of her other brother, looking around as if he was hiding under the table or something.

"He went to pick up Max from the sitter's." James wagged his phone at her. "And don't even think about talking him into giving you Art. He needs help finishing up those cabinets."

"I had no intention of talking Eddie into anything," she said primly. "It's not my fault my favorite brother agrees with me in most situations."

"Don't worry, Jimmy boy," Leo called, frowning at the video game. "You're still my favorite brother."

James stared at him blandly. "That means…surprisingly little."

"Don't mention it."

"I'm surrounded by boneheads," Maddie murmured.

"Look," James told her, "I know it's a pain in the ass and you have a lot of work to do on the bed-and-breakfast, but this is how it has to be. And I promise, as soon as I'm done at the Simpsons', I'll put in at least a week with you. Deal?"

She dropped her arms. "What choice do I have?"

He pretended to think that over. "None?"

"That's what I thought. In that case…sure. It's a deal." Besides, if James said he'd help her out, he would. He never broke a promise.

The door opened and their mother came in. "Madelyn," she said with a smile, a straw hat on her head, a basket of herbs and green onions on her arm. "This is a pleasant surprise."

Rose gave Maddie a one-armed hug. Could Maddie really be blamed if she held on a moment too long? She'd had a really crappy day so far and some days, a girl just needed her mom.

Even if that girl was a mother herself.

When they stepped apart, Rose studied Maddie's face but only said, "Leo? Did you stop at the store like I asked?"

"Have I ever let you down?"

She removed her hat and ran a hand through her chin-length hair, the dark color now thanks to her hairstylist instead of nature. "Shall I start a list?"

"Ouch," he said cheerfully.

"Bagged salad?" Rose asked as she pulled items out of the cloth grocery bags on the counter. Her sigh was a pure work of art, one Maddie hoped to emulate someday. "Have I taught you nothing? You should've gone to Pineview Market. They have the best produce."

"I did go to Pineview." Leo walked over to stand between his mom and his sister. "What's the problem? You open the bag, add some dressing, toss it a few times and voilà! You're done." He shook his head sadly. "You really should be thanking me. I saved you both time and energy. You know, in case you wanted to throw together a batch of those peanut butter brownies the guys at the station all love."

Maddie put a container of feta cheese into the refrigerator. "Wow. Subtlety, thy name sure ain't Leo Montesano."

Subtlety has never been one of your strengths.

She slammed the door shut harder than necessary. Hated that after all these hours of trying to forget Neil was in town, his voice still lingered in her head. Hated even more that she hadn't been able to hide her reaction when he'd touched her.

Stupid hormones.

"I'm sorry," Rose said, neatly folding the bags and placing them back into the bottom drawer, "but I already promised your father I'd teach him that new computer program tonight."

Maddie turned to find Leo sending her a pleading look. "Uh-uh. Not going to happen. Make your own brownies."

"Don't do it for *me*," he said. "Do it for the guys who serve this town so honorably. So selflessly. They give their time and risk their lives with little pay and even less gratitude, all for the people of—"

"Okay, okay. I'll do it." She turned to her mother, who'd started humming softly along with Leo's words. "'The Battle Hymn of the Republic'?"

"Such a grand and heartfelt speech deserves a bit of background music."

"You'd better make two batches," Leo told Maddie. "Some of the guys are real pigs."

Maddie frowned at her mother. "This is all your fault. You had three boys running around but was it enough for you? No," she continued when Rose opened her mouth. "It wasn't. You had to try for a girl one more time. Did you even consider the trauma they'd inflict upon me?"

"You survived," Rose said, shoving plates at Leo so he could set the table. "And grew up strong, independent—"

"And able to kick any poor sap's ass," Leo added as he headed into the dining room.

"Not quite what I was going to say." Rose shrugged. "But overall, an apt description."

"I'm sending you the bills for my therapy sessions," Maddie muttered as she checked her phone. Nothing. She slid it back into her pocket.

Rose sent her a knowing look. "Honey, stop worrying. She's fine."

"Stop reading my mind. It freaks me out." She leaned against the counter and crossed her feet at the ankles. "So obviously you're aware that Bree is spending the night at the Pettits'?"

"I saw Big Leo while I was in the garden and he told me."

"Did he tell you that she didn't want to go? That when I told her Neil was in town and wanted her to spend the night, she asked me if she could stay home?"

More like begged Maddie to let her stay home. Like she had back in April when Neil had wanted Bree to fly out to Seattle for a few days. Unlike then, this time Maddie hadn't given in.

"I made her go," she said softly, running her thumbnail along the rounded edge of the quartz counter. "Maybe I shouldn't have."

"Neil is her father. He has every right to want his daughter to spend the evening with him."

"He hasn't seen her in six months. Six. Months. I'd say any rights he had are null and void now."

At the sink, Rose rinsed off the onions. "I'm not sure a judge would agree."

Leave it to her mother to bring logic into the conversation.

Maddie curled her fingers into her palms, her nails digging into her skin. Sure, technically, *legally*, Neil had partial custody of Bree and was entitled to have her every other Christmas, one month in the summer and one week four times a year. But he'd rarely taken advantage of the agreement they'd made when Maddie was still pregnant.

"I just want to protect her from getting hurt," she said.

"Do you really believe Neil would hurt that child?"

"Not purposely," she admitted grudgingly. Neil wasn't a monster, after all. Just a rat bastard. "But that won't make it any less painful for Bree."

"Seems to me, both you and Breanne can learn something from this situation."

"Thanks, but I've had enough of those pesky life lessons."

"Sorry, not how it works." Rose shook water from the onions and set them on the counter then dried her hands. "This is an opportunity for Breanne to learn that loving someone doesn't necessarily mean they always meet your expectations."

Wasn't that the truth?

"And you're learning one of the toughest lessons there is for a parent," her mom continued as she cupped Maddie's face in both hands, her palms damp, her skin smelling of dirt. "We can't always protect our children from pain. No matter how much we want to."

FAY HADN'T COME down for dinner.

For what must have been the hundredth time since he'd sat down at the glossy dining room table with his family, Neil glanced up. But his sister didn't suddenly materialize, smiling and happy and whole, in the doorway.

She'd been fine at lunch, he reminded himself as he sipped his water. His mouth tightened. Maybe *fine* was a slight exaggeration. More like she'd been...coping. She may be unsteady on her feet, but at least she was still standing. He'd take comfort in that. And make sure she stayed that way.

"Isn't that nice, Neil?"

He blinked at Gerry. "Yeah. It's great."

"You have no idea what we're talking about, do you?"

Not a clue. But if the conversation he'd zoned out was

anything close to what he'd already endured since sitting down to dinner with Carl, Gerry, Bree and his nephews, it probably centered around Carl's golf game, local gossip or Elijah's favorite TV show.

At Gerry's arch look, Neil shifted, realized that he was squirming like a guilty ten-year-old and stilled. "Sorry."

She set her fork onto her plate with a soft clang. "We were discussing Bree's award."

"Award?"

"I came in third," Bree said, her hands in her lap. "It's not like I won or anything."

Gerry smiled at her granddaughter. "Still, it's a huge honor and we're very proud of you."

"What award?" Neil asked.

"To Breanne," Carl said, raising his water glass.

Elijah climbed onto his knees and held up his plastic cup. "To Bree!"

Glasses clinked against each other. Elijah hit Bree's glass so hard, milk sloshed over the side.

"What award?" Neil repeated. Loudly.

Loud enough that everyone went quiet. Even Elijah stopped talking and Neil was starting to wonder if that was even possible without knocking the kid out.

"You didn't tell your dad about the contest?" Gerry asked Bree.

Across from him, Bree lifted a shoulder. "I guess I forgot."

He waited but she stared at her plate. It was like pulling teeth with his own kid. Worse, he was in the spotlight, all of his shortcomings as a father on display for his family.

"Why don't you tell me now?" he asked.

"It's no big deal." She rubbed at a spot of gravy on the tablecloth. "My English teacher sent in one of my short stories to a contest in Pittsburgh and it got third place."

He'd known nothing about it. Hadn't even known she wrote short stories.

"Good job." He managed to squeeze the words out through the tightness in his throat, feeling as if they were wrestling with what he really wanted to say.

Why didn't you tell me?

"Can I have another roll?" Elijah asked, practically landing in Bree's lap as he reached across her for the basket of homemade rolls.

Next to Neil, Mitchell kicked his feet against the wooden high chair. *Thump. Thump. Thump.*

"Dinner was, as always," Carl told Gerry, "excellent."

It was. She'd made roast beef, mashed potatoes and green beans with bacon and pearl onions. Neil's favorites. He could afford the fanciest meals, ate out at the best restaurants and still, there was nothing like Gerry's cooking. He was probably biased due to the fact that, up until the time Carl and Gerry took him in, Neil's meals had come out of a box, a can or a drive-through.

"Oh, honey," Gerry said to Bree with a tsking sound Neil had heard often growing up. "Are you sure you want another helping of mashed potatoes? Oftentimes we think we're still hungry but that's only because it takes our brains twenty minutes to get the message that our bodies are really full."

Bree froze, a spoonful of potatoes hovering over her plate. She blushed, color creeping from her neck all the way to her hairline. Then she looked at him but he had no idea what she wanted. Permission to eat more? His opinion?

Because his opinion was that she needed to cut back on her carbs. Maybe incorporate more cardio into her exercise routine. She'd always been on the chubby side, but she was noticeably heavier than when he'd last seen her.

"If you're still hungry," he said, "you could have more salad. Or green beans."

She slowly put the spoon back into the serving bowl and sank back into her chair. Then she shot him an accusatory glare before averting her gaze to her plate.

What the hell had he done now? He'd given her a good compromise, hadn't he?

He couldn't win with his daughter.

"She's a growing girl," Carl said, taking matters into his own hands by plopping a small amount of potatoes onto Bree's plate. "I'm sure she knows when she's full and if she's hungry for potatoes or salad."

She sent her grandfather a grateful look. But she didn't eat any more, only dragged the tines of her fork through the food a few times.

"May I be excused?" she asked, setting her fork down.

"Of course," Gerry said quickly, seemingly relieved none of those potatoes had passed Bree's lips.

Elijah leaped to his feet: "Me, too, me, too!" He bounced on his toes. The kid was nonstop energy. If his feet weren't moving, his mouth was. "Come on, Bree, let's go outside and play."

"Clear your place first," Gerry called as Elijah ran toward the door.

He kept right on going. Then again, he may not have heard her, seeing as how he was yelling like Mel Gibson's character in *Braveheart*. All that was missing were the bad Scottish accent and a rousing cry of "Freedom!"

"I'll get it," Bree said, taking Elijah's still-full plate along with her own as her cousin slammed the kitchen door shut behind him.

She'd no sooner disappeared into the kitchen when Mitchell let out a howl of displeasure that had Neil's teeth aching. No wonder Fay preferred to spend so much of her time in bed.

Gerry lifted the baby from his high chair. His little body was rigid, his head back, his cheeks streaked with tears, his face turning an interesting shade of magenta. Might help if he stopped screaming long enough to take a breath.

Bree came back into the room and, as if a switch had been flipped, the wailing stopped.

Pretty neat trick, that.

"You want to come outside?" Bree asked Mitchell, as if the baby understood her. Could answer her.

Mitchell babbled and bounced up and down. Guess that was a yes.

She took the baby and he gazed at her adoringly.

An odd pang of longing settled in Neil's chest. Bree used to look at him like that, as if he hung the stars just so she could see them shine.

He missed it.

Worse, he hadn't even appreciated it at the time. He'd actually resented his daughter's clinginess. Had wished she'd give him breathing space instead of always demanding so much of his time and attention. Her devotion had made him feel guilty, as if he didn't do enough for her. As if he was as bad a father as his old man had been.

But he wasn't, Neil assured himself as he watched Bree carry Mitchell outside. He hadn't abandoned his child, hadn't left her to fend for herself in foster care. He busted his ass every day so he could give her the things he'd never had.

Wasn't that enough?

"Those boys adore Bree," Gerry said with a smile as she carried dishes into the kitchen. Neil grabbed a couple of serving bowls and followed her. "I'm so glad Maddie let her come over tonight. The last few times we've called about having Breanne spend the night, Maddie has made excuses—"

"They weren't excuses," Carl said, carrying in the tray of leftover roast beef. "And it was one time. Bree already had plans with her friends," he told Neil. "She's growing up and would rather hang out with kids her own age instead of her old grandparents."

Gerry set her hands on her hips. "Who, exactly, are you calling old?"

"Only myself," Carl assured her. Then he kissed her cheek. "Since Neil's here to help clean up, I'll just go out and water the garden."

Through the window over the sink, Neil watched Bree help Mitchell walk around the yard. What was Maddie doing, keeping his daughter away from his family? She'd always been more than fair about letting Carl and Gerry be a part of Bree's life before. What had changed?

"I'll talk to Maddie," he said. "About not letting Bree spend the night."

He already dreaded it.

Gerry loaded plates into the dishwasher. "All of this would be so much easier if you played for a team on this coast."

"The Knights have been good to me." He was team captain, had made a name for himself in Seattle. And he fully expected them to renew his contract when it came up for negotiation next year. He started his career as a Knight and he'd finish his career as one.

"I'm thrilled you won the Cup with them, but you've been away for so long and Bree's growing up so fast. Before you know it, she'll be a teenager and then she'll be off to college." Laying the dishcloth on the sink, Gerry faced him. "You've already missed so much of her life. I'm afraid you'll regret it."

He wouldn't. Couldn't. If he did, it'd mean every decision he'd made, every choice as a father, had been wrong.

"My relationship with Bree is fine." It had to be. He didn't know how to change it. How to be any different.

"Your daughter needs you," Gerry said, her words quiet and reproachful.

Guilt was like a knife twisting in his gut, sharp and ruthless. "I'm right here."

"For how long? A few days? That's not enough. She deserves more. You both do."

"She seems fine to me." She had Maddie and the Montesanos and his parents and sister.

She didn't need him. She'd never needed him.

"You must have noticed how much weight she's put on," Gerry said in a whisper, as if afraid someone would overhear. "All she does is read and watch TV."

"She plays soccer."

"Only because Madelyn told her she needed to do something active this summer. I swear, if Breanne wasn't pushed to move, she'd sit all day lost in some book. It's not healthy for her to be so heavy and it's not good for a young girl's self-esteem, either."

"What do you want me to do?" he asked, unable to keep the frustration from his voice. He didn't know what his daughter needed from him. "Send her to one of those fat camps?"

Gerry looked ready to hit him over the head with the pot she was scrubbing. "Of course not. I just think that with some positive attention from you, we can nip this problem in the bud."

If something was wrong, Gerry charged in to fix it. She never put up with excuses or accepted anything less than pure victory.

The door opened and Elijah raced in, his skinny legs

poking out from under a long pair of shorts, Bree following with Mitchell in her arms. Elijah opened the freezer door and pulled out a box of ice cream sandwiches, handing one to his brother and then Bree.

Bree put Mitchell on his feet then unwrapped his ice cream for him. When she tugged at the paper on hers, Gerry clapped her hands.

"Wouldn't you rather have fresh fruit?" she asked, her tone overly cheerful. "How about some strawberries? I picked some up at the store this afternoon."

Neil raised his eyebrows. Strawberries or ice cream? He knew which one he'd pick. But what could he say? Gerry meant well. Besides, he didn't want to take sides, not against the woman who'd taken him in, loved him and given him a future.

Bree held her treat out to Gerry. "I'm not very hungry."

Smiling, Gerry hugged Bree. "That's a good girl."

"I don't feel well." Bree stepped out of her grandmother's embrace, kept her eyes on the floor. "I want to go home."

"Oh, but you and your daddy were going to have so much fun tonight," Gerry said with such disappointment, you'd think his kid had just admitted she wanted to be a serial killer when she grew up. "He's been looking forward to seeing you. Here, let me see if you have a fever."

Before the back of Gerry's hand could make contact with Bree's forehead, Bree jerked back. "I want to go home," she repeated, as stubborn as her mother, as quietly insistent as him when he wanted something.

"You can stay here," he said, his voice rough when he'd meant to sound comforting but, damn it, he was only in town for two days. He wanted to spend some time with her. "We'll get you set up on the couch in the TV room. I'm sure Grandma Gerry has some ginger ale or saltines—"

"Of course I do," Gerry said, already heading to the

walk-in pantry. The way she liked to stock up at the warehouse store, she probably had enough crackers in there to keep each family in town alive in case of Armageddon.

"See?" he asked Bree, who'd yet to look at him. He knelt in front of her and checked her complexion—and hoped like hell she didn't throw up. "Why don't you go upstairs, get your pajamas on while I find us a movie to watch?"

"I don't want to stay here." Her voice broke. She raised her head and his stomach cramped to see tears in her eyes. It killed him when she cried. "I want my mom."

He flinched. Her real meaning as clear as if she kicked him in the teeth then spit in his eye.

I don't want you.

He exhaled heavily and straightened. "Then I guess I'd better take you home."

CHAPTER SIX

MADDIE LIFTED HER HEAD when headlights illuminated her darkening kitchen. They were here. Thank God. She closed her laptop, then stood and padded across her kitchen to the back door, the wood floor cold under her bare feet. She no sooner opened the door when Bree came at her like a missile.

"Whoa," Maddie said, catching her balance as Bree wrapped her arms around Maddie's waist with enough force to make a python envious. "Hey, hey." She rubbed Bree's back. "What's the matter?"

Against Maddie's chest, Bree shook her head.

"You aren't sure?" Maddie asked, used to her daughter's head shakes, shrugs and I-don't-knows. "Or you couldn't possibly say?"

"She's not feeling well."

Maddie looked over Bree's head to find Neil filling the doorway, Bree's pink backpack small and incredibly girlie-looking in his hand. Wish she could say the same for the man holding the bag, but he was too big and broad to be considered either.

"I got that much from your phone call." The one he'd made fifteen minutes ago as she'd stepped out of the shower. He'd told her he was bringing Bree home. "You can just leave her bag on the table. Thanks," she added, in case he missed the hint that she didn't want him hanging around.

He stepped inside far enough to put the bag on the chair closest to him then turned around. But instead of taking off—his usual M.O. when things didn't go his way—he shut the door. Leaning against it, he crossed his arms, his expression set in a way that made it clear she'd need something more drastic than a snide hint to get him moving.

She brushed Bree's short hair from her forehead. "What hurts?"

Please, God, don't let it be strep throat again. When Bree had it last September, it'd been so bad, she'd cried herself to sleep. Maddie had cried right along with her.

Bree met Maddie's eyes briefly. Scratched her right eyebrow. "My stomach," she finally mumbled to a point somewhere over Maddie's left shoulder.

Her stomach. Uh-huh.

Maddie studied her daughter's face. Her cheeks were pink but she wasn't feverish. It wasn't the flu, food poisoning or a twenty-four-hour bug. No, her eyebrow scratching and gaze averting meant only one thing.

Bree was lying.

She sucked at it, though Maddie supposed she could give her daughter points for effort. And she *had* fooled Neil.

Then again, he didn't know Bree. Not as well as Maddie did.

"Stomachache, hmm?" Maddie asked, noting the mix of guilt and defiance on Bree's face as she nodded.

Maddie should call her on it. Have Bree apologize for lying to her father and making him bring her home. She should force her daughter to spend at least a few more hours with him, if not the entire night.

But Bree was looking at her as if she'd been sentenced to burn at the stake and Maddie was the only person in the entire world with a working hose.

Why did being a parent have to be so hard sometimes? Maddie knew what her own parents would have done. But it was different for them. They had each other to rely on, to lean on. When it came to their kids, they'd made every decision, good or bad, together. Despite the tall, brooding man taking up too much space in her kitchen, Maddie was on her own as a parent. All she could do was what she'd always done—trust her instincts.

And remember that Neil had been the one who'd left.

"Why don't you change into your pajamas and get in bed," she said to Bree. "I'll bring you some ginger ale in a few minutes."

If Bree's sigh of relief—one that ruffled Maddie's damp hair—didn't clue Neil to the fact that he'd been duped, the grateful hug she gave Maddie should have. Seriously, her kid was terrible at lying. Maddie just hoped she didn't get any better. At least not until they'd both survived Bree's teen years.

Bree walked toward the doorway separating the kitchen from the living room.

"Hey, now," Maddie called. "Didn't you forget something?"

Though her back was to Maddie, it didn't take a genius or some sort of supermom to know Bree was giving an impressive eye roll at being called on her bad manners.

Taking her sweet time, she faced Neil. "'Bye."

"Good night," he said in his low voice, his gaze intent on their daughter. "Feel better."

Maddie narrowed her eyes at his bland tone. Maybe Bree hadn't fooled him, after all.

"You're leaving town soon, right?" she asked, her words rushed and, to Maddie's mind, hopeful.

By the tightening of Neil's lips, he noticed that part, too. "Saturday. But I'll stop by to see you before I leave."

"You don't have to."

And that tone had been a little too bratty. Even if Maddie secretly thought that was what Neil deserved.

"Breanne," she said, using the stern tone she so rarely had to employ when dealing with her usually sweet-natured, even-tempered daughter. "Your dad wants to see you before he goes back to Seattle."

"It's okay if he doesn't. I mean, we can just say goodbye now." She met Neil's eyes, the look in hers daring him to fight her on this. To prove to her that he cared enough to fight her. "Then he won't have to worry about seeing me again."

But Neil, stubborn, stoic Neil, didn't even blink. The man was made of stone and completely clueless when it came to realizing what his daughter was doing. What she wanted from him.

"I'll be back to say goodbye properly," he stressed, closing the distance between him and Bree so she had to tilt her head back to maintain eye contact, "before I go back to Seattle."

"Whatever," Bree muttered before stomping out of the room.

A minute later, the door to her bedroom slammed shut.

Maddie pressed the heels of her hands against her temples. "If that was a preview of what the next seven years of my life are going to be like, I think I'd rather just skip ahead to her high school graduation." She dropped her hands. "Want to tell me what brought all of that on?"

He shoved his hands into his pockets. "Hormones?"

"Funny how men say that when it's usually something they've brought on themselves."

"She's pissed at me." He slid her an unreadable look. "Like mother, like daughter."

"Ha-ha. So glad to see all those years of getting hit upside the head with hockey sticks haven't ruined your witty sense of humor." She crossed to the door and opened it. "Well, whatever it is, I'm sure she'll be over it the next time you see her."

Maybe. Bree had never been the type to hold a grudge before, but then, she'd never been very mouthy before, either.

Because he hadn't moved—and she desperately wanted him to—she waved the door back and forth. "Look, I hate to be rude—"

"No, you don't," he said quietly. "You hate to be pushed into a corner, coming in second place and being told what to do. But you don't mind being rude. Not if you think the other person deserves it."

Damn him. How could he know her so well after all these years when she didn't know him at all? When she never had.

"You're right." Nerves may have been jumping in her stomach but her voice was steady. That, at least, was something to be thankful for. She shut the door then brushed past him.

"So, let's just get to it. What do you want?" she asked as she searched a bottom cupboard for ginger ale. Not finding any, she grabbed a cola and straightened. And caught him staring at her. After her shower she'd put on cotton shorts and a sweatshirt that fell off her shoulder. Now she wished she'd donned sweatpants, that her hair wasn't down, curling slightly as it dried. "Other than to check out my ass?"

He, of course, was unabashed. He wasn't charming, never had been easy with his smiles or laugh, but he'd always had that whole sexy, dangerous bad-boy vibe. He was…smoldering. Yeah, the man smoldered and you couldn't help but get burned a little by his heat. Those sharp eyes, that handsome face, the way he looked at a woman made her feel as if she was the center of his world. As if nothing mattered to him more than her next breath, her next word.

What bullshit.

"It's a fine ass," he said.

She lifted the can in a silent toast. "Right again."

Not that she bought the heat in his eyes, the interest. He was playing with her, much like he played hockey. Strategizing. Sizing her up, trying to find her weakness, to figure out how to get past her defenses. The man had affairs with models, actresses and pop stars. Did he really think she was so naive that she'd buy his lame attempt at a come-on? That she'd melt in a puddle at his feet?

Idiot.

He lightly touched the petals of the tulips she had in a vase on her table. For a moment, one stupid, weak moment, Maddie imagined his fingertips tracing her skin. Maybe he wasn't the only idiot in the room.

"Gerry mentioned that Bree hasn't been spending much time with them lately."

Maddie shrugged. "She's been busy."

"Are you sure that's all there is to it?"

In the act of reaching for a glass on the top shelf, Maddie froze and looked over at him. "What do you mean?"

Neil's gaze was hot on her bare legs. She set the glass on the counter with a sharp slap then pointed two fingers at her face. "Eyes up here, buddy."

When he dragged his gaze slowly up her body, as real and heated as a touch, she wished she'd kept her damn mouth shut.

"Are you keeping Bree away from my family as a way to get back at me?" he asked.

He used that calm, complacent tone just to bug her. Too bad it worked. "I can't believe you'd even ask me that."

Worse, she couldn't believe how much it hurt that he'd think that of her.

"If there's a problem between you and my family—"

"There's not." She tossed ice into the glass then opened the can and poured the soda. "Like I said, Bree's been busy. I'm sure she'll spend plenty of time with your parents over the summer. If that's all, I'm going to check on my daughter. You can see yourself out."

"Gerry's worried about Bree," he said, easily blocking her way. "About her weight."

Heat engulfed her but she pushed back the spike of temper. "Bree's fine. She's a preteen going through adolescence. Her body is changing and, as you mentioned, her hormones are spiking—"

"She's overweight." He glanced pointedly at the soda. "And giving her all that sugar isn't helping her."

Maddie's fingers tightened on the can, denting it. "You've got some nerve, I'll give you that. Coming here after not seeing your daughter for six months—"

"I told you—"

"Six. Months." She shook her head. "God, you are unbelievable. Bree is healthy and happy and that's all that matters. Once she hits puberty, she'll grow taller and that baby fat will melt away."

"I'm concerned about her," he said, sounding stiff and angry. Good. Why should she be the only one who was mad? "I just want what's best for her."

"What's best for her is to have a father who loves her for who she is." Her voice shook, her hands trembled and she set the soda and can down. "Not for what she looks like."

"That has nothing to do with it," he said through barely moving lips.

"You can't even say it, can you?" she asked quietly, her

heart breaking for her daughter. Knowing Bree was paying for Maddie's mistakes. "You can't even say you love her."

"Of course I do."

But he hadn't said the words. And Maddie had had enough.

"I want you to leave," she said, surprised she could push words out past the tightness in her throat.

He looked as if he wanted to say something but then just nodded. Walking away once again. "I'll stop by tomorrow to see how Bree's feeling."

"Don't bother," she told him as he stepped onto her porch. She followed him, held on to the doorjamb on both sides, her fingers gripping the wood so tightly, her hands ached.

He stopped, his back rigid, and slowly faced her. "I take care of my responsibilities, Maddie. You know that."

She did. God help her, it was part of the reason why she'd fallen so hard for him all those years ago. Why she'd done what she did.

"Bree doesn't want you to think of her as a responsibility. All she wants, all she's ever wanted, was for you to spend time with her. Pay attention to her. To want to be with her."

The same things Maddie had wanted from him. Like her daughter, she'd only wanted Neil to love her back, to say the words. But he wasn't capable of that depth of feeling. Something she'd found out too late.

She'd be damned if her daughter had the same fate.

"Stop pretending you're the father Bree needs," Maddie said, wishing her words had a snap to them, that she sounded confident and strong instead of defeated. "And go back to pretending we don't exist."

THE NEXT MORNING Neil forced himself to jog up the steps to Maddie's house instead of turning around, like he wanted, and heading back to Carl and Gerry's place. Or better yet, driving to the airport and grabbing the first westward flight he could get.

But there'd be no escaping Shady Grove. Not yet, anyway. He was there for the duration. He was there for his sister who, according to Gerry, never came out of her bedroom last night. Mostly, he was there for his daughter. Whether she or her mother liked it or not.

He knocked on the door. Birds chirped loudly, some cheerful song that set his teeth on edge. A chipmunk raced onto the sidewalk then rose onto its hind legs, its nose twitching. At the edge of the lawn, where the green blades sparkled with dew, two rabbits nibbled on grass.

It was like being in a freaking Disney movie. Next thing he knew, one of those birds would land on his shoulder and all the woodland creatures would break into a dance routine.

Cupping his hands, he peered through the glass of the door. The kitchen was dark. And empty. He knocked again, this time using the side of his fist. The rabbits startled then darted into the underbrush. But the birds kept right on chirping.

The rising sun broke through the shroud of fog, made it look as if God Himself was shining His holy light down on what Neil thought of as the Montesano Compound. Across the street, Rose and Frank Montesano's two-story brick home towered over Big Leo's place, a small cottage they'd built on the front corner of their property. From what Gerry said, Eddie Montesano and his son lived on this street as well.

The Montesanos always did like to stick close together.

The door opened. Maddie, a cup of coffee in her hand, blinked at him. Blinked again.

"Morning," he said, edging his foot forward to stop the door in case she decided to slam it in his face.

A distinct possibility, given the scowl she aimed at him.

"It's six-fifteen," she said.

"Yes."

"In the morning."

"I didn't wake you." It wasn't a question since she'd already made coffee and had on a pair of faded jeans and a black tank top.

He told himself he wasn't disappointed she no longer wore those tiny blue shorts from last night.

"That's not the… Oh, never mind." She exhaled heavily, which did some really interesting things to that tank top. "Why are you here?"

It wasn't easy for him to share his thoughts, to put everything he had on the line for others to use against him. But this, this was easy. Because it was right.

"I'm here for my daughter."

"Your daughter is sleeping. And is, as far as I know, unaware that you two had plans this morning."

"We don't. Have plans, that is. But I'd like to see her."

Maddie leaned against the doorframe. "Why?"

Damn it, she couldn't make this easy, could she? She wasn't about to let him in, not until she got what she wanted—for him to open up, to share what was on his mind. She'd always demanded too much from him. As if she'd had a right to his every thought, to know what he felt at any given time just because they'd been a couple. But they weren't together now, hadn't been in a long time. And he was getting mighty tired of always toeing that line she tossed out for him.

It didn't help his equilibrium that he hadn't been able to get her out his head, had even fantasized about her as he fell asleep. Her and those damn shorts, her tanned legs smooth and bare, her hair tumbling around her face.

Today was somehow worse. Her shirt accentuated the curve of her waist, clung to her breasts. Her neck was long, the muscles in her arms defined but still feminine. The strap of her bra—black, to match the shirt—slid down her arm. She ignored it, was way too busy glaring at him to slide it back into place.

It was all he could do not to slip his finger under the silk and do it himself.

Hell. He was losing his mind. Either that or he'd regressed. Right back to his eighteen-year-old self, the kid who'd been crazy for her. Who'd known, even then, that she had the power to bring him to his knees.

When all he'd ever wanted, all he'd needed, was to stand on his own two feet.

"I thought about what you said last night," he said.

Watching him over the rim of her cup, she sipped her coffee. "That's it? You supposedly had some big paternal epiphany and that's all you're going to tell me?"

He nodded once.

She straightened. "Sorry. Not good enough."

And, as he'd predicted, she made to shut the door on him. To shut him out, of her home and their daughter's life.

For a moment, he considered letting her. Just…walking away. But he couldn't. Bree was his daughter, too. His responsibility.

The door hit his foot and it took all he had not to kick it a few dozen times. He pushed it open, held the edge so she couldn't shut it. "What do you want from me, Maddie?"

"Right now," she said, her lips barely moving, "I just want you to let me close my own damn door. God, it is way too early in the morning for this."

But she didn't give in. Not Maddie. She turned and

put her back into it, trapping his foot between the door and frame.

"Shit," he muttered, wishing he had on steel-toed boots instead of sneakers. Was that a bone he just felt crack? Grimacing, he shoved, giving himself enough room to wiggle his foot free but not letting up so much that she won.

No way he'd let her win. Not today.

She grunted and yanked the door open so suddenly, he fell forward. "Fine," she said as he caught his balance. "You want to know what I want. How about some honesty."

"You want honesty?" he repeated.

"It'd be a nice change of pace."

He shut the door behind him with a quiet snick. See? He was still in complete control, of himself and the situation. "You were right."

She smirked. "Well, that's nothing new. It's also nothing I didn't already know."

Christ, but she was something. An arrogant, cocky smartass.

He shouldn't find it appealing. Shouldn't let his appreciation for the way she tackled challenges push him into giving her more than he could risk losing.

But this wasn't about Maddie. It was about Bree. And his daughter deserved for him to admit the truth.

"Last night," he said, choosing his words carefully, "I couldn't stop thinking about what you said, about Bree needing more from me. You were right."

"So now you're here, at the crack of dawn, to bond with her?"

"I want to spend the day with her."

Maddie raised her eyebrows. "And you wanted to get a jump start on that?"

He stood with his legs apart, his hands clasped behind his back. "I thought we'd go for a run."

She choked on her coffee, coughed to clear her throat. "You want to train with your eleven-year-old daughter? Oh…I get it," she said softly, her eyes flashing with enough heat to set him aflame. "This isn't about you having some crazy yen to spend quality time with Bree. You want to fix her." Maddie glanced at the doorway leading to the hall as if checking to make sure Bree hadn't magically appeared out of thin air. "All that talk about Gerry being worried was bull. It's you. You're embarrassed about her weight."

Not true.

Was it?

He gave a mental head shake. Didn't matter. He was doing this for Bree. She needed him.

"I'm concerned for her health," he said. "Childhood obesity is a real problem in this country and overweight kids are at risk for heart disease—" he ticked off items on his fingers "—high blood pressure and diabetes. Plus, teens with weight problems often have low self-esteem—"

"Well, telling her we think she's fat," Maddie whispered harshly, "should be great for her self-esteem."

"She needs to lose weight to be healthy. Did you know eighty percent of kids her age who are overweight become obese adults?"

"Someone spent last night on the internet."

"I read up on a few things," he said, sounding defensive. "And it convinced me that the sooner we tackle this problem, the better it'll be for Bree. It's important for girls her age to have a healthy self-image and to love their bodies."

Maddie set her cup down onto the table with a sharp crack. "And you think the way to accomplish that is to show up at the butt crack of dawn, drag her out of bed and force her to exercise?"

He saw where Bree got her dramatic streak. "It's a mile

or two, Maddie. Not the Boston Marathon. Or the Bataan Death March."

But Maddie, stubborn as always, shook her head as if amazed he'd be worried about their daughter's mental and physical health. "Just when I thought you couldn't stoop any lower, you prove me wrong."

"What the hell does that mean?"

"It means that Bree doesn't need a personal trainer. And she sure as hell doesn't need you. Go back to Seattle, Neil. Leave us alone."

A roaring filled his head, muted the hum of the air conditioner, amplified the sound of his own breathing. Before he knew his intention, he'd closed the distance between them, trapping her between the table and his body. He didn't touch her, though. Didn't trust himself, not when his emotions were roiling, anger building. "You're not keeping me from my daughter."

"You must've forgotten who you're dealing with." Looking him up and down with an expression that would have cut a weaker man off at the knees, she smiled thinly, a bring-it-on grin that promised he'd have one hell of a fight if he did. "You don't scare me, Neil, and I'm sure as hell not intimidated by the size of your ego, your checkbook or what you carry around between your legs."

She leaned closer, her eyes locked on his, her voice vibrating with rage, heat emanating off of her. "Bree is my world, my entire world. I'm the one who's been here, every day. Every. Single. Day. Taking care of her. Protecting her. Loving her. And I'll do whatever it takes to make sure nothing and no one ever hurts her. Are we clear on that?"

"Crystal."

"Good."

She tried to get past him, her smug expression sliding away when he blocked her escape.

"Now let me make something clear to *you*," he said, not letting any of his own bitterness coat his words. "I came here hoping you and I could work together and do what's best for Bree. I don't want to fight you. But if you try to keep me from my daughter, you and I will do battle." He edged closer until her scent filled his nostrils. "And I will win."

"Threats?" She snorted and tossed her head. "That's beneath you."

"Maybe you don't know me as well as you thought."

From her expression, that idea didn't sit too well. "I know that Saturday you'll get on a plane and fly back to your real life, the one you chose. That this time next week, you'll be too busy with your career and your skinny blonde models to remember you even have a daughter, let alone call her or want to see her."

"Wrong again," he told her and had the satisfaction of seeing her swallow visibly. "I'm not going back to Seattle. I'm staying in Shady Grove."

CHAPTER SEVEN

"For how long?" Maddie asked, not caring that she sounded scared and freaked out.

She *was* scared and freaked out.

"A few weeks. And I'd like to spend the majority of that time with my daughter."

"What about the commercial for the sports drink?"

He lifted a shoulder. "It'll have to wait."

Maddie's throat got tight. Her skin hot. Neil wasn't leaving Saturday.

Oh, God.

And he still hadn't backed up. He was too close, so close she couldn't even take a breath without inhaling his scent. She couldn't think. Damn it, she needed to be reasonable and rational. To rely on good sense. Instead, panic built inside of her, prodding her to make decisions based on her emotions. Her fears.

Just like when she'd been sixteen.

"I don't think that's a good idea," she said, her voice a croak.

He watched her steadily, all calm and confident. She wanted to shove him, push and push and push him until he showed some real emotion. To prove she wasn't the only one at a loss, fumbling between the past and the present.

"That's not what you said last night," he said.

"Last night I was just trying to…to…"

He raised his eyebrows, his blue eyes knowing. "To lay out my flaws?"

"Pretty much. I didn't really expect you to listen." Or that her words would get him to change his plans and stick around town longer. Not when they'd never mattered to him before.

Crap. What had she done?

More important, how could she get out of this? When backed into a corner, there was only thing to do. A full-fledged frontal assault.

"No," she said, firming her mouth and her resolve.

"No?"

"No, you can't spend time with my daughter. Not when all you want is to browbeat and nag her about her weight."

"It's not enough for you that I'm here, is it?" he asked, his voice a low rumble. "That I want to do what's right for Bree, that I'm trying to be a better father. No matter what I do, it's never enough." Edging closer, he set his hands on the table on either side of her, his forearms brushing her hips. "How long are you going to keep punishing me, Maddie?"

She flinched and prayed like mad he didn't notice. But this was Neil. Watchful, quiet, intense Neil. Of course he noticed.

"I'm not punishing you," she said, cursing the breathlessness that made it sound like a lie.

But it wasn't, she assured herself. She was protecting her daughter. Neil might not set out to hurt Bree and he certainly wouldn't mean to, but that's what was bound to happen. Was it really so wrong of Maddie to try to stop that?

His arms now pressed against her, his bare knee touching her outer thigh, the warmth of his skin burning through her jeans. "Then what is it?"

"Move back," she said, her voice low and dangerous, her legs trembling. "Now."

Slowly—so slowly it was all she could do not to scream—he lifted his hands in mock surrender and stepped back. She stalked to the coffeepot and, just to have something to do with her hands, poured more into her cup.

"You think I don't know what's going to happen?" she asked, yanking open the refrigerator. "I can already see how this is going to end up. You'll play daddy for a few weeks, give Bree all the time and attention she's ever wanted." Maddie dumped milk into her coffee then waved the carton at Neil. "And just when she's gotten used to having you around, you'll go back to Seattle."

Bree would start trusting him. Get attached to him. Believe he'd always be there for her.

And then he'd leave her.

Like he'd left Maddie.

No. No, no, no. She refused to let her daughter make the same mistakes she'd made. She couldn't let Bree count on Neil. Depending on him to be in her life for the long haul was nothing but a fairy tale.

"My job is in Seattle," he said.

"I, more than most people, realize how important your job is to you." Without bothering to stir her coffee, she took a sip. "All I'm asking is that, for once in your life, you put your wants aside and do what's best for someone else."

"I always do what I think is best," he said, sounding irritated, as if *she* was the one getting on *his* last nerve. His expression was hard, his eyes cold and flat. "But you never see that. All you see is that you're not getting your own way."

"Ouch," she whispered, hating that his words had the power to hurt her. Hating more that there was the possibility he was right.

He rolled his head from side to side. Exhaled. "Believe it or not, we're on the same side here. Can't we be partners in this? For Bree?"

Maddie didn't need him to be her partner. She'd been a single parent for the past eleven years. She was used to calling the shots, making all the decisions. She was used to going it alone.

She didn't want or need him. Not anymore.

But Bree did.

Maddie was the one who was here for Bree every day. She'd raised her with equal doses of indulgence and discipline, surrounded her with family—grandparents and aunts and uncles—and it still wasn't enough. Maddie wasn't enough.

It killed her.

Because all her sweet, bright, sensitive daughter wanted, all she'd ever wanted, was her daddy.

Lo and behold, here he was, claiming he was ready to finally, *finally* be the father Bree needed him to be. Maddie couldn't deny her daughter the chance to have something she'd been missing, been craving, her entire life.

"We'll let Bree decide," Maddie said, clutching her coffee cup, but her fingers remained cold and numb. "It'll be up to her when and how much time she wants to spend with you."

He nodded. "Thank you."

She didn't want his gratitude. Couldn't handle the way it amped up her guilt. Made her wonder if he was right. She was punishing him for walking away. That she was at least partly responsible for the distance between him and Bree.

"I'll go wake her up," Maddie said, heading toward the hall. "Help yourself to coffee."

He seemed so shocked by what was nothing more than

a polite offer, she bit the inside of her lip. Okay, so maybe she could tone back the resentment a bit.

Be his partner in parenting? Only when he played hockey in Hell. But she could at least stop fighting him every step of the way.

For her daughter's sake.

She stepped into Bree's room and was hit with a blast of arctic air. No wonder her electric bill was through the roof. Crossing the room, Maddie rubbed her hands over the goose bumps on her arms. Shut off the AC unit in the window. Seemed they needed to have another talk about lowering their energy consumption, the high cost of utilities and being financially smart.

The joys of being a parent. Lectures and bills and constant worry.

God, sometimes being the adult sucked.

Bree slept soundly, a heavy, purple comforter pulled up to her nose. Sitting on the edge of the bed, Maddie brushed back Bree's bangs.

"Honey?" Bree stirred, stretching her legs—and giving Maddie's hip a solid kick. She shifted out of range. "Honey, wake up. Your dad's here. He wants to see you."

Bree blinked. Yawned. "He's here?" Though heavy with sleep, there was no disguising the surprise in her voice. "Now?"

"He's waiting in the kitchen."

Moving faster than Maddie had ever seen her—especially before 7:00 a.m.—Bree kicked off the comforter and got to her feet. In silky pink pajama pants and matching T-shirt, her hair sticking up on the side, her round cheeks flush from sleeping, she looked so young. Vulnerable. And completely filled with hope and joy that her dad was there for her.

Maddie's heart squeezed. No, she wouldn't fight Neil on this. But that didn't mean she wouldn't continue to watch out for her daughter. She'd do whatever she had to in order to protect Bree.

And if that failed, she'd be there to pick up the pieces when Neil left.

WHEN MADDIE AND BREE entered the kitchen hand in hand, Neil felt something, some unnamed tugging in his stomach. They were so similar—same golden skin, same dark hair. The shape of their brows, the way their mouths turned down at the corners as they studied him. They were connected. A unit. A family. He had no idea where he fit with them. If he wanted to fit at all.

They, more so than his debt to Carl and Gerry or his loyalty to his sister, kept him tied to Shady Grove. To his past. And no matter how hard he tried not to, he resented them for it. For always reminding him of what he'd come from. Of the mistakes he'd made.

He didn't know if he could get past it. But he was going to try.

"Good morning," he said to Bree.

She sidled closer to Maddie. "Hi."

"How are you feeling?"

Now she and Maddie had matching frowns. But then Bree's expression cleared as if remembering she'd been so ill last night, she'd had to be rushed home. "Better," she told the floor.

Better. Right. "That's good." He didn't see any point in calling her on lying to him. The way Gerry had treated her, he couldn't even fully blame Bree. "I'm heading out for my morning run. Do you want to come with me?"

Bree looked at Maddie. "It's up to you," Maddie told her.

Bree seemed to turn the invitation over in her head.

He scratched the scar under his eye. Shifted his weight from his right leg to his left. This was nuts. He was as nervous as a rookie starting his first professional game all because his daughter hadn't jumped at the chance to spend time with him.

Neil's heart slammed against his chest. What if she refused?

"Uh…I guess I could go with you," she said, looking unsure, sounding about as unenthusiastic as someone could get and still be breathing.

Still, he'd take it. "Do you have sneakers?"

"Yeah."

"Why don't you get dressed," Maddie said, giving Bree a reassuring smile, as if she was one hundred percent on board with Bree hanging out with Neil. "I'll get your breakfast ready."

"I appreciate this," he told Maddie when Bree left.

"What's that? Our little truce?" He nodded. "It's the right thing to do," she said simply, brushing past him. "And it's important for Bree to make up her own mind about you."

Maddie set a bowl and spoon on the breakfast bar. Got out milk and a box of cereal.

"She can't eat that," he said, eyeing the happy pirate on the box. "She needs a balanced breakfast, one with lean protein, healthy fats and complex carbs."

"This is what she always has."

"It's empty calories."

Maddie sat at the bar and opened the box, helping herself to a handful. "Tasty empty calories. What are you doing?" she asked when he opened her fridge door and pulled out the carton of eggs.

"I'm making her a healthy breakfast. It wouldn't hurt you to eat better, too," he said as she poured Cap'n Crunch into the bowl and added milk. "Set a good example for her."

Maddie spooned up a nice-sized bite of the sweet cereal. His teeth hurt just thinking about all the sugar in it. "I believe in all things in moderation," she said, with a lofty wave of the spoon. "Including healthy eating."

And he believed actions spoke louder than words.

He grabbed the bowl as she was going in for another bite.

She leaped off the stool, held the spoon out like a weapon. "Hey—"

"It's junk." He dumped the cereal into the sink. Then, knowing her as he did, swiped the box before she could pour another bowl. "Junk in, junk out."

He dumped the contents into the garbage.

She squeaked, like a chew toy being stepped on. "I just opened that yesterday. Do you know how much a box of empty calories costs? And what does that even mean? *Junk in, junk out?*"

"It means you are what you eat."

"What are you, some sort of professional cliché spouter? And for the record, let me state that I wouldn't mind being a pirate."

"Mrs. Cap'n Crunch?"

"Please," she said with a sniff. "I have higher standards. More like Mrs. Jack Sparrow." Joining him at the sink, she glared down at the mess. "You are so lucky I have a garbage disposal or you'd be paying a plumber to clean out my pipes."

He hadn't even considered that. He scratched the back of his neck. "Is that a euphemism?"

Her lips twitched. "No. But it's not a bad one."

Then she smiled. At him. A real smile, one with warmth and humor.

It about knocked him on his ass.

As if realizing she was sharing a joke with him, that

they stood so close, their arms brushing, she stiffened and slid to the side. "Well, I guess since you tossed my breakfast down the drain, you can just double whatever it is you're making for Bree."

"No problem."

He pulled some cold-cut ham and a block of cheddar from the fridge, along with a small package of mushrooms and a tomato.

"Bree doesn't like mushrooms," Maddie said, taking her coffee with her back to the bar.

"But you do." He remembered her ordering them on pizza when they'd been together. "Right?"

"Right," she said, looking as if she'd like to deny it just on principle. She sipped her coffee. Tapped her fingers against the mug. "Bree said Fay wasn't at dinner last night."

He washed and dried his hands. "She wasn't feeling well."

"Seems to be a lot of that going around at your parents' place," Maddie said drily. She sighed. "I think she needs to talk to someone."

"She will," he said, slicing mushrooms. "When she's ready."

"I don't mean one of us. I mean a doctor."

He paused, the knife hovering over the last mushroom. "Like a shrink?"

"A psychiatrist, yes."

"No."

Hell no.

"Why not?"

Because his sister wasn't crazy. She didn't need some stranger pumping her full of prescriptions to get through this. She needed Neil.

"She can get more involved in the bed-and-breakfast.

Help pick out paint colors and furniture, plan the menus, get a computer system up and running." He cracked an egg on the side of the bowl. "She just needs something to do, something that gives her a sense of purpose."

"She has two sons who give her plenty to do. And believe me, being a mother comes with its own sense of purpose."

Not for everyone. It hadn't been enough for Annie. "Some women prefer to work, to have something outside of motherhood."

The look Maddie sent him could have frozen a bonfire. Good thing he was used to the cold. "Oh, pretty please, tell me more about being a mother. A working mother. Because obviously, I would know nothing about that."

She didn't have to work. The support he sent for Bree was more than enough for both of them to live on. And he wasn't so stupid that he'd actually point that out. "Having a job brings with it a sense of satisfaction. Of independence."

That's what Fay needed most of all, he thought, adding three more eggs to the bowl. The means to be able to take care of herself and the boys. To learn how to rely on herself and put her own wants and needs first instead of pinning all her hopes, dreams and happiness on someone else.

Maddie leaned forward, helped herself to a mushroom slice. "I can't argue that a job would do Fay good, but when did she decide running a bed-and-breakfast was what she wanted for her life's work?"

"Probably right around the time I suggested it."

"Ah. I should've known you were behind this."

"It's not a conspiracy," he said, pouring the beaten eggs into a heated pan. "I saw an opportunity to invest in some real estate and start a business in my hometown. I wanted to do something to give back to the local economy."

"Aren't you quite the altruist?"

He looked up from the eggs. "Yes."

"Hey, as someone who's benefiting from you playing Donald Trump, I'm not complaining."

"Could've fooled me."

"I'm just saying that I'm not sure this is what's best for Fay. Forcing her to run a business—"

"Forcing?" he muttered. "Christ."

"—she knows nothing about. Look," Maddie continued, her voice gentling, "I know she's your kid sister and you want to take care of her, but if she's spending more time in bed than on her feet, she needs something more than just being kept busy."

"Weren't you the one who told her she should stop wasting time crying over Shane and move on with her life?"

"Unfortunately, she hasn't heeded my excellent and wise advice. And there's a chance, a small one, mind you, that I was wrong about that. The longer this goes on, the worse she gets. For God's sake, she dragged her sons to the gas station to parade them in front of her husband's lover—"

"Damn it," he said roughly, his palms on the counter. "I said no. No doctors."

Maddie leaned back. "You have something against psychiatry in general? Or maybe you're just worried word will get out. Can't have that sparkling reputation of yours tarnished now, can we?"

He felt as if she'd tossed the contents of her coffee cup in his face then whacked him on the head with it. "Is that what you really think of me?"

She blushed. "No. No," she repeated softly, almost regretfully, as if she wished it was. "That's not what I think of you."

What do you think of me?

He snapped his lips together so the question wouldn't leap out. It didn't matter what she thought of him as anything other than a father. And she'd made it clear he lacked greatly in that capacity.

Getting to her feet, she started gathering items off the counter—mail, empty cups, what looked to be some sort of fancy wrench. She'd always had a problem being still, had preferred to be moving, doing, all the time. Especially when something was bothering her.

"I know it doesn't seem like it," Maddie continued, putting the glasses into the dishwasher, "but I'm starting to get really worried about her."

"She'll be okay."

"Because you're tossing money around?" Maddie's dark eyes were steady. Expectant. Waiting for more.

Damn it, he had his reasons for feeling the way he did and they were just that. His. Just because they'd agreed to this temporary truce didn't mean they were confidants. Or even friends. They were coparents, ones who usually only spoke to each other about their daughter.

But she was worried about Fay. Loved her, as much as Neil did.

Turning the heat to low, he stirred the eggs. "Did Fay ever tell you about our mother?"

Maddie frowned. "About Gerry?" Her expression cleared and she straightened. "No, not Gerry. You mean your biological mother?"

He nodded curtly. "Annie. She was…sensitive. Like Fay. But mostly she was…emotionally dependent on our father, I guess you could say. He was her entire world. All that mattered to her was keeping him happy. Keeping him with her. When he cheated on her, she was crushed."

"Your father had an affair?"

"Many and often."

Maddie's expression soured, her mouth twisting.

"Go ahead," Neil said softly. "Say it."

She straightened, wrapped her hands around her coffee cup. "Say what?"

Setting the spatula down, he met her eyes. "Say how I take after my old man."

MADDIE BLUSHED SO HARD, she considered sticking her head under the faucet, turning on the cold water and giving herself a good dousing.

"I wasn't going to say that," she told Neil, her chin lifted in the perfect picture of an affronted female.

But it was a lie. Her first instinct *had* been to lash out. To hurt him.

The way he'd hurt her all those years ago when he'd called and confessed he'd been unfaithful with some redhead he'd met in a bar.

And, dear Lord, what did that say about her?

"Whenever Dad…Sam…cheated," Neil said, staring at the tomato as if it was a mirror to his past, "Annie was always shocked, as if she couldn't believe he'd do that to her. Again. Then, when she confronted him, they'd fight…." He shook his head as if shaking off a memory. "Eventually, things would settle down. He'd apologize and promise to change and she'd forgive him. She always forgave him."

Neil's mouth was tight, his shoulders rigid, but his tone remained cool.

How he managed to be so detached was beyond Maddie. But she wouldn't mind taking a lesson on it from him. Especially when she found herself softening toward him. Thinking of how horrible it must have been for him as a boy, witnessing his parents' dysfunctional marriage.

What it must be like for him to see his sister making the same mistakes as his mother.

How he must have hated himself for following in Sam's footsteps.

She stepped forward, realized she meant to lay her hand on his back. To soothe him. Offer him comfort. She stayed rooted to her spot, her hands curled into fists at her sides. "And you think Fay is doing exactly what your—" No, she couldn't think of that woman as his mother. Not when the only mother she'd ever known him to have was Gerry Pettit—even if he didn't feel the same. "What Annie did? That she'll take Shane back?"

"That's up to her. I just…I want her to have options. Like the means, the financial means, to take care of herself and the boys."

Maddie chewed her lower lip but she couldn't stop herself from asking what worried her most. "What if she's not strong enough to take care of herself?"

"She is," he said, as if there was no way Fay would dare prove him wrong on that. As if he couldn't afford to believe otherwise.

Maddie hoped he was right.

God, how messed up was that? Her wishing Neil Pettit was right and she was wrong? This entire morning had been one surreal moment after another—Neil declaring he was staying in town and wanted more time with Bree. Maddie agreeing.

And those moments just kept coming, piling on top of each other like dominoes.

Crossing her arms, she pinched the inside of her elbow. Hard. It hurt. This was, indeed, her current reality. Neil Pettit taking over her kitchen, his movements graceful despite being too big, too masculine, the play of the muscles of his shoulders and back distracting. Irritating. He sliced and diced, tossing ingredients together like some contestant on *Top Chef.*

It was too weird, having him in her house, too intimate

having him cook in her kitchen, his shorts and T-shirt showing how different he was now, how muscular and hard.

Maddie snorted, sent him an innocent look when he glanced over his shoulder at her. Who was she kidding? He'd always been hard. Hard, closed off and brooding.

She had been a fool to think she could soften him.

She would be an even bigger fool to believe that just because he'd shared a tiny piece of his past with her—after all these years—that he'd changed. Was capable of changing.

Okay, so it was the first time he'd talked with her about his biological parents. Ever. But Maddie had already known his and Fay's life with Sam and Annie Douglas had been horrible.

Fay had told Maddie long ago about her parents' fights, the shouting and name-calling. Annie would fly into a rage, slapping and kicking Sam, screaming that she hated him. Wished he was dead. Sam would throw things— plates, chairs, even the TV once—swearing and threatening to leave forever.

Then they'd make up and things would settle down. Until the next fight.

So it wasn't as if Neil had opened up to Maddie. He still hadn't admitted how he felt about growing up that way. How Annie's death and Sam's abandonment affected him. How hard it'd been for him to be put into the foster care system, separated from his sister for almost a year before the Pettits—who already had Fay—took him in.

He'd given Maddie the facts. Just enough to prove why he was right about buying Bradford House for Fay. He hadn't revealed any deep truths, thoughts or feelings. Everything important Maddie knew about Neil's past, she'd learned from her friendship with Fay.

She couldn't soften toward him or let her guard down around him just because he'd tossed a few sentimental scraps her way. It was too dangerous, made it too easy to confuse the past with the present. Neil had cheated on her. He'd abandoned her. Her and Bree. She couldn't forget that.

Wasn't sure she could ever forgive it.

CHAPTER EIGHT

FIVE MINUTES LATER, in an effort to avoid making eye contact with Neil, Maddie had loaded the dishwasher, wiped off the already clean table and lined up the chairs with military precision. If Bree didn't get in there soon, Maddie might break out the mop next and start scrubbing the damn floor.

"Breanne Rose," Maddie called down the hall. "Put the book away and get dressed already."

There was a moment's pause where, if she had to guess, Bree marked her place in the story before answering, "Okay."

"How did you know she was reading?" Neil asked.

"A mother always knows," she intoned somberly.

"Which is why you people scare the shit out of us mere mortals."

"Just doing our best to keep that maternal mystique alive."

"It's working." He plugged in the toaster. "I don't suppose you have any wheat bread?"

"Sorry," she said, not in the least bit apologetic. "Only refined carbs for us Montesano girls. And before you start reciting facts about the benefits of whole grain, let me say that I like white bread."

She grabbed the loaf from the fridge and tossed it to him.

He caught it easily. "Peanut butter?"

"Second shelf on the left," she said with a nod toward the closet she'd converted into a pantry.

He came back with a half-empty jar of peanut butter. "Not much in there."

"I haven't been to the store in a while." A while. Three weeks. Same difference. "Actually, I don't cook often."

She refused to feel guilty about it. So she wasn't Martha Stewart—who somehow seemed to run a multimillion-dollar corporation and cook, bake and decorate with wild abandon. Maddie didn't have Martha's bankroll or legion of workers doing grunt work.

"Not enough time for it?" Neil asked, putting two slices of bread into the toaster.

"I'm a single mother." Of course she didn't have enough time. "A single *working* mother—though that term has always seemed redundant to me, but that's not the point," she continued, waving her hand as if to rid the present of her last words. "I prefer to spend what little time I have with my daughter doing things other than chopping, mixing, cooking and washing dishes."

She often turned to convenience and fast foods. Sue her. They gave her a few extra minutes for everything else on her always-growing to-do list. Laundry. Paying bills. Working on estimates for jobs. Yard work. House maintenance and cleaning. Running Bree to various activities year-round.

"You and Bree could spend time cooking together," Neil said.

"Thank you for that Solomon-like wisdom."

Though she supposed he had a point. Not that she was worried about Bree's weight. Maddie had been on the pudgy side when she was Bree's age. But then puberty kicked in, she'd grown four inches in six months and voilà.

The pudge had melted off. She was sure the same thing would happen to Bree.

She supposed, for the sake of having a healthy lifestyle, they could cut back on the trips to the drive-through and stop stockpiling frozen dinners. Take some long walks after dinner a few times a week. How hard could it be to work ten to twelve hours a day, maintain a home, keep up with all of Bree's activities, exercise several times a week and prepare a home-cooked meal each day?

Throw a cape on her back and call her Supermom.

"Now that I'll be in town longer," Neil said, "I can get that tour of Bradford House."

She narrowed her eyes. "You're not going to be one of those customers who tries to micromanage things they have no clue about, are you?"

"I trust you to do your job."

His words, sincere and quiet, warmed her. She shoved the fuzzy feeling aside. "Thanks."

"You have a lot of work left to do."

"Restoring an entire house takes time."

He sent her one of his no-need-to-get-all-riled-up looks. "Just making conversation."

She refused to blush. Or to admit, even to herself, that there was the possibility she'd sounded a tad defensive. But that's what he did to her. Put her back up. Made her realize what a fool she'd been for him when all she needed to remember was how far she'd come without him in her life.

"Yes," she said through gritted teeth, "I have a lot of work to do."

"You doing that work alone?" When she frowned at him, he added, "There wasn't a crew there yesterday."

"Only because they were needed elsewhere. They'll

be there next week." They'd better be or else she'd take a hammer to James's head for real.

"I thought by now you'd be on your own. Wasn't that your plan? To have your own company by the time you were twenty-five?" The toast popped up and Neil set the slices on a plate, spread peanut butter over them. "You used to be good at going after what you wanted."

She had no idea what he meant by that. There was a time back when she was young and naive and so completely, helplessly, foolishly in love with him that she knew his thoughts better than he did.

Now she wanted him to keep those thoughts, and those searching looks, to himself.

"I still go after what I want," she assured him as she heard Bree coming down the hall. "I just have more patience now."

Bree appeared in the doorway, looking both relieved and wary to find her father still there. She had on dark blue sweats and a white T-shirt with a huge sparkly red heart on the front. Her hair was combed back and red stones twinkled in her ears. Maddie smiled. Her kid loved bling.

And she loved her kid. So much more than she'd ever expected.

Emotion swamped her, had her feeling as if the walls were closing in on her. "Perfect timing," she said, her voice high and overly bright. "Your breakfast is almost ready. And I'm late for work." She plucked a piece of toast out of Neil's hand. "I'll call Pops and tell him you'll drop Bree off later this afternoon. Lock up when you leave."

She kissed the top of Bree's head, grabbed her keys and phone and went out through the back door. It wasn't until she was on the porch that she let her faux cheerful expression slide away.

You used to be good at going after what you wanted.

True. So very, very true.

Back then, if she wanted something, she went out and got it, no holds barred and damn the consequences.

Then she'd gone after Neil.

And those consequences were still coming back to bite her in the ass.

SHE WAS DYING.

Bree squinted against the sun as she ran down the sidewalk. Her lungs burned. Her legs hurt. Each slapping step jarred her knees, made her body shake. She wanted to stop. Wished like mad she still had on the roomy sweatpants that hid her body. But no, her dad had insisted she'd be too hot, that she needed to change into shorts.

The shorts that showed everyone how fat her legs were. They rode up, giving her a massive wedgie, leaving nothing between the skin of her thighs as they rubbed together.

"Doing okay?" her dad asked from beside her.

He wasn't even breathing hard! And his steps were smooth and easy, as if he could do this all day. As though he enjoyed sweating and running until it felt as if his legs could just fall off.

"Fine," she gasped.

But she wasn't. Shouldn't he notice and…well…do something? Her mom would. Her mom would know Bree was lying, that she needed to stop. To rest, just for a few minutes.

Her dad jogged faster.

Bree wanted to cry.

She wouldn't. Not over him. Not anymore. She quickened her pace to match his. He probably ran ten miles a day, practiced hockey for eight hours then lifted weights.

The boys in her class loved to tell her how awesome her dad was. How cool. They knew everything about him. His favorite workout, what he liked to eat to keep in shape and his stats as a player—including how many minutes he was on the ice and how often he got put into the penalty box.

They thought they could be like him. A famous hockey player. They all loved when he came to town.

She wheezed in a burning breath. She liked it when he stayed away.

Oh, when she was little, she used to dream of him coming back to Shady Grove, of being with him every day. She imagined they'd do all those things that dads and daughters did together, like…like…

Well, she wasn't sure exactly what sort of things they'd do. Only that her dad would be here for her.

Except he never was. So she stopped dreaming about it. Stopped wishing for him.

At the corner, he jogged in place as they waited for a car to go by. Bree stopped and wiped the back of her hand across her forehead. It was wet with sweat. Gross.

"What time is soccer practice?" he asked.

"Ten," she managed to respond, having forgotten all about it. She'd never survive practice, not after this. She wondered if she could use the upset-stomach bit again.

"We'll be back in plenty of time." He gestured ahead. "We'll circle that second block, then head back."

A whimper escaped her throat. Go back? All the way they'd just come?

He really was trying to kill her. Then he wouldn't have to come back to Shady Grove or make those stupid phone calls every week where neither one of them knew what to say.

He had no interest in her. In what she was doing at school or with her friends or even what she liked to do.

She could give him a hint. It didn't involve running.

Her stomach felt funny. For real. The contents were sort

of sloshing around in there, threatening to come back up. She swallowed. Swallowed again. Maybe she shouldn't have guzzled that big glass of orange juice when her dad went out onto the porch to take a phone call from his agent. But she'd been hungry still. She'd been so nervous during breakfast, with him watching every bite she ate—as if he wished he could snatch half the food from her mouth— that she'd only nibbled at the eggs and toast he'd made.

"How about we race?" he asked, his sunglasses hiding his eyes, his arms muscular. People honked and waved or yelled out the windows of their cars and he always lifted a hand or nodded.

But he never smiled.

"First one around the block wins," he added.

It took her two tries to get enough breath to ask, "Wins… what?"

He didn't hear her. He increased his pace, going faster and faster until she fell behind. No matter how fast she ran, how hard she tried, her arms and legs pumping, she couldn't reach him.

He didn't notice, didn't even glance back. Not once.

He crossed the street and in what seemed like a few seconds, disappeared around the corner at the second intersection. She'd lost him.

Panic coated her throat, made it raw. She glanced up the street at the intersection, saw the car approaching, but it was far enough away that, if she hurried, she could make it across. Pushing herself, she sprinted toward the road, staring straight ahead, at the spot where she'd last seen her dad. She could make it. She would make it.

But her toe caught on the curb and she fell, landing hard on her hands and knees. The car swerved, the driver laying on the horn. Yelled something out his window but she couldn't make out the words.

Slowly, shakily, she got to her feet, limped over to the corner and slid to the cool, damp grass in front of a brick house. Her face was hot, her skin clammy. She wrapped her arms around her bent legs and lowered her head, her breath coming out in gasps. In sobs.

She hated this. Hated running. Hated getting up early and having to eat eggs when all she'd wanted was a bowl of cereal.

Sometimes, she thought she might even hate her dad.

A car pulled to a shrieking stop, the door slamming as the driver got out. She kept her head down, her eyes squeezed tight in case it was the driver come back to yell at her.

"What the hell were you doing?"

The voice was very male, very angry and very, very familiar.

Bree raised her head, blinked back the moisture from her eyes as her uncle Leo stormed toward her. "I fell."

She sounded like a baby but he didn't call her on it, just knelt in front of her.

"You could've been killed. When I saw you darting out in front of that car—" His hands shook as he grabbed ahold of her upper arms. He swore, then hugged her. "What were you doing, running across the road like that?" He leaned back, a scary frown on his face as he looked around. "Where's your mother?"

"She's working." Bree's own voice sounded strange, as though she was going to cry or something. She sniffed and wiped her nose on her sleeve. "I'm with my dad."

If possible, his frown got darker. Scarier. And he went really still, like a cartoon that'd been shot with a freeze ray. "Your dad?"

Staring at her sneakers, she nodded.

Uncle Leo sighed. "You sure you're okay?" he asked, this time sounding nice like he usually did.

"My knees and hands just sting a little," she said, though they hurt worse than that.

He whistled lowly. "They don't look so good."

As a firefighter, Uncle Leo knew all about cuts, bruises, burns and broken bones. Bracing herself, she glanced at her legs. Felt woozy. No. They really didn't look good. Her knees were bleeding, the skin torn away. Her palms were scraped, bits of dirt and tiny pebbles embedded in the fleshy part.

"Can you stand?" he asked.

"I think so."

He straightened and helped her get to her feet. Kept his hand on her shoulder. "We need to get those cuts cleaned and—"

"Is there a problem?"

Uncle Leo's fingers tightened briefly on Bree's shoulder but he smiled at her before facing her dad. "She's hurt," he said, gesturing to her legs. "She fell."

Her dad took off his sunglasses and, though he was never one to notice much about her, blinked at her torn-up knees. "What happened?" he asked, not sounding quite so mean as he had a moment ago.

"I was trying to catch you." She tried to be cool, as if it was no big deal, but instead she sounded like a little kid who was about to start bawling any second. As if she blamed him for what happened. "I tripped on the curb."

"She ran out in front of a car," Uncle Leo said, giving her shoulder a squeeze as if that somehow made him tattling on her all better. "She didn't even look down the street."

Her dad stared at her for so long, she squirmed. "Is that true?"

"I did look," she whispered. "I thought I could make it."

"I thought you were old enough to cross the street by yourself." He sound confused and looked surprised, as if he really didn't know what she could and couldn't do.

"I am," she insisted.

"I'll take her home and help her get cleaned up," Uncle Leo said into the silence. "Wouldn't want to take you away from your training."

Her dad put his hand on her other shoulder. "I've got this."

Bree glanced between them, feeling unsettled and… nervous…she guessed. Both her dad and Uncle Leo were pretty big—her dad was wider but her uncle was taller—but that's where any similarities ended. Uncle Leo cracked jokes and smiled all the time.

Well, she thought, biting her lip as Uncle Leo glared at her dad, he usually smiled all the time. He wore jeans and a black Shady Point Fire Department T-shirt, his dark hair neatly combed, his face smooth. While her dad was… sweaty. He must have run around the block really fast. He had wet spots under his arms and his shirt clung to his stomach and back. His hair was messy and his cheeks and chin were covered in whiskers.

"Do you know each other?" she asked then winced. Duh. Of course her dad and her uncle knew each other. Didn't they?

Uncle Leo nodded once. "We went to school together."

"So, were you friends?" she asked.

"No," they said at the same time.

"Leo always had a problem staying out of other people's business." Though her dad's voice was quiet, his words were still sort of scary.

Uncle Leo stepped forward, pressing Bree closer to her dad. "My sister is my business." He smiled but it wasn't his regular smile. It was mean. "Tell me you wouldn't have done the same thing if some loser had gotten your sixteen-year-old sister pregnant."

Bree's eyes widened. They were talking about her mom?

"I wouldn't have needed two of my buddies to help get my point across," her dad said. "I would've handled it on my own."

They were quiet, staring at each other in a way that made Bree feel funny. She wanted to tell them to knock it off, except they weren't yelling or fighting or anything. But it seemed as though they were about to.

"Come on," her dad said to her, his voice rough. "Let's get you home."

But Uncle Leo didn't let go of her shoulder. "You're going to make her walk all the way home? She's hurt. I'll drive you."

"I don't want to walk home," she said when it looked as if her dad was going to say no. She shifted closer to Leo so that her dad's hand fell away from her. "I'm tired."

His jaw twitched, as if he was chewing on something. Then he nodded.

They got in Uncle Leo's car, her dad in the back, her up front. The ride home was quiet. Tense. And couldn't end soon enough.

As Leo pulled to a stop in her driveway, his radio went off. He listened to the call—car accident on the highway—responded, then swore under his breath. Her dad got out of the car and waited for her on the porch. "I have to go," Uncle Leo said as she climbed out of the car. "Will you be okay?"

"Yes." What else could she say? That she didn't want to be alone with her dad? That she wanted to go with him even if it meant spending the rest of the morning at the fire station? "Thank you for the ride."

"No problem. I'll call to check on you first chance I get." He smiled but it seemed forced. "Watch out for those curbs from now on."

"I will," she promised as she shut the door.

Standing with her arms crossed as he reversed out of the driveway, she bit her lip to stop from calling him back.

"IT'S NOT A SEVERED ARTERY," Gerry said in her no-nonsense way.

Neil squeezed the cell phone, glanced at Bree sitting on the bathroom vanity, watching him out of guarded eyes. His eyes. Maybe she took after him in a few ways after all.

"I know," he told his adoptive mother. He'd called her for help. Medical instructions. Not smart-ass replies. "But what if she gets an infection?"

"You are not taking that child to the emergency room for a couple of banged-up knees. Clean and bandage them. She'll be fine." In the background, someone sent up a wail. "Elijah!" Gerry scolded—right into the phone. Neil flinched and held it away from his ear. "Stop that this instant. I have to go," she said in a lower volume, her tone frustrated. "Elijah just hit Mitchell with a block. I swear, that child thinks the baby is his own little punching bag."

The line went silent before he could thank her. Or beg her to come over and handle this for him. But she couldn't. She was too busy taking care of his sister's kids while Fay stayed holed up in her dark bedroom. He should be there, trying to cajole Fay back to the land of the living.

One crisis at a time, he told himself as he put the phone back into his pocket.

"Grandma Gerry thinks I can handle this on my own," he told Bree.

She didn't look convinced.

Hell, he wasn't convinced of it, either.

"We could call Pops," she said.

They could. But Neil had already spent more than enough time with one Leo Montesano today. He'd rather not spend another minute of what had already been a shitty morning with another one.

He wet a washcloth with warm water, knelt and pressed it against her left knee.

"Ow."

"Sorry," he murmured, his hands only slightly unsteady as he gentled his touch, wiping away the dried blood.

He should have taken her to Carl and Gerry's after she'd eaten. They could have gone on their run from there. But he'd hoped to pick out a route Bree was familiar with, one she could do on her own after he went back to Seattle.

Cleaned, the scrapes didn't look so deep, but they must have stung like hell. He straightened and tossed the washcloth into the sink. "Antibiotic cream?"

She pointed to the medicine cabinet.

He took out the tube and squeezed a dab onto his finger. If one dab was good, two must be better. With that rationalization in mind, he smeared enough ointment on her knees to have any germ or piece of bacteria sliding right back off again. He smoothed on square bandages, crumpled the wrappers and tossed them into the garbage can beside the toilet.

"Let's see your hands," he said.

She held them out and he pressed his lips together. They were worse than her knees, the skin on the heels of her palms torn and red.

He turned on the water, checked to make sure it wasn't too hot, then tugged on her wrist. She cringed and pulled her hand back.

"We have to wash them," he said.

"It'll hurt."

She looked so scared. So little sitting there with her smooth cheeks and sweaty hair sticking to her forehead.

"Only for a minute."

"I don't want to."

"We all have to do things we don't want to," he said, unable to keep his growing impatience out of his tone. He inhaled and counted to ten. Reminded himself he was dealing with a little girl and not one of his teammates. Exhaled and tried again. "I'll be as quick as possible."

With a greater deal of reluctance than the situation called for, she slowly held out her hands. His head bent, his jaw tight with concentration, Neil washed the cuts, brushing away bits of pebbles and dirt. Though he tried to be as gentle as possible and Bree didn't complain or cry, he knew it still hurt her.

He swallowed. He'd been bruised, banged up and received more stitches than he could count. None of it ever fazed him. But seeing his daughter's hands torn up while she tried so hard to be brave?

He'd rather take a slap shot to the mouth.

After patting both palms dry with a clean towel, he repeated the routine of smearing on antibiotic cream and applying a bandage. Then, some latent paternal instinct must have kicked in, because he kissed her hands, one then the other, above the bandage.

Rolling her eyes, she tugged free. "I'm not a baby. You don't have to kiss it and make it better for me."

Heat crawled up his neck. Was that what he'd been doing? Damned if he knew. All he was certain of was that he sucked at this. Was completely inept and unprepared to deal with Bree and this minor crisis.

Worse? She knew it. And she wasn't cutting him any slack.

"It won't happen again," he said.

But then she looked disappointed, as if he'd said the wrong thing. Again.

"I can't go to soccer practice." Her words were rushed, her mouth set in a mulish line. "My knees hurt too much."

If she'd been a boy, he'd have told her to rub some dirt on her knees and walk it off. That sometimes athletes get hurt but they keep playing.

But she wasn't a boy, a son he could relate to, could understand. She was a female, with all the contradictions, emotions and sensitivity of her kind.

Neil put away the antibiotic. "You'll have to call your coach and tell him you won't be there."

Picking at the corner of the bandage on her knee, she shrugged.

"Did you hear me?" he asked.

She sighed and dropped her hands. "Yeah."

"I thought we'd go to the rink," he said, sounding as if he was asking her permission. Feeling like an idiot for it.

"If I don't go to practice, I shouldn't go ice-skating."

Shit. Good point.

"You could bring a book and read while I do some drills. Then we'll go to your grandparents' house and you can play with your cousins."

And he could hit the home gym in the basement, do the workout the team trainer had emailed him last night. Just because he was staying in Shady Grove for a few weeks didn't mean he could slack off. He had to stay in shape, keep his edge. At thirty, and already considered an old man in a league of twenty-year-old superstars, he had to constantly push himself to be stronger and faster, to play smarter, harder than anyone else.

"No, thank you," Bree said, polite as if he was one of her teachers or some stranger instead of her father. "I'd rather stay at Pops's."

She hadn't treated Leo this way, Neil thought, bitterness coating his throat. Hadn't looked at him as if he was something slimy and smelly that'd been dredged up from the river. No, she'd gazed at him as if he was her savior.

The bastard.

Neil should have knocked his teeth down his cocky throat when he'd had the chance eleven years ago.

"So?" Bree asked in such a snotty tone, he raised his eyebrows. "Can I go to Pops's house?"

"Sure." What else could he say? She didn't want to go with him. Didn't want anything to do with him.

And he had no idea how to change it, how to fix this. If he should even keep trying.

CHAPTER NINE

SOMEONE POUNDED ON the kitchen door, rattling the windowpane. At the table working on an estimate for a bathroom remodel, Maddie jumped, her heart racing. She was halfway out of her seat when the door opened.

"Where's Bree?" Leo asked.

Maddie sat back down slowly. "In the shower. Wha—"

He stormed into the kitchen followed by James and Eddie. James held the door and Zoe, his German shepherd/husky mix, padded in, her pointy ears perked, her tail wagging.

"Well now, don't be shy," she drawled. "You all just come right on in."

Eddie, a Pittsburgh Pirates cap covering his short hair, sawdust clinging to his faded jeans, crossed to the fridge and opened it.

"No, really," she continued, hooking her arm around the back of her chair. "Please help yourself to anything you'd like. What's mine is yours."

He opened the crisper drawer. Shut it again. "These idiots kidnapped me before I could have supper."

"Don't blame me," James said as he leaned back against the counter. He nodded toward Leo. "He's the one with the bug up his ass."

Leo paced from one end of the kitchen to the other muttering under his breath, his strides long and angry. He was either working off a good mad or worried about something. Or both.

They all ignored him.

"There's leftover chicken, rice and asparagus in plastic containers," she told Eddie. "Second shelf."

"You cooked?"

"Don't sound so shocked. It doesn't take a gourmet chef to throw chicken on the grill."

She rolled her eyes when he peeled the lid off the container of chicken and gave a cautious sniff. Wimp.

If her brothers thought it strange she'd prepared a meal without it being a special occasion, they kept further comments to themselves. Thank God. The last thing she wanted was to explain about Neil's mini-lecture on healthy eating. How she'd given in to it.

Maddie bit into one of the chocolate chip cookies Pops had sent over yesterday. "I take it you're not here just to raid my refrigerator."

Glowering, Leo stalked over to her. "This is an intervention."

She stilled. "You can't cut off my cookie consumption. Taking away a woman's right to chocolate is just wrong. Not to mention possibly illegal."

And she took a huge bite.

"This isn't about a damn cookie," he growled, swiping his hand through the air as if to brush aside her words. "This is about you making another stupid mistake. We stood by last time, but not now."

"Did you suffer a brain injury?" she asked, finishing off the cookie. "What have we told you about sliding down the fire pole headfirst?"

"I warned you years ago. I told you Neil Pettit was nothing but trouble. That he'd hurt you." He stopped and tossed his hands in the air. "But did you listen? No," he snapped when she opened her mouth. "You didn't. And look what happened."

"I take it this is about your little run-in with Neil and Bree this morning?" she asked.

Bree had called Maddie that morning to tell her she was spending the rest of the day at Pops's house. It wasn't until Maddie had picked her up there that she'd learned about Bree getting hurt while out with Neil.

And Leo coming to her rescue.

Now he was here, all irritated and in full big-brother, defender-of-weak-willed-baby-sisters mode. She should have expected this little visit, Maddie realized with an inner sigh. Her brothers loved her and Bree. Wanted to protect them.

She wished that one day they'd get it through their thick heads she was more than capable of taking care of herself.

Zoe nudged Maddie's knee and she stroked the dog's silky head. "Yes," Maddie said, "you warned me. But unless you happen to have a DeLorean that you've tricked out into a time machine, there's not a whole lot I can do to change the past."

Wasn't sure she'd do anything different even if she did get some magical do-over.

Leo's mouth tightened, the skin around it turning white. "How long is he in town?"

She blinked at the vehemence in his tone. Out of all her brothers, Leo had always had the biggest problem with Neil. "I'm not sure. A few weeks, I guess."

He stood with his legs apart, his arms crossed. "You can't let him spend time with Bree. Not after everything he's done."

Her blood heated. Her hands curled into fists. She stood, her body trembling with the need to haul off and punch Leo in the nose. "Excuse me?"

Zoe whimpered and hid under the table.

James sighed. "And here we go."

"You heard me," Leo said. "Tell him he can't see her again."

"Pettit's Bree's father," Eddie interjected before Maddie could calm down enough to gather her thoughts. "He has a legal right to see her."

"Screw his legal rights."

Eddie snorted. "Say that when it's up to the courts to decide whether you get to see your kid or not."

Eddie had full custody of his son, Max, but his ex-wife had been making noises about wanting to be a bigger part of Max's life. Maddie knew Eddie's biggest fear was losing his son in a custody battle where the courts usually favored the mother.

"This isn't about you," Leo said. "It's about Neil Pettit being no good for Bree."

Eddie pointed his fork at Leo. "That's not up to you to decide."

Leo, his eyes narrowed to slits, stalked over to Eddie, all cocky and aggressive. "I'm her uncle. I care about her."

"We're all her uncles and care about her, you moron," Eddie said.

"Who are you calling a moron?" Leo asked, pushing Eddie's shoulder.

Eddie's face darkened, his eyes flashed.

"Are you going to stop this?" Maddie asked James as Eddie set his food aside.

James shrugged. "Nah. Leo's been itching for a fight. Might as well let Eddie give him one."

"I'm calling you a moron," Eddie said, using both hands to shove Leo back two steps. "Moron."

There was a beat of silence—the calm before the storm—then, sure enough, Leo snarled and charged. Eddie neatly sidestepped and gave Leo a sharp crack to the back of the head as he went by.

And it was on.

Zoe barked, her tail thumping against the table leg. But she kept her distance, her body vibrating with excitement. Leo bent his head like a bull and tried again, this time wrapping his arms around Eddie's waist.

"You have to go in low on Eddie," James told Maddie as if imparting some hard-earned wisdom, "or you'll never have a chance of taking him down. He's built like a tank."

"Didn't I say you were boneheads?" she grumbled. "All three of you."

Eddie and Leo wrestled, each trying to gain the upper hand. Leo was taller and wiry, but James was right—Eddie was pure muscle. They crashed into the island. Leo grunted, swore, then tried to sweep Eddie's feet from under him. When that didn't work, he used his longer reach to pop Eddie on the chin hard enough to have his teeth snapping together.

They were evenly matched. Too evenly matched. And Bree would be getting out of the shower any minute.

Maddie crossed to the sink, turned on the cold water full blast and grabbed the spray hose.

And doused them both.

They sprang apart, roaring like a couple of idiot bears.

"What the hell was that for?" Leo yelled, his arms out, his hair dripping. To her left, Eddie shook like a dog, his shoulders hunched.

"That," she said in a decent impersonation of her mother's most regal tone, "was for fighting in my kitchen. And this—" She sprayed Leo's face. He sputtered and held out his hands. "—is for asking such a stupid question."

She shut off the water, stalked over to him, grabbed his ear and twisted.

"Who do you think you are," she asked as she dragged him toward the door, "coming here, telling me what I can and can't do? Did you really think I'd take orders from a man who still plays video games, thinks *Mob Wives* is quality television and jumps off of cliffs for the hell of it? Huh?" When he didn't answer, she twisted harder. "Well?"

"Ow. Damn it, Maddie. I'm only trying to help."

"If I need your help, I'll ask for it." Opening the door with her free hand, she shoved him onto the porch. "Until then, whatever happens between me and Neil is none of your business."

His expression darkened. She was surprised the water on him didn't turn to steam. "Nothing better happen between you two. Not again."

"I didn't mean it that way. But if you're seriously worried about keeping my virtue safe from Neil Pettit, you're twelve years too late." Turning, she faced Eddie. "You can leave under your own power, or I can escort you out the same way I did this bozo," she said with nod at Leo. "Your choice."

"I'm going," he said. It wasn't until he'd hurried past her that she realized he had her leftovers in his hands.

"You'd better bring those containers and my fork back," she called after him.

Walking down her driveway, he lifted said fork in salute.

She slammed the door shut. While Zoe sniffed at the water on the floor, Maddie got the roll of paper towels out from under the sink, tore off several then tossed the roll at James. He bobbled it, then hauled it into his chest.

"Come on," she said, squatting to sop up water. "Since you didn't stop them from wrestling like a couple of overgrown children, the least you can do is help clean up."

Why hadn't he stopped them? she wondered, throwing wet towels into the garbage can. James could usually be counted on to be their family's rock. Solid, steady and dependable. Besides keeping Montesano Construction running smoothly, he also kept the peace within the family, and kept Eddie and Leo from killing each other.

Usually.

"How's Bree?" he asked, wiping water off the cupboards.

"She's fine. Just a couple of skinned knees."

"No, I meant emotionally. Leo said she was pretty upset about Neil leaving her behind like that."

Neil left Bree behind? Seemed her daughter conveniently managed to forget at least one key point when she'd told Maddie what had happened. But she wasn't going to get into any of that with James. As much as she appreciated her family helping her out with Bree—and always being there for them—Maddie needed to handle this… situation…with Neil on her own.

"I'll talk to her about it," Maddie said, ripping off several more towels. "I'll take care of it."

James touched her arm. "You sure about this?" he asked quietly.

She didn't need to ask what he meant. Was she sure about letting Neil be a part of Bree's life? Was she sure she wasn't making a big mistake, one that could potentially hurt her daughter?

No. She wasn't sure at all.

"I'm sure." She forced a smile. "It's only for a few weeks. And what Eddie said was true. Neil has the right to spend time with his daughter."

As long as that's all he had the right to, she could handle it, she assured herself. Neil had never wanted more than the opportunity to see Bree several times a year. Just because he thought he wanted to play dad for the next few weeks didn't mean any of that had changed. Bree still belonged with Maddie. Belonged to her.

Only her.

BREE WAS LAUGHING.

The sound, light and cheerful, innocent and pure, washed over Neil like the evening breeze. Warm. Comforting. He stood at the end of Maddie's driveway, the door to his rental car still open, and just listened. She giggled louder and his mouth twitched. He'd started to wonder if he'd ever hear that sound again.

Hadn't realized how much he'd missed it until now.

It almost didn't even matter that she hadn't so much as cracked a smile at him since he'd been in town.

Almost.

The sun had dipped behind the tree-covered hills, staining the sky in pinks and golds. Still, Neil reached back into his car for his sunglasses, slammed the door shut then put them on before walking toward the back porch.

Toward the sound of that laughter. Toward his daughter.

He crossed to the porch, frowned at the scene before him. Bree, Maddie and James Montesano at the table playing cards. Smiling. Laughing.

Bree noticed him first, her laughter, then her smile dying away.

"Neil," Maddie said, following their daughter's gaze, her tone wary as she slowly stood. "Something we can do for you?"

He wasn't sure. He'd come there for a reason, but seeing this little cozy, domestic scene made him feel edgy and anxious, as if his skin was too tight. As if he couldn't take a full breath. Bree sidled closer to James and he put his arm around her. She leaned into him, laid her head on his shoulder.

It was like taking an elbow to the gut.

He was jealous.

Him. One of the best hockey players in the league. He'd accomplished every goal he'd set from the time he was sixteen, had amassed wealth, success and security for himself and his family. And still jealousy gnawed at him. Sharp and ruthless, it pushed him to storm onto the porch, grab his daughter. Demand that she look at him that way. Smile at him.

Want to be with him like she used to.

"I didn't mean to interrupt your game," Neil said, hating how stiff and pissed-off he sounded. Hating that they were a unit. A family. That he was the one out of place.

Hating that it bothered him.

"Actually, we were just finishing up," Maddie said. "And you still haven't mentioned what you're doing here."

He'd come to see Bree. Had just gotten out of the shower when he'd realized he hadn't spoken to her since dropping her off at Big Leo's that morning. That he should have at least called her to see how she was. Tried to spend more time with her.

But he hadn't known he needed a reason to want to see her.

"I thought," he said to Bree, trying to come up with a plausible excuse, "that since you missed soccer practice, we could go to the park. Kick the ball around."

Bree stared at the table. Clearly being with him wasn't her idea of fun.

"It's late," Maddie said.

"Not too late for a card game. Or company," he added quietly, nodding at James, who watched him steadily. Studying him, as if trying to figure out what Neil was doing there, what he wanted from his niece. And his sister.

Neil wasn't sure he knew himself.

But unlike Leo, James had never treated Neil with any outward animosity, and Neil had nothing against him.

"It's too late for Bree to play soccer," Maddie said. "She's already had her shower."

Only now did he notice Bree was in her pajamas, her feet bare.

"Uncle James," she asked, her head still on his shoulder, "can we play another game?"

Neil had nothing against James. Until now.

"Sure," James said. "But why don't we take it inside?"

Bree gathered the cards, never once so much as glancing Neil's way. James collected the cups then straightened. He touched his sister's shoulder. "I'll be in the kitchen if you need me," he told her.

Keeping her eyes on Neil, Maddie nodded.

Bree slipped her hand into her uncle's and they walked inside. She didn't say goodbye. She didn't even look back. The door shut, the sound loud in the quiet night.

"Maybe next time," Maddie said, linking and unlinking her fingers together, "it'd be better if you called first instead of just dropping by."

"Right," he managed to say. "Wouldn't want to put you or your family out."

He turned on his heel and headed back toward his car, anger—unreasonable and uncontrollable—threatening to drown him.

"Neil," she called. "Neil! God, could you wait a minute?" she asked in exasperation when he kept walking.

He forced himself to stop while she carefully made her way down the gravel driveway. Like Bree, her feet were bare, her hair was down. In a pair of yoga pants that ended just below the knee and a stretchy V-neck T-shirt, she was toned and curvy. And beautiful. She'd always been beautiful to him.

Damn it, she made him forget why he'd left. Made him want her. Want the life he'd left behind.

"What, exactly," she asked, her arms crossed, her hip cocked, "is your problem?"

Tension tightened his spine, had him closing the distance between them. "You want to know my problem?" His tone was low, his words rough. "I'm tired of you dictating when I can and can't see my daughter."

"I'm not *dictating* anything," she said, laying her hand on her chest, the perfect picture of affronted female. He wasn't buying it.

"Bullshit. You love this, don't you? You love having all the control, being the one in charge, making all the decisions. But it's not enough for you that I have to ask for your permission before I can take Bree anywhere, do anything with her. Now I can't even see her without making a goddamn appointment while your family gets to be with her whenever the hell they want?"

She gaped at him. "Oh, my God. That's what this is all about? You're jealous?" Her laugh was breathless, humorless. "Unbelievable. All that fame and fortune you worked so hard for, that you wanted for so long, is no longer enough for you?"

He couldn't even deny it. Not when he was afraid she was right. "This isn't about my career."

"It's always about your career. Always has been about your goals." She whirled around, took three steps away before turning back to him, her hair whipping around her face. "How dare you come here and act like you're the injured party? How *dare* you stand there and pretend that it bothers you not to be the one playing cards with your daughter, the one who'll tuck her into bed tonight? You didn't want that, remember?" she asked, her voice soft now and shaking, though no less vehement. "You didn't want to be tied down with some ordinary life in Shady Grove, didn't want a wife or kids holding you back. You had plans to follow and big dreams to chase. And unless I'm mistaken, neither those plans nor those dreams included Bree. Or me."

Her words hit him, landing like two quick right jabs to his solar plexus, stealing his breath and his ability to defend himself. To protect himself. To stop from admitting more than he could risk her knowing.

"You're right," he growled, whipping off his glasses and edging closer. Her throat worked as she swallowed but she lifted her chin, kept her eyes on his. Maddie always met your eyes. Always let you know where you stood with her. She put it all out there, made herself vulnerable. That openness and honesty had been a big part of what had drawn him to her.

Even as it'd scared the hell out of him.

"I didn't want a wife or a kid," he continued. Still stalking her, barely recognizing that for every step he took forward, she took two quick ones back, the words ripped from his throat. "I didn't want to be stuck here. Not when I'd worked so hard to make something of myself. To prove I was—"

Cursing himself, he clamped his lips shut, his breathing ragged.

"Prove what?" she whispered, watching him in that way that had always made him feel as if she was looking for something inside of him. Something more than who he was, than what he could give.

"I may not have wanted it," he said, "but I still stood up. I did the best I could to take responsibility, to be a father even if I couldn't be with my daughter every day. And because I wasn't here, because you were, because I felt so guilty about that, I gave in to you."

"Gave in to me? Oh, this should be good," she said, tossing her head in that way that irritated the hell out of him. "Why don't you tell me, exactly, how you gave in to me all these years?"

"You're always so stubborn. So certain you're right. And why wouldn't you be? You just roll over anyone who disagrees with you. And I made it so easy on you. I never fought you. About anything. Not Bree's last name or visitation rights or you having her for every holiday. When I wanted her enrolled in that preschool program—"

"She was three. And she went the next year."

"She went when you wanted her to go. But I didn't question it. I never questioned any of your decisions. I never fought you," he repeated, his voice all the more dangerous for its softness. He opened his car door. "Maybe it's time I did."

"WHERE'S BREE?" Elijah demanded as he let himself into Maddie's house.

Finishing the dinner dishes, Maddie raised her eyebrows. "What happened to 'Hi, Aunt Maddie, so good to see you. You're awesome as always'?"

He giggled. "Hi, Aunt Maddie. You're awesome as always."

"Better." She nodded toward the hall. "Bree's in the living room," she said, the last word barely out of her mouth before Elijah made a beeline that way.

Letting the water out of the sink, she dried her hands as Fay came inside.

"Hey, buddy," Maddie said, taking Mitchell from Fay and placing the baby on her own hip. "Are you going to hang out with us Montesano girls tonight? Huh?" Completely in love with the little butterball, she gave him a bounce. Then another. He clapped his hands then shoved his fist into his mouth. "Now, that's the kind of response a woman likes to get from a guy."

Her baby radar in full swing, Bree came into the kitchen. "Hi, Mitch." Mitchell squealed and held his arms out. Bree took the baby and cuddled him close. "Hi, Aunt Fay."

"Hi, honey. How are your knees?" When Bree looked at her quizzically, her sweatpants covering her scabbed-over knees, Fay added, "Your dad told us about your accident."

"They're better," Bree said, her face darkening.

Maddie didn't blame her. Every time she thought of Neil she felt like a storm cloud herself. One ready to explode and rain down like the wrath of God on Neil at any moment.

I never fought you. Maybe it's time I did.

Bastard. He wanted her frightened. Scared to make a move or a decision about her daughter without his say-so. Not going to happen. She and Bree had gotten along perfectly fine without him in their lives, without his opinions. It was too late for him to be playing *Father Knows Best* now. Even if he had seemed sincere.

Even if part of her, a small, secret part, wanted to give him another chance.

Another chance with Bree, she assured herself. To be the kind of father their daughter deserved.

"Can I take the boys outside?" Bree asked. "Elijah wants to play in the sandbox."

"Sure." Fay kissed Mitchell's cheek. "'Bye, baby. See you later."

Mitchell did the baby wave—his chubby fingers opening and closing—as Bree carried him out of the room.

"Are you sure you don't mind watching the boys?" Fay asked. "I know it was late notice and—"

"It's not a problem." Maddie used the dishcloth to wipe

away a spot of dried milk from the counter. "You know we love having them."

Fay unzipped the diaper bag she'd set on the table. Zipped it again. "I know. It's just…" Unzipped it. "If you're busy or have something else to do, I can ask Gerry."

"I'm glad you asked us." But Fay kept up with the zipping and unzipping. Talk about trying to drive someone crazy. Tossing the dishcloth into the sink, Maddie crossed to the table and covered Fay's hand—and the damn zipper—with her own. "I've missed you. Still mad at me?"

"I was never mad." But she didn't meet Maddie's eyes. "I've just been busy—"

"Busy being pissed at me. It's okay. I'm just glad you're over it."

Glad she had her best friend back. And it did, indeed, seem as if Fay was back.

In fact, gone were the baggy sweats, roomy T-shirts and dirty flip-flops. Tonight Fay had on dark skinny jeans that showcased her long legs—and exactly how much weight she'd lost the past few months—a deep green, sleeveless top with a ruffle at the bodice and strappy, high-heeled sandals.

"You look great. Really great. And your hair's different. Lighter," she added, hoping Fay didn't notice how suspicious she sounded. As if being a bleached blonde was some sort of crime against humanity.

Fay lifted a hand to her hair. "Just a few highlights. They're not too much, are they?"

"No," Maddie said slowly. "It looks really pretty. My question would be why?"

"Why what?"

"Why the highlights? Jeez, a few days ago you weren't even washing your hair regularly and today it's all—" She waved her hands. "Fluffy and cute. And…" She leaned forward, noted the shine to her friend's mouth, the subtle color that made the blue of Fay's eyes stand out. "You're wearing makeup." Maddie narrowed her own eyes. "What did you say you were doing tonight?"

"Oh." Fay blinked. Several times. "I'm, uh…not sure I mentioned it, actually."

"Well, then, why not lay it on me? And for God's sake, stop all that blinking before you have some sort of seizure."

Fay's eyes stayed open. Her gaze landing everywhere but on Maddie. "Book club," she blurted.

"Excuse me?"

"I'm going to a book club meeting."

"You don't belong to a book club."

"I'm thinking of joining one and thought I should attend a meeting before I committed."

Maddie shook her head. "God, I cannot believe you're lying to me. Right to my face. If you don't want to tell me where you're going, what you're doing, all you had to do was say so."

"I'm sorry," Fay cried, twisting her hands together. "I don't want to lie to you, it's just…"

"It's just what? Hey, come on. This is me. You can tell me anything."

"No. I can't. Not if it's something you don't agree with. Then all that happens is you tell me what I'm doing is wrong and then you get disappointed and upset when I don't do what you think I should."

Maddie froze, too stunned to move or argue. Too hurt to take a full breath.

You're always so stubborn. So certain you're right. You just roll over any opposition.

Dear Lord, was that really how people saw her? Was that really how she was?

She swallowed but the painful lump in her throat remained. "You're meeting Shane."

"He wants to talk. See if we can try and work things out. And I knew you'd think that was a bad idea."

A bad idea? How about a horrible, rotten, the-worst-idea-ever?

What was Fay thinking? Why was she doing this to herself? Maddie wanted to remind her of Shane's lies, of all the ways he'd hurt her over the past few months.

She swallowed it back, every last word, feeling as if she was choking on them. "I don't want you to get hurt."

Didn't want her fragile spirit crushed, her heart broken again. It was too painful to witness. And only served to remind Maddie how close she'd been to being that weak, that willing to give up her pride when Neil had left her.

"If it means getting my husband back, my family back," Fay said, sounding sure and determined, "I'm willing to risk it."

"You can forgive him?" Maddie asked, thoroughly confused as to how someone could willingly put their heart on the line again and again. "It's that easy?"

"Not easy but worth the effort. I know you think I'm stupid—"

"Never," she said heatedly, appalled that Fay would even consider that. "Not even once."

"I love him, Maddie. I still love him. And whether that's right or wrong, I'll do whatever I have to so we can be together again. Forever."

Maddie winced. Hadn't she had the same thought twelve years ago about Neil? She'd done everything in her power to make Neil love her. To want her. Her forever had been short-lived, her heart broken, her pride crushed. But she'd picked herself up, brushed herself off and moved on. She'd become stronger, smarter because of it. She'd survived.

"I hope," Maddie said, "for your sake, that things work out between you two. Just...be careful, okay?"

Fay gave one of her heartbreakingly sweet smiles then hugged her hard. "Don't worry. Once I have Shane back, my family back, I'll be fine."

Holding on to her best friend, Maddie prayed she was right.

CHAPTER TEN

"WE'RE NOT GOING to have enough potato salad."

By the alarm in Gerry's voice, you'd think they'd run out of air to breathe.

Neil shut the kitchen door on the sounds of conversation, laughter and music outside.

"There's not another potato famine," Carl said, coming up behind Gerry to wrap his arms around her waist. "Didn't you make pasta and macaroni salads? And what about that stuff with the beans and peppers?"

"Yes, yes, we have those." Turning, she frowned at him. "I didn't say we didn't have enough food."

"I could ration it," Fay offered with a smile, a bag of chips in one hand, a bowl of taco dip in the other. "Make sure everyone gets a quarter cup of it and not one potato cube more." When they all stared at her, her smile faded and she shifted. "What?"

"You made a joke," Neil said. And she was dressed in real clothes—white shorts and a bright orange shirt.

Her fingers must have tightened on the bag because it made a crackling sound. "I have made jokes before."

"Not lately."

"What your brother is trying to say," Gerry said, shooting him a for-the-love-of-God-be-quiet look, "is that we're all glad you're…feeling better."

"No," he said, helping himself to a cherry tomato from

the vegetable tray on the table. "What I was trying to say was 'What's going on?'"

She blushed, her gaze on the dip as if she could see her future in the mix of sour cream and taco seasoning. "Nothing. I'm happy." Now she glanced at the three of them. "Isn't that what you all wanted?"

Gerry offered up a cheery smile that was so forced, Neil was surprised her face didn't crack. "Of course it is. Now come on," she added to Fay, smacking Neil's hand as he went in for a cucumber slice, "let's take these out to the food table."

Neil shut the door behind them and hoped none of the guests decided it might be a good idea to come inside. Corner him. Force him into stilted, polite conversation. He'd had all the conversation he could take for the day.

And the picnic had only been going on for an hour.

His hands in his pockets, he peered out the window over the sink at the people milling around the yard. There were shouts as someone did an impressive—and what had to be a stinging—belly smack into the inground pool. The tables under a large canopy were filled, the bartender Gerry had hired kept busy at the makeshift bar, pouring wine, mixing cocktails and opening beer bottles. Teenagers shot hoops in the fenced-off court while a group of younger kids played street hockey on the paved rectangle behind the garden shed.

A car door slammed and he straightened, squinted at the two figures walking up the driveway. A man and woman. Not Bree. Not Maddie.

"'Just a small get-together,' she told me," Neil muttered, remembering how Gerry had conned him into this picnic just yesterday morning. "'To celebrate the Knights winning the Cup, so people can congratulate you in person.' I hadn't realized you two even knew this many people," he said to Carl. "What'd she do? Put up flyers around town? Post an open invitation on her Facebook page?"

"She does love that Facebook." Carl opened a package of hot dogs and added the links to the pile already assembled on a cookie sheet. "She did do her best to keep the guest list to a minimum. But you know how it is. Word spreads and suddenly people we haven't spoken to in years are calling, asking if it's okay if they drop by to see you while you're in town."

Neil snorted. "It's not me they want to see. It's the Cup."

Each player on the championship team got the Stanley Cup for a day. For his day, Neil had the Cup brought to Shady Point. That morning he'd taken it to Shady Grove Memorial Hospital before attending a ceremony at City Hall in his honor. Now the Cup sat on a table in the corner of the huge deck, where people could see it up close, touch it, take pictures of it.

"It's both," Carl said. "Though we all know you'd rather be anywhere else but out there, posing for pictures and being fawned over."

It made him nervous, having someone else knowing him that well. "The fawning's not that bad."

Carl laughed. "You're doing a good thing," he said, taking a tray of raw hamburgers and T-bone steaks out of the refrigerator, "letting Gerry throw you this party. Letting people see you and the Cup up close." He clapped Neil on the shoulder. "You're a good man, son. Your mother and I are proud of you."

A damn lump formed in Neil's throat. He didn't know what to do. What to say. Luckily, Carl wasn't the type for long, sentimental conversations. He squeezed Neil's shoulder and then carried the meat outside, leaving the door open.

His adoptive father's words meant a lot to Neil, more

than he wanted to admit. But he couldn't get hung up on what other people thought, couldn't base how he felt about himself on how others viewed him. That way led to a lifetime of trying to keep that high opinion. Of spending all his time trying to make other people happy and of relying on them to make him happy in return.

"Daddy!"

The word, shouted outside, carried easily into the kitchen. Neil spun around looking for Bree, expecting to see her barreling toward him, a huge smile lighting up her face.

But it wasn't his daughter calling out to him in excitement, throwing herself into his arms like she used to. It was Elijah. His nephew attached himself to Shane's legs, looked up at him, his mouth going a mile a minute. Guess that explained Fay's turnaround.

"I'm not sure that's a good idea," Neil told Carl as he came back into the kitchen.

Carl joined him at the window, where they watched Fay join Shane and Elijah. "Not for us to decide. Your sister's a grown woman. She needs to make her own decisions. And her own mistakes. Here," he said, handing Neil a cold beer. "Take this, and those hot dogs, out to the grill. If you're going to hide out you might as well do something useful."

"I thought you threatened to shish-kebab anyone who touched the grill?"

"I'm granting you special access for today only. But you'd better get out there. The steaks are already on the fire and if they burn, Geraldine will have your ass."

That was true—and terrifying—enough that Neil grabbed the tray of hot dogs and hurried outside. Luckily, the grill had been set up at the edge of the party. Close enough to keep an eye on the action, far enough away that few people would make the trek over.

If he played this right, he'd have a good twenty minutes to himself.

He opened the grill lid, leaned back as a rush of flames and steam poured out. The steaks and burgers sizzled, scented the air. Sipping his beer, he checked the steaks. Carl thought the knobs on the front were for decoration purposes only, which meant everything he grilled ended up looking and tasting like charcoal.

After adjusting the heat, Neil shut the lid, swept his gaze over the crowd. At a table near the pool, the mayor sipped a glass of wine and listened to the president of the school board. Mrs. Leslie, Neil's seventh-grade English teacher, laughed at something Gerry's dentist said.

The free booze must have been a big draw. Local politicians, business owners and professionals mingled with grocery store clerks, factory workers and cops. It seemed as if everyone Neil had ever been in contact with—from Carl's old coworkers at the refinery to the women Gerry used to clean house for—were there.

Everyone except his daughter.

He pulled out his phone and pressed the button for Maddie's house. It rang. And rang. When the machine picked up, Maddie's husky voice telling him to leave a message at the beep, he disconnected and turned back to the grill. He'd already left two messages. One yesterday when he'd called to invite Bree to this impromptu picnic. Another this morning when he'd checked to see if she'd gotten his first message.

His daughter was ignoring him.

It was unacceptable. And, more than likely, all Maddie's doing. She was pissed he'd stood up to her. Questioned her. She hated that he wanted to be a bigger part of Bree's life after giving in to her for so long.

It was partly his own fault, he realized. Maddie hadn't

so much pushed him out of Bree's life as nudged him out.
He was the one who'd stepped back. He'd let her get away
with her excuses for why Bree couldn't visit him, had
given in to her every whim and wish where their daughter was concerned.

He hadn't wanted to make waves, hadn't wanted to
cause problems. Had thought—hoped—that by keeping
the peace, it'd make up for hurting her. Would assuage the
guilt he felt about not wanting to be a father.

Now his daughter didn't return his calls and acted as
if she'd rather wear bacon-scented clothes and be tossed
into a pen with rabid dogs than hang out with her father.

"You shouldn't press down on them."

He stilled at the familiar voice. She was here.

About damn time.

Bree stood a few feet from the grill frowning at him in
a pair of bright pink sweatpants and a tie-dyed T-shirt at
least two sizes too big.

He stepped toward her, wanting to pull her in for a hug,
but she stiffened and took a small step back. His stomach
dropped. He should tell her how glad he was that she'd
made it. That he'd been thinking of her the past few days.
That he missed her.

"Hey" was all that came out. "You got my message.
About the picnic," he added.

"Uh…yeah. I mean, I'm here, aren't I?" she asked, not
sounding too happy about it.

"I didn't think you were going to make it. You didn't
call me back."

"I was at my soccer scrimmage."

He groaned inwardly. Her scrimmage. The one she'd
invited him to.

The one he'd totally forgotten about.

Shit.

His fingers tightened on the spatula, ached with the urge to whip it across the yard. "I had to do this thing at City Hall," he told her, "or else I would've made it to your scrimmage."

She lifted a shoulder. As if she couldn't care less if he watched her play or not.

He cleared his throat. "What were you saying about not pressing on the burgers?"

"If you press on them, all the juice squirts out. And you should only flip them once." She lifted her chin. "That's how Uncle James does it."

"Yeah? You think that'll help from turning these into hockey pucks?"

She eyed him as if trying to decide if he seriously wanted her opinion or not. Studied him as if she could see inside his head and read his thoughts, judge them and then decide if he was worthy or not.

Just like her mother used to do.

He wanted her to smile at him, just once. Look at him like she used to, with respect and adoration and a bit of awe, as if he was some superhero. *Her* hero.

"It should," she finally said, stepping closer to him. "Plus, you have the flame low enough that they'll cook all the way through." She edged even closer, glanced around then lowered her voice. "Papa Carl always keeps the heat up too high."

"Carl's not much of a cook. He used to ruin peanut butter and jelly sandwiches."

She nodded, not a hint of a grin in sight. Tough crowd.

"You do a lot of cooking?" he asked.

"No, but Mom said we're gonna start making dinner at home more and that I can pick something to make by myself once a week. I like to bake stuff, though. I brought chocolate cupcakes I made myself."

Maddie had actually listened to him? He hadn't expected that. Had figured he'd have to fight her every step of the way about every damn thing.

Score one for him.

"Chocolate, huh? That's my favorite."

"It is?"

Did she have to be so suspicious of everything he said? "It is. Since you know so much about burgers, why don't you help me with these?" he asked, holding out the spatula.

After what seemed like an eternity, she took it and stepped up to the grill.

"Don't get too close," he warned.

"I won't." Her tongue between her teeth, she checked one of the burgers then carefully flipped it. Flames leaped, grease sizzled. But she wasn't burned and her hair hadn't caught on fire.

"How come you call Papa Carl 'Carl' and not Dad?"

About to take a drink of his beer, he froze. Slowly lowered his arm. Where the hell had that come from? "He's not my dad. Not my real dad."

"But he and Grandma Gerry adopted you and Aunt Fay because your real mom died and your real dad left you."

Leave it to a kid to be that succinct. "Yeah."

"A girl in school was adopted from Russia and she calls her adopted mom 'Mom.' And Aunt Fay calls Papa Carl and Grandma Gerry 'Dad' and 'Mom.'"

"That's Aunt Fay's choice." It'd been easier for Fay, two years younger than Neil, to bond with the Pettits. To think of them as her parents.

To forget about the people she'd come from.

"I'm sorry your real mom died," Bree said softly, laying her hand on his forearm. "I guess I never told you that, but I am."

Her hand was small, a bit clammy and incredibly warm.

He studied her. His child. Intellectual, polite, nonathletic…
she was the complete opposite of everything he was, of
everything he was familiar with. Comfortable with. He
didn't know what to do with her, how to connect with her.
Ever since he'd been in town, he'd had the feeling that she
was mad at him. That she hated him.

And yet here she was, offering him sympathy.

He wondered if his biggest mistake wasn't getting Maddie pregnant or sleeping with that redhead.

But in staying away for so long.

"Bree!"

Her heart racing, Bree hunched her shoulders and shoved
a dip-laden Dorito into her mouth before turning.

But Grandma Gerry wasn't looking at her with disappointment as she climbed the steps to the deck. No, she was
smiling at her. A wide smile that showed lots of her teeth.

Bree's stomach sank. She didn't like that smile. It usually meant Grandma Gerry was going to tell her something
bad. For her own good, of course.

"What are you doing over here by yourself?" Grandma
Gerry asked. "Why aren't you having fun with the other
kids?"

"I was on the trampoline with Elijah." That was fun. She
didn't feel so heavy on the trampoline. When she bounced
on it, when she was in the air, she felt as if she could do
anything. Even flips. Plus, it counted as exercise because
she'd been jumping. A lot.

Leaning over the table, Grandma Gerry rolled down
the top of the Dorito bag.

How did she know? It must be a mom thing—even
though she wasn't her dad's real mom, she'd still raised
him and Aunt Fay for a long time, so maybe she got some
of that mom stuff that way.

Or maybe, she thought with a sigh as she glanced down at her hands, Grandma Gerry had spied Bree's stained fingers.

Stupid fake cheese flavoring. Why did it have to be so… orange? And so delicious?

"You should be playing with kids your own age. Aren't any of your friends here?"

"No," Bree muttered.

"Well, then, let's see what we can do to make you some new friends, hmm?" Grandma Gerry said in a determined voice. "Look, there's Ryleigh from your soccer team. Ryleigh?" she called to the other girl.

Bree couldn't breathe and her head felt itchy and prickly, as if her hair was trying to crawl away. She couldn't draw in even the slightest bit of air. Her lungs burned. She was going to pass out. She was going to pass out and die, right then and there.

And when her grandma waved and smiled that scary, toothy smile at the best player on Bree's team and said, "Honey, could you come up here for a minute?" she wished she was already dead.

Frantic, Bree scanned the crowd for someone to save her, preferably her mother. Luckily, she was there because Aunt Fay had invited her to the picnic, too.

The second time Bree looked from the pool to the garage, she spotted her mom with some woman in jean shorts and a flowy top. Her dad…where was her dad? Chewing on her lower lip, she rose onto her toes and searched until she saw him sitting on a lawn chair with Papa Carl. But he wasn't looking at her grandpa. He was looking at… her mom.

Maybe he was staring because he wasn't used to seeing her in a dress, even a casual sundress and wedges. Or maybe it was because she was laughing, her head thrown back, the tail of her braid trailing down her back.

Whatever it was, it made Bree feel funny, the way he watched her mom, his jaw tight, his eyes narrowed. Sort of like how Edward looked at Bella in the first *Twilight* movie. As if he was mad. As if he wanted to kill her.

As if he wanted to kiss her.

She swallowed and forced herself to turn away.

"Ryleigh," Grandma Gerry said, putting her arm around the blonde's shoulders, "do you remember Bree? From soccer?"

"Sure," Ryleigh said, her own smile friendly. "Hi, Bree."

"Hi."

"Were you heading to the pool?" Grandma Gerry asked.

Ryleigh, wearing her swimsuit and carrying a beach towel, nodded. "Mr. Pettit set up a net so we can play volleyball in the water."

Grandma Gerry's eyes gleamed. "That sounds like fun. Doesn't that sound like fun, Bree?"

Standing in the water getting splashed while a bunch of kids—skinnier kids, more athletic kids—hit a ball back and forth?

"Sure," she said.

"Maybe Bree could join you?" her grandma asked, as if that was just the best idea ever.

Bree's face burned. Why didn't she just say, *Hey, could you play with my fat granddaughter? Oh, and be sure to teach her how to be more like you and less like herself.*

"Yeah, that'd be great," Ryleigh said, as if she really meant it.

Even though she was a year older than Bree, she always said hi to her at practice and even told her "Good job" when Bree did well—which wasn't often.

Ryleigh truly was nice. One of the nicest girls on the team.

Nice and pretty and skinny and popular and good at sports.

Her grandma and dad probably wished they'd had her instead of getting stuck with Bree.

"I forgot my suit," Bree said.

Ryleigh didn't seem to know what to say. And she kept glancing at the pool. Where her real friends were.

"Oh. Well, maybe when you're done swimming, you two could get on the trampoline," Grandma Gerry said. "Or play badminton."

"That'd be great. I'll come find you when I'm done," Ryleigh said to Bree.

"Okay."

She'd just have to make sure she couldn't be found.

"Why don't you borrow one of my suits?" her grandma said after Ryleigh left. "I bet we could find one that fits you."

Yes, because wearing one of her grandmother's bathing suits wouldn't be embarrassing at all.

"No, thank you," Bree said.

"Are you sure? Maybe your mom would run back to your house and pick up your suit."

"No," Bree said quickly. "I mean…I'm not really in the mood to swim."

Wasn't in the mood to put on her one-piece—currently tucked into the bottom of her bag on the floor of her mom's truck—and be around Ryleigh and all her friends in their bikinis. They all had flat bellies and skinny legs, were already growing boobs. They looked great in their suits, like models.

Bree just looked stupid with her big stomach and flat chest. And she had these dimples on her upper thighs that never went away no matter how hard she rubbed at them.

"Dad's asking about your cupcakes," Aunt Fay said to

Bree as she came up the stairs. Her aunt hadn't been very happy lately, but today she was smiling and laughing.

Probably because Uncle Shane was there, paying attention to her and the boys.

It made Bree feel kind of mean inside. Seeing her uncle with his family. Knowing he'd probably just leave them again. Like her dad always left her.

"We could start bringing out the desserts," Grandma Gerry said.

"I'll get them," Bree said.

"That's sweet, honey," Aunt Fay said, running her hand over Bree's hair. "Thank you."

She went inside before her grandma tried to get someone else to play with her.

Carrying two rectangular containers, she came back out to the deck. After clearing off a space at the end of the long table under the living room window, she set the cupcakes on the silver tray her mom had brought.

"Hey," a deep voice to her right said. "How's it going?"

Bree turned...and froze. She may have squeaked but only a little. It was him. *Him.* The shirtless boy she'd seen earlier playing basketball except now he had on one of the Knights' play-off shirts, his hair damp with sweat.

She blushed. He was even cuter up close. And tall. Almost as tall as her dad.

He raised his eyebrows. And he smiled. "Mind if I have one of these?"

"Yes." She blinked. "I mean no," she blurted. "I mean... you can have one. If you want."

Ducking her head, she squeezed her eyes shut. *Well, of course he wanted one, you dummy. Or he wouldn't have asked.* Since it was easier to think, to speak, when she wasn't looking at him directly, she kept her head down, watched his hand as he reached for a cupcake then un-wrapped it.

A moment later, he reached for another one. "You make these?" he asked. She nodded. "They're really excellent."

She lifted her head, her eyes widening slightly as he ate the cupcake in two bites. He leaned toward her. "You won't tell anyone if I have another one, will you?"

She shook her head. "I promise," she said, her voice barely a whisper.

"Great." But he didn't take a third cupcake, he offered her his hand. "I'm Luke Sapko."

Bree laid her hand against his, hoping her palm wasn't all sweaty and gross. "I'm Bree...." She bit her lip, once again noted the T-shirt. "Bree Pettit," she said, only feeling a little bit guilty that she wasn't telling the truth, that her mom's feelings would be hurt if she found out.

In the midst of shaking her hand, he stopped, just sort of...holding her hand. "Yeah? You related to Neil Pettit?"

"He's my dad."

"Cool." Luke let go but her palm was all tingly. She curled her fingers, hoping to hold on to that feeling for a few more minutes. "You're lucky. Your dad's awesome."

She didn't know how to respond to that so she didn't say anything. Seemed safest.

But he didn't seem to notice. Or care. "He's offered to give me some pointers about skating and hockey." He nodded toward the Stanley Cup. "One day, I'll bring the Cup back to Shady Grove."

"And when you do," a redheaded girl his age said as she came up behind him and wrapped her arms around his waist, "I'll throw you a party like this."

He turned and slung his arm over her shoulders. "That's a deal. Hey, this is Bree. She made the most incredible cupcakes. Bree, this is Kennedy."

"Nice to meet you," Kennedy said.

"Hi," she mumbled.

Kennedy was tall and thin with light blue eyes and long hair that was so straight, it was as though someone had ironed it. Her shorts were supershort and Bree could see the tops of her boobs sticking out from her tank top. Plus, her skin was pale—almost white—and so pretty it made Bree wish she didn't tan so easily, that her own arms and legs weren't so brown. That her pants weren't so dumpy-looking, that she hadn't spilled mustard on her shirt when she'd had a second hot dog.

Made her wish she was someone else. Someone pretty, thin and confident.

"I claimed the ball court," Kennedy told Luke. "You up for a little one-on-one?"

"I think I can take you." He looked at Bree. "What do you think, B?"

B. He called her B. Like a nickname, something between the two of them. Feeling brave for a moment, she met his eyes. "I think you can, too."

He winked. "That's my girl."

But she wasn't his girl. Because she wasn't the one he held close to his side and walked off with.

She was the one he left behind.

"JAMES SAYS YOU'VE GOT a long way to go at Bradford House, baby girl," Frank Montesano said to Maddie as they sat on her parents' patio.

The setting sun cast shadows across her parents' neatly trimmed backyard, early summer flowers blooming in her mother's gardens. A warm breeze caressed Maddie's bare shoulders, reminded her of a lover's touch.

Neil's face floated into her mind. She shoved it right back out again.

"James is the king of stating the obvious." She dragged a cracker through the bowl of hummus her mother had brought out. "Next thing he'll be telling us the color of the sky and the boiling point of water."

Frank sipped his red wine, his thick eyebrows lowered over eyes the same color as Maddie's. "Does he exaggerate?"

She sighed. Bit viciously into the cracker. "No."

"Tell me."

"The parlor's almost done. We ran new electrical, insulated the outside walls and hung and taped the drywall. Next week the bricklayers are coming to refinish the fireplace."

"The same fireplace I told you was unsalvageable?"

She smiled. Tossed the remainder of the cracker into her mouth. "Yep."

"What did you do and how much did it eat into our profit?"

"I raised the fireplace." She'd had to. It was sinking into the floor. But there was no way she could get rid of it. Marble and original to the house, it was a work of art. And worth every penny she'd spent making sure it stayed that way. "I rented a lift and shored up the beams in the basement and added new support columns. And it didn't cut into our profit for the job because Neil Pettit has more money than he knows what to do with."

"Now that sounds like sour grapes," Rose said as she carried out a tray of thinly sliced meats and cheeses and cut fresh fruit.

"It's not," Maddie insisted. Her parents exchanged a loaded glance. "I hate when you do that," she muttered.

Rose set the tray on the glass-topped table. "Do what?"

"Communicate without saying a word. It's freaky."

"It's the only way we could get a word in edgewise," Frank said. "We were outnumbered two-to-one, you know."

"Whose fault was that?" Maddie asked, wrapping prosciutto around a slice of cheese.

He pulled Rose onto his lap. "Your mother's. She never could keep her hands off me."

"So true," Rose said, wrapping her arms around her husband's neck. "So very, very true."

They kissed. Pulled back and kissed again.

"Hello?" Maddie said. "I'm still sitting here. Right here." They kissed once more. "I've got a front-row seat to this and am about to gouge out my eyes if you don't knock it off."

Still holding on to Frank, Rose leaned back. "I think you'll survive. It's not the first time you've seen your parents be affectionate."

No, it wasn't the first time, or even the hundredth. Maddie and her brothers had been firsthand witnesses to their parents' love. The secret smiles they had for each other. The way their gazes would lock and hold. How their dad would brush their mom's hair back, his touch gentle and reverent. How she'd cup his cheeks each morning after she kissed him goodbye, her fingers trailing across his jaw as they stepped apart.

It was that sort of relationship, that bond, that Maddie had wanted so badly for herself. She'd imagined her and Neil as parents, their own children running around, their own little house. Their family.

"Thank you," Maddie said, her throat clogging with emotion.

"For what?" her dad asked.

"For loving each other. For showing us all what a healthy, loving, passionate relationship looks like."

"Oh, honey," Rose said with a soft laugh. She slid off of Frank's lap, knelt in front of Maddie. "What's wrong?"

"Wrong? What could be wrong?" Maddie picked up a cracker, set it down again. "My life is great. Practically perfect, really. I mean, sure, I'm a single, twenty-eight-year-old woman and I'm spending Saturday night watching my parents make out but other than that I have it all. A bright, beautiful, healthy daughter. Loving parents. Three pain-in-the-ass brothers. What more could I want?"

Rose grasped Maddie's hands. "Did something happen at the Pettits' picnic?"

"Did that boy do something to upset you?" Frank asked with one of his fierce scowls.

Maddie couldn't help it. She laughed. "*That boy* is over six feet tall, thirty and a multimillionaire."

"So?" her dad grumbled.

Maddie shook her head. "No, Neil didn't do anything."

Except stare at her. Every time she'd glanced at him—and, God help her, she hadn't been able to stop glancing at him—she'd caught him watching her with an intensity that had stolen her breath, made her skin heat. Reminded her of when she first fell for him, when her feelings for him were so new and exciting. He'd watched her then, too. As a teenager, he'd averted his gaze when she looked his way.

Tonight he'd held her gaze, his blue eyes glittering with interest and intention. Blatant. Sexual.

It'd been too much. And not because it'd been reminiscent of the way they used to be, but because it'd been tempting, to see what it'd be like to be with him now. So she'd done what any reasonable, intelligent woman would do.

She'd run like hell.

"And Bree was okay?" Rose prodded. "She was having fun?"

"She was," Maddie admitted, her tone grudging.

Now it was Rose's turn to laugh. "There's no need to sound so upset about it."

"I'm not. It's just…Neil let her cook the burgers and then he taught her how to lay the wood for the campfire."

"And…?"

"And he was…good with her. He paid attention to her, sat next to her while we ate, played kickball with her and Fay's boys…"

"Those are good things," her mom said. "Didn't you want him paying more attention to her?"

"Of course. I just don't want Bree to get too attached to him, that's all."

Rose squeezed Maddie's hands. "He is her father. I'd say any attachment was already formed, wouldn't you?"

"Yes, but she might start to believe he'll always be around, but he won't. In a few weeks, he'll go back to Seattle. He's going to leave. That's what he does."

"Seems to me, his leaving was the best thing for you and Bree," Frank said gruffly as he got to his feet. "He never was near good enough for my girls."

He kissed the top of her head, ran his hand over Rose's hair then went inside, shutting the French door behind him.

"Don't listen to your father," Rose said. "I'm sure Neil will do his best to be a better father to Bree."

"You never say anything bad about him," Maddie said thoughtfully to her mother. "To dad he's always *that boy*—said in the same vein as *that rat bastard*. My brothers all want, to varying degrees, to wipe the floor with his face. Even Pops threatened to break Neil's kneecaps when he found out he'd gotten me pregnant. But not you. I don't think I've ever heard you say one ugly word against him."

"Would it make you feel better if I was angry with him?" her mother asked softly.

"Yes. No." Maddie tugged on her braid. "God...I don't even know anymore. All I know is that if I stop being mad at him, what's left?"

"Forgiveness?"

"I don't know if I can forgive him." Didn't know if she wanted to.

Rose pulled Frank's chair closer and sat on it, took Maddie's hands in hers once again. "I hate what Neil did to you and Bree. Hate how he hurt you." Reaching out, she smoothed back a loose strand of Maddie's hair. "But, honey, we've all made mistakes. Haven't we?"

Maddie's gaze flew to her mom's, her heart thumping painfully. But she saw no censure in Rose's eyes, no judgment. Only understanding. Acceptance.

She wanted to lay her head in her mother's lap, confess what she'd done, purge herself of the lies, the guilt.

But there was only one person she needed to tell. She wasn't brave enough.

So she sniffed back the tears clogging her throat. Tried to smile. "You hate what he did, but you don't hate him, huh? Looks like, other than Bree, you're the only Montesano who doesn't."

"Oh, I think we both know there's one more Montesano who doesn't hate him," Rose whispered. "No matter how much you want to."

CHAPTER ELEVEN

MADDIE OPENED HER kitchen door. And almost slammed it shut again.

Which Neil must have sensed because, just like the last time he stood there, he braced the door open with his foot. "Please," he said, "I'm begging you. Let us in."

Well, he did look a little…disheveled. And wild-eyed. "Actually," she said, "I'm having second thoughts about this—"

"Mom," Bree said with an impressive eye roll. "Let us in."

Maddie stepped aside while they entered—Neil carrying a sleeping Mitchell in one arm, the diaper bag and a backpack in the other, Bree and Elijah holding hands, looking as if they'd survived a war.

Maddie knelt and tapped Elijah's purple mustache. "Grape juice?"

"Popsicle," he said, giving her a sleepy grin.

Pressing her lips together, she straightened. "Your sister so owes me," she told Neil darkly.

Fay had called her not forty-five minutes ago and asked if Maddie could keep the boys overnight.

"She knows." He set the bags on the table and lifted Mitchell higher. The baby stirred, raised his head for a second then put it back on Neil's shoulder. "She says you can have anything you want. Including her firstborn."

"Funny but she never offers him up when he's clean and smells good and is cuddly—"

"Does a time like that even exist?" Neil murmured.

"I only get him when he's been rolling in the mud— literally, from the looks of it," she added, taking in the streaks of dirt on his bare legs, the grass stain on his shorts. "And has—" Frowning, she peered at Elijah's head. "Is that melted marshmallows in his hair?"

Bree nodded and helped Elijah peel off his sweatshirt. "And chocolate. Papa Carl let him make his own s'more."

"My marshmallow burneded, Aunt Maddie," Elijah said. "So I threw it into the fire and it got big and ex- ploded!"

She flinched at his loud tone. Mitchell, God bless him, kept right on sleeping. "That must've been very exciting," she whispered, hoping Elijah would follow suit. "But it's late and you and Bree need to get ready for bed."

Elijah yawned so widely, Maddie was surprised his jaw didn't crack. "I'm not tired."

"I can see that," she said. "Unfortunately, it's after ten and what's the rule when you spend the night at mean old Aunt Maddie's house?"

"No staying up late."

She flicked his nose. "Winner, winner, chicken dinner." He giggled and leaned into her, his body warm, his hair sticky. "Let's get you into the tub before you fall asleep standing up. Honey?" she asked Bree. "Can you take him into the bathroom and help him get undressed? I'll be in in a minute."

"Okay." Bree took Elijah's hand again then faced Neil. "Thank you for the ride home."

"You're welcome," he told her just as solemnly. "Good night."

"'Bye."

"Can't you just douse the kid with the hose?" he asked Maddie when they were alone. "It'd save you a lot of trouble."

She couldn't tell if he was serious or not. "What's life without a little trouble?"

"Peaceful."

He said it so sincerely, so seriously, she couldn't help but ask, "Is that what you want? A peaceful life?"

Was that why he hadn't wanted Bree? He hadn't wanted the ups and downs that came with parenting. Emotional highs and lows, the loss of sleep and privacy. The worry and stress.

"Isn't that what everyone wants?" he asked.

"I have no idea. I only know what I want." She picked up Elijah's sweatshirt, wrinkled her nose at the smell. Looked as though she'd be doing a load of laundry tonight. "While peace ranks up there with good wine and expensive chocolate, if that's all you had, it'd get boring pretty quickly."

"You always did like the excitement and drama of chaos and confusion," he said. "Of a good cry. Or a good argument."

She inclined her head in agreement. "And you always hated it. You didn't get sad, happy or angry. No emotional ups and downs for the great Neil Pettit. Must be nice, not having to deal with something as irritating and messy as all those pesky human feelings."

When they'd been together, he'd never argued with her, even when she did her best to piss him off. She'd tried, so hard, to get him to prove she was worth fighting for, that *they* were worth fighting for.

I never fought you.

No, he'd never fought her and not just over their daughter. Even when they'd been kids themselves, he'd walked away from arguments. She wondered if his threatening to fight her now was just ironic or a truckload of bad karma come to park in her driveway.

"Mom?"

"Coming," she called back to Bree. She reached for the baby. "Here, I'll put him to bed."

"I'll do it."

She froze, her arms still out. "You?"

"I have put a baby down before."

Sure he had. A few times. And always when Gerry or Fay was there with him and Bree. "I don't want to keep—"

"You're not," he said, already heading toward the hall. "Where's the crib?"

"I have a portable one set up in my bedroom." Her bedroom where she hadn't made the bed or picked up her clothes in, oh…two days now. "Really," she said, hurrying after him, "you don't have—"

He turned. "Maddie. You have your hands full. Let me help."

She didn't want his help. Not tonight, not with his nephews, not with their daughter. She had to do everything herself. It was the only way she could protect herself from getting hurt again.

"Mom!" Bree cried over the sound of Elijah screeching.

No, Maddie thought again, she didn't want his help. But maybe she could accept it. Just this once.

"It's the last room on the right," she said, gesturing at her closed bedroom door. "I left the lamp on. You can just see yourself out when you're done."

"I'll wait."

"That's not necessary." And not what she needed after a very long day.

He met her eyes over the baby's head. "I'll wait."

Damn him for being so immovable. But she wasn't

going to argue with him, wouldn't give him the satisfaction of acting like a shrew—again.

"Fine." See? He wasn't the only one who could be calm, cool and collected. "I'll be out as soon as I can."

Except she wasn't. Out as soon as she could have been, that was. She took her sweet time, drawing out what should have been a ten-minute deal into twenty. Would have taken even longer but she'd no sooner tucked Bree and Elijah into Bree's bed when they were both asleep. Still, she checked on Mitchell, only slightly mollified to find him safe and sound in the portable crib, a blanket covering him.

It wasn't until she was literally dragging her feet down the hallway that she realized she was stalling. But that wasn't what really got her goat, oh, no. What was so much worse was why she was stalling.

She was nervous. Neil Pettit made her nervous, made her palms sweat and her pulse race. Made her want to run and lock herself in her bedroom until he got tired of waiting and left.

And that would not do. None of it.

Head high, shoulders back, she stepped into the kitchen only to have her stomach jump to find him sitting at the table, his legs stretched out, his shoulders broad, his shirt clinging to his chest.

It was just Neil. Her stomach, and other parts of her, stopped jumping for him a long time ago.

What right did he have to be sprawled out like that, completely comfortable and at ease, looking for all the world as if he owned the damn place? This was her place. Her home. Just as Shady Grove was her town.

She was the one in control, of the situation, her feelings and her reaction to him.

Hey, if a girl couldn't lie to herself, who could she lie to?

"All settled?" he asked, getting to his feet.

"Hopefully." She crossed to the fridge. "Do you want a drink?"

"No, thanks."

She didn't, either, but grabbed a beer anyway. Opened it and took a sip. "Let's go out to the porch. I don't want to wake the kids."

Or have a repeat of that cozy domestic scene they'd had in her kitchen a few mornings ago.

Outside, she lit the lantern on the table, more to keep mosquitoes away than for light, and sat on the bench to the right of the door—and immediately realized her mistake. The night surrounded them, thick and silent, the flame from the lantern illuminating the harsh planes of Neil's face as he sat next to her. The sky was a dark canvas dotted with glowing stars and a brilliant moon, the air soothing and still and expectant, as if the night itself was holding its breath.

And Neil, the sharp scent of wood smoke clinging to him, sitting so close that his thigh, his warm, solid thigh, brushed hers.

Crap.

"Nice night," she said and inwardly cursed how breathless she sounded. She cleared her throat and oh-so-casually shifted, putting as much distance as the bench—and her pride—would allow. "How'd you get roped into bringing the boys over here?"

"I volunteered."

She glanced at him, watched the flicker of light flash across his profile. "We'll have to get you the Mr. Helpful Award."

He lifted a shoulder. "I wanted to see Bree home. It only made sense that I take the boys, too."

"What did you do, toss them in the trunk?"

"I took Fay's minivan since she and Shane were going in his car. Looks like they're getting back together."

Though she tried, she really did, she couldn't stop a snort from escaping.

"You don't think that's a good idea?"

She thought Fay was a fool for giving Shane the chance to hurt her again. "I'm keeping my opinion to myself from now on."

She felt his surprise. "Really? How's that working for you?"

"It's killing me."

But Fay had made it very clear she didn't want or need Maddie's most excellent advice. Maybe Neil was right. Maybe she did roll right over people. The thought made her throat hurt, so she took another drink and settled against the back of the bench. Hopefully the shadows would swallow her, hide the fact that her hair was coming out of her braid, her mascara was smudged under her eyes and the rest of her makeup had long ago melted off.

All of which she was sure Neil, of the eagle eye, had noticed. Not that she cared. It was just that she was tired. And quickly heading toward grumpy.

Why wouldn't she be? It was late and she'd just wrestled forty pounds of wiry boy into the tub, scrubbed him, washed his hair three times and wrangled him into a pair of *Cars* underwear—the only clothing she could get on him. Even dried off the kid was slippery.

Maddie's shirt was soaked and stuck to her skin. She had a blister on her pinkie toe thanks to those stupid wedged sandals she'd worn to the picnic, and all she wanted was to slip into a cool, silk nightgown and crawl into bed. Not hang out on her porch like some all-you-can-eat bug buffet.

But she refused to ask Neil why he'd insisted on staying, refused to let him think she was curious or concerned or interested in the slightest in his reasons.

Proud of her self-restraint, she lifted her beer in a silent toast to herself then took a drink.

If he didn't say something—recite the alphabet or break into song or spout hockey stats…God…anything and soon—she was going to scream.

"Thank you," he said after what felt like an hour, but was probably closer to a few minutes. "For bringing Bree to the picnic."

Anything but that.

She bobbled the bottle in her hand, set it between her thighs before she dropped it. She didn't want his gratitude. Didn't deserve it. Not when she'd erased his message, the one he'd left yesterday. Not when she'd planned on forgetting all about it. On not telling Bree that he'd called, that he'd wanted her there.

It was a mistake. Another one. She'd been angry…God… it felt as if she was always angry. She'd spent the past twelve years letting fury and resentment control her when she'd promised herself never to let any emotion do that to her again.

She'd wanted to hurt him. To prove that she was in charge. Shame filled her, made the beer in her stomach sour.

"Since Bree wasn't there when you won the Cup," Maddie said, admitting only what she could, what couldn't come back to haunt her, "she needed to at least be a part of the party celebrating that win."

Neil needed her to be there.

For the first time in a long time, Maddie had put his needs before her own.

It scared her. Even if it was the right thing to do.

He lifted a shoulder as if it was no big deal that he'd

reached the pinnacle of his career. That his dreams had come true.

"You should be proud," she said slowly, forcing the words out. "Winning the Cup is a huge deal."

He touched her, just his hand on her wrist, but the contact swept over her like a memory. His warm, rough fingers a reminder of all the times he'd touched her, of how she could reach for his hand at any time and count on him to be there. Strong. Steady.

Hers.

"Do you mean that?" he asked in his quiet voice, his eyes searching.

She didn't try to free herself, didn't want to give him that much satisfaction, as if having his skin on hers was too much for her to handle. "Of course."

His fingers tightened momentarily and she thought, hoped, he'd release her, prayed he couldn't feel the erratic beat of her pulse. But when his grip loosened, he didn't pull away, just traced the rough, calloused tip of his forefinger along the delicate skin of her inner wrist.

"Did you watch?" he asked.

She blinked at him. Couldn't think, could barely breathe. "What?"

"Did you watch the last game?" He dragged his finger over the heel of her hand, his nail lightly scraping her palm. "Did you see when I raised the Cup?"

After winning the championship, it was tradition for the players to take turns hoisting the Cup on the ice.

"No," she said, sliding her hand away from him. She'd avoided TV while the games had been on, hadn't even so much as glanced at the sports section of the paper. Wouldn't let him back into her life in any way, shape or form. "I didn't see it. I didn't watch any of the games."

His mouth tightened and he nodded, as if understanding why she'd had to protect herself. "I always thought you'd be there."

Her throat dried. Her mind spun, took her back to when they'd been together. For as long as she'd known him, he'd wanted to win the Cup, to have that shining moment on the ice. They'd talked about it, dreamed about it together. Of how it'd feel, how she'd be there, cheering him on. Celebrating with him.

Maddie wanted to rail at him, to scream and hit him. To leap to her feet and make one hell of a grand exit. She sat there, unable to speak or move.

Neil linked his hands together between his knees, stared at the flickering light on the porch floor. "As I raised the Cup, I looked into the stands. I saw Gerry and Carl but I kept searching. I wasn't even sure what I was looking for...who I was looking for...until I got home that night and it hit me."

"Don't," she told him sharply. Succinctly.

Don't drag me into the past. Don't get to me with your sad eyes and somber words. Don't make me care about you. Not again.

Holding her gaze, he lowered his voice. "I was looking for you."

NEIL'S WORDS HUNG in the air between them, quiet and honest. He wouldn't take them back, no matter how much trouble they caused him.

He'd thought of her that night. They'd won the last game at the Knights' rink and the place had gone wild. When he'd held the Cup above his head, tens of thousands of fans had erupted into riotous cheers, stomping their feet, screaming his name over the music pumping through the PA system. He'd been beyond himself, his battered body exhausted, his entire being filled with a sense of euphoria, of pride and accomplishment, unlike anything he'd ever experienced. It was, without a doubt, the greatest moment of his career, the moment he'd worked so hard for. It'd been perfect. And he'd looked for Maddie. Had wanted to share it with her.

With the girl he'd left behind.

"I'm honored," Maddie said, her flat tone and crossed arms a good indication that she was lying through her teeth. "Although I am surprised I crossed your mind at all."

"You did." Too often. After all these years, he still thought of her, and he hated it. Hated how, when his defenses were down, she slipped into his mind. Into his dreams. "What we had, it…meant something to me." He exhaled softly. "You meant something to me."

Her mouth dropped and she blinked. "Wow," she breathed, shaking her head slowly. "Wow. Thank you, so much, for that incredibly patronizing, completely dispassionate declaration. Meant something to you," she muttered, lifting her beer to her mouth only to lower it again without taking a drink so she could skewer him with one of her scathing looks. "Your lucky socks meant something to you. Your conditioning coach and the lunch lady who always gave you extra dessert meant something to you. I loved you."

Her voice was whisper-soft, her words as intoxicating, as powerful, as they'd been all those years ago when she'd so freely told him of her feelings. Repeatedly. Endlessly. Until those three words had suffocated him, constantly prodding him for a response. One he'd been unable to give.

"I loved you," she repeated. "More than that, I trusted you. And you showed me exactly how you felt about me by screwing someone else."

She started to rise and his control cracked, threatened to crumble under her mocking words, her disdainful glare.

He swiveled, bracketing her with his arms on either side of her hips, his knee pressing against her thigh. His heart pounded, his muscles tensed. She had no right, no goddamn right, to throw his words back at him. Not when words never came easily for him. When his tongue felt clumsy, his brain muddled and stupid.

"I was eighteen," he said roughly, ignoring how huge her eyes were, how she was probably getting ready to hit him over the head with her beer bottle. "When you told me you were pregnant I was terrified."

Scared all of his plans were ruined, that he'd end up back in Shady Grove, tied down with a wife and baby. That he'd turn into his father, trapped with a family he hadn't planned on, one he could barely afford to support.

One he hadn't wanted. Not yet.

The resentment he'd seen on his father's face had already taken hold of Neil. Resentment, confusion and anger. How had it happened? They were so careful, had always used birth control. But somehow, Maddie had ended up pregnant anyway.

Two weeks after Maddie told him, when Neil had gone out with some of the older guys on the team and a slinky redhead five years his senior had come on to him, he'd seen it for what it was. An opportunity. A way to get back his freedom, to push Maddie away, to kill her love for him once and for all.

"Telling you what happened..." His throat clogged. He cleared it. "Admitting to you what I'd done was the hardest thing I'd ever had to do."

She laughed harshly. "Yeah? Believe me, it wasn't easy for me to hear, either."

"I know." He remembered how stricken she'd been. He'd come back to tell her, had known that he had to look into her eyes and confess his sin. He'd expected her to tell him off, to yell and call him names. To end things between them.

He hadn't expected how crushed she'd be. How much he'd hurt her.

"I messed up," he said, unable to stop himself from edging closer, from sliding his arms in so that her hip warmed his skin. "I hurt you. And for that, I'm sorry."

"I always knew you'd come back someday begging for my forgiveness," she said with a sneer, but her voice trembled, the pulse at the base of her throat fluttered.

Christ, but she was caustic and defensive. He should have washed his hands of her a long time ago. He shifted, bracing his weight on his right hand, bringing their faces even closer. He laid his left hand on her waist, and she inhaled sharply but didn't push him away.

Thank God.

"Are you going to grant it?" he asked. "Will you forgive me, Maddie?"

All those years ago when he'd admitted to cheating on her, he hadn't apologized. Just told her the truth, accepted her anger as his due and he'd gone on his way. Back to his new life, his goals, without ever seeking absolution. Now he wanted it, needed it, more than his next breath.

Her throat worked. "It doesn't matter—"

"It does to me." He inhaled deeply, searched for the right words. "You think I never got mad at you because I didn't yell or hit things, that I wasn't happy with you because I didn't jump for joy, but you're wrong. You pissed me off plenty." He lowered his voice, couldn't stop himself from touching the loose strand of hair by her ear, rubbing it between his fingers. "And you made me happy."

Happier than he'd ever thought possible. Happier than he'd thought he had a right to be.

She leaned back so that her hair slid through his fingers. "You want forgiveness? Okay. I forgive you. Satisfied?"

"Satisfied?" Her scent filled his nostrils, her heat beckoned him. "Not even close."

She licked her lips and his gaze dropped, followed the movement. "I know I'd be a lot happier if you'd back up."

"You looked really good in that dress at the picnic." The words came out a husky growl, as raw as if they'd been ripped from his throat. She stilled, seemed to even stop breathing. "Different. Soft. Touchable."

"I'm not yours to touch."

He held her gaze, watched the play of light in her eyes. "You used to be."

"Times change. I'm not that girl anymore."

"No," he said, taking note of the changes time had made on her face, "you're not that girl. You're a woman. And you're so damned beautiful, Maddie. You take my breath away."

She'd always done that. Always took his breath and his thoughts, occupied so much space in his head. In his heart. He'd been afraid she'd take over.

"Tell me," she said with a thin smile, "do those lines ever actually work? Because I have to say, being on this side of the pickup, I'm sort of shocked you ever get lucky."

"They're not lines." He wished they were. Wished he was spouting bullshit to some stranger he'd met, his only concern getting laid. That his gut wasn't a tangled knot, his chest not tight with want, his hands aching to feel Maddie's skin. "You always wanted to know my every thought, my every feeling. Here they are. I couldn't take my eyes off of you today."

"Like I said," she snapped, her shoulders going rigid, "times change. Now, it's late and—"

"You must have felt it, felt me watching you," he continued, his fingers tightening on her waist. "No matter what I was doing I could hear your laugh. You'd smile and I remembered how you used to smile at me, how you used to look at me. I wondered if your hair still smelled the same—" He rubbed the end of her braid between his fingers, the strands like silk. "Like lavender. If your skin was still as soft. If you tasted the same." He trailed his fingers from the line of her jaw down around to cup her neck. His other hand slid under her shirt to caress the curve of her hip. "If you still trembled when I touched you."

She did. Lust shot through him, settled hot and heavy in his groin.

"It's just memories." Her eyes were wide, her tone desperate. "It's just the past getting confused with the present. It's not real."

"Maybe not," he said, the words barely a rumble in his chest. He tugged her slowly toward him, triumphant and grateful when she didn't resist. "Let's find out for sure."

CHAPTER TWELVE

SHE SHOULD DO SOMETHING, Maddie thought, frantic. Shove him on his ass or dump her beer in his lap. All viable options, options she should take. Instead she let him pull her, oh, so slowly, toward him. It was shock, she told herself, that had her thoughts fuzzy, her chest tight. Not anticipation. Not hope or excitement. Certainly not fear.

His eyes, hot with want, dropped to her mouth. Her lips parted. Her throat dried. Oh, God. She stiffened but his fingers delved into the hair at the nape of her neck and he held her head. Just like he used to. His hand large and warm, his thumb brushing against the sensitive skin on the underside of her jaw. And he was looking at her as if she was the only woman in the entire world, the only one who mattered.

The only one he wanted.

It was a lie, one she'd fooled herself into believing years ago. One she couldn't afford to believe now.

His face filled her vision, his head blocking the light from the lantern. He became her focus, all she could see was the blue of his eyes, all she could feel was the warmth of his breath on her mouth. He hesitated, his lips a hairbreadth from hers, and that feeling she'd insisted wasn't anticipation built until she was afraid she couldn't take it anymore. That if he didn't close the distance between them, the unthinkable, the unfathomable, would happen.

She would.

He saved her ego and her pride, let her keep believing the lies she told herself, by brushing his mouth against hers. Her breath stuttered out, her heart pounded, the sound echoing in her ears. She froze, her hands clenched in her lap, as his lips settled against hers, warm and firm. He kept the kiss gentle. Sweet. Like their first.

Like their last.

Tears stung her eyes, made her throat burn, but she kept her gaze on his as he eased back.

She tipped her head. "Like I said, just memories."

Her voice was cool. Calm. There was no way he'd suspect her palms were sweating, that there was an odd and unwelcome fluttering in her stomach.

Wouldn't know what it'd cost her not to kiss him back.

"You can't blame a guy for trying," he said, shifting so that he was crouched in front of her. Then, with a self-depreciating shrug, he smiled.

The tips of her fingers tingled. Her cheeks heated.

Crap.

She lunged at him, toppling her beer to the floor with a dull thud. He grunted softly and caught her, somehow managing to keep them both upright. Wrapping her arms around his neck, she arched against him and fused her mouth to his. She tasted his shock, his hesitation, before his arms tightened around her and he stood, keeping her in his arms.

He kissed her back. Deep, wet kisses, his tongue rasping against hers, his five-o'clock shadow scraping against her chin and upper lip. He felt…God…he felt so good. Too good. Solid and hot. His chest bigger, his shoulders broader, his entire body harder than what she remembered. He didn't kiss her like the sad-eyed boy she'd loved— softly and reverently and carefully. He kissed like a man with one intention. Seduction. Long, slow, mind-numbing kisses that threatened to drag her under his spell. Put her completely in his control.

He slipped his hands under her shirt, skimmed them across her lower back, then settled them on her waist, his thumbs rubbing circles on her stomach as he walked her backward. Lifting his head, he guided her to the far corner of the porch on the other side of the kitchen window, pressed her against the side of the house and slid his knee between her thighs.

He dragged her shirt up, the backs of his knuckles brushing across her ribs. Bunching the material under her arms, he reached behind her and undid her bra, pushing the cups up before he lifted his head and stepped back. He cupped her, the skin of his palms rough against her breasts, his eyes glittering in the darkness.

"Still soft," he murmured, caressing her lightly, trailing his fingers down the slope of her breasts to circle her areolae. Her nipples tightened. Her core contracted. He pinched her left nipple, rolled the tip between his thumb and forefinger.

He bent his head, touched his tongue to her right nipple. Looked up at her. "Still tasty," he said, his voice husky, his breath hot on her.

Then he sucked her into his mouth.

Maddie shut her eyes and concentrated on how good it felt to have his mouth, warm and wet on one breast, his fingers firm and sure on the other. Need settled heavily in her stomach, moisture pooled between her legs. She ran her hands over his shoulders, down his arms and up to hold his head, her fingers sifting through the cool strands of his hair.

Neil slid his hand down her side, across the waistband of her pants. She inhaled sharply, her stomach muscles quivering. Back and forth his hand went. Back and forth.

He straightened, kissed her again, one hand again holding her head, the other now slipping under the stretchy material of her pants and underwear to barely, just barely, graze her curls.

Longing, need, unlike any she'd ever experienced, filled her, deep-seated and burning.

All because Neil was kissing her. Touching her. Neil. Always Neil.

Only Neil.

Panic suffused her, had her wrenching her head back with enough force that she whacked it against the house with a sharp rap.

"Easy," he said, reaching for her.

She slapped his hands away, but when she spoke, her voice was thin. Needy. "Don't. Just…don't touch me."

He lowered his arms, the flickering light casting shadows on his face. "You didn't seem to mind a second ago."

That'd been the problem. Was still the problem. She craved his touch. More than that, she wanted to touch him back, to see if she could still make his breath quicken. If she could still make him quiver when she took him into her mouth.

She licked her lips, crossed her arms to cover herself. To hold herself together. "I don't want this."

His eyes flashed. "Liar. You may not like it, you may wish you didn't, but you still want me. Just as much as I want you." He edged closer, his mouth tense. "I tried to forget you, to be free of you, but you're always there. In my head. In my dreams. Goddamn it, Maddie," he said harshly, his voice unsteady, "you're always there."

"I know," she whispered. It was the same for her. "I know."

He inhaled sharply, leaned down to kiss her. Sanity and clarity resurfaced and she stiffened, set her hands on his chest to push him back. To push him away. Neil shook his head, one quick shake. Their gazes locked. Held.

Her heart raced. She couldn't catch her breath. Oh, God, Neil was right. She was nothing but a liar.

They moved at the same time, their mouths melding together. Gone was any resistance on her part, any finesse on his. His kiss was hard and angry, his hunger fueling her own until she writhed against him. Desperate for his heat, seeking his skin, she reached between them, tugged his shirt up. He leaned back, yanked it over his head and threw it aside, the muscles of his chest and arms contracting with his movements.

He was beautiful, his body a work of art, a testament to the grueling hours spent training and on the ice. It was as if he was a Greek god, carved of stone. Perfect. Inhuman.

But when she placed her hands on his waist, his skin was soft. Warm. Not stone, she thought, but flesh and blood. She traced her fingertips over the ridges of his stomach and his muscles quivered. She slid her hands up, combed her fingers through the crisp hair covering his chest before laying her palms flat against him. His heart beat strong and steadily. Not inhuman. Spreading her fingers, the edge of her pinkie rubbed over the raised edge of a scar.

No, he wasn't perfect. He was just a man. Just Neil.

Her eyes on his, she lowered her hand and cupped him through his jeans. Flesh and blood.

With a low growl, he shoved her back, trapping her between the side of the house and his body. Her breasts were crushed against his chest, her beaded nipples scraping against his skin. His arousal, hard and unyielding, pressed against her center.

He rolled his hips. Once. Twice. She gasped. Grabbed his waist to steady him. To stop him. Then she slid her hands into his back pockets, her fingers curling into his ass. And she rubbed against him. Electric shocks coursed through her, heating her blood, clouding her mind. Moaning into his mouth, she did it again. And again.

He tore his mouth from hers and stepped back. Before she could protest, though, he was shoving down her pants. The night air washed over her for a moment and then Neil's hand was on her. She lifted her hips, rocked against him and he quickened his pace. He worked her faster. Harder. Her breathing grew ragged. Pleasure built, sweeping through her body like a firestorm, heating her skin. Neil's other hand went to her breast. He rolled her nipple between his fingers.

Spark after spark blasted through her, rising higher and higher until her climax exploded through her. She shut her eyes and let the flames consume her.

NEIL'S BODY ACHED, his chest burned. He couldn't take his eyes off of Maddie. She was so beautiful as she came, her lips parted, her head thrown back. Her body trembled under his fingers, her scent filled the air, made him dizzy. The image of her was imprinted on his mind, the feel of her embedded in his skin.

Days, weeks from now, this would be just another memory he wouldn't be able to escape, one that would come to torture him in his sleep. Remind him of all he'd lost, of all he'd given up. But now, right now, it was real. In this moment she wasn't a memory, wasn't a dream, she was warm and soft and wet for him.

In this moment, she was his once again.

He wrapped her braid around his fist, held her head for his kiss, his other hand on the roundness of her hip. He swept his tongue into her mouth and she jerked against him. Kissed him back just as deeply, as voraciously, as if she needed this, needed him, as much as he needed her. She wiggled her hands between them, found the button on his jeans. He shifted, giving her more room to work the button free, drag the zipper down.

Maddie laid her palms flat against his hips, slid them under the heavy cloth of his jeans, the waist of his boxers, pushing his clothes down until his erection sprang free. It jutted out, brushing the silken skin of her lower stomach. He pressed his forehead against hers, his chest rising and falling rapidly. They both watched as she trailed a finger up his length. He hissed out a breath. Moisture beaded at the tip, clung there until she rubbed the pad of her thumb over it, spreading wetness across the head.

His fingers tightened on her, digging into her skull, her hip bones. Sweat broke out on his upper lip, the back of his neck. Then both her hands were on him, soft, seeking. Stroking. Driving him to madness.

He dug his wallet out of his back pocket, pulled out a condom and sheathed himself in record time. His hands on Maddie's waist, he lifted her, bracing her against the house as he reached beneath her thighs, wrapped her legs around his waist. Leaned back to look at her, pliant and open for him. Beams of moonlight broke through the clouds, casting her body in an unearthly glow, gold touching her face, the slope of her full breasts, the curve of her stomach. Lust, primitive and animalistic, roared through him, drowning out every thought except being inside Maddie.

He stepped forward, his arousal rubbing against her slick folds. Something, some latent sense of reason, had him pausing. Just for a moment. Long enough to meet her eyes. To make sure she wanted this, too.

Setting her hands on his shoulders, she tightened her legs and tilted her pelvis forward so that he was at her entrance. He slid into her, gritted his teeth against the urge to plunge into her. But she felt so freaking incredible, her body tight and wet surrounding him, her eyes dark with passion, her mouth red and swollen from his kisses. As always, she stole his breath, but for the first time he didn't resent her for it. For the first time he let himself wish that things could have been different between them. Let himself wonder, just for a second, if he'd made the wrong choice all those years ago.

Then she rolled her hips, taking him in even deeper, and held him there, buried to the hilt. And she smiled at him, a small, feminine smile that told him she knew exactly the power she held over him.

His heart slammed against his ribs. The nape of his neck prickled with apprehension. Denial rushed through him. He cupped her butt, pressed his face against the curve of her neck and drove into her. She made this completely sexy sound, as though it was the best thing she'd ever felt. Her fingers clenched, her nails dug into his upper arms as she met him thrust for thrust. He pounded into her again and again and again until his skin was coated with sweat, his muscles trembling with fatigue. Until Maddie tightened around him, her body shuddering with her release. Until his own orgasm swept over him and he emptied himself inside of her.

But with his body satiated, his blood cooling and his head clearing, he couldn't pretend, could no longer hide from his thoughts. And the truth that at this moment, here with Maddie, for the first time since he'd left Shady Grove, he'd finally, truly come home.

THE BREEZE PICKED UP and gooseflesh rose on Maddie's arms. She shivered. Her body was pleasantly sore, her back rubbing against something cool and rough. She inhaled deeply—and breathed in the familiar scent of Neil's skin, his sweat. And sex.

She slowly raised her head. Her stomach turned and she swallowed down the beer rising in her throat.

Oh, God.

She was clinging to Neil, her legs wrapped around him, her ankles pressing into his lower back. He held her under her thighs, his breathing ragged, his whiskers tickling the side of her neck. He was still inside of her.

Ohgodohgodohgod.

Rearing up, she shoved at his arms and chest, kicked her legs. Her toe connected with his shin and pain shot up her leg. He grunted softly then shifted back and slid his hands to her waist. He lifted her, setting her on the floor as if she weighed next to nothing.

And though he more than likely saved her from falling on her naked ass, she hated him in that moment for his athlete's strength and grace.

She turned her back on him and hooked her bra then tugged her shirt down. But she was shaking so hard, it took her three tries to shimmy back into her underwear and pants. Once dressed, she tipped her head back and gulped in air. Well, it was official. She'd lost her ever-loving mind. That was the only answer for why she'd had sex—quick, hard, semirough sex—on her porch with the one man she'd sworn she'd never let lay so much as a finger on her again.

Remembering exactly where his fingers had been, what they'd done to her, she covered her face with her hands.

"Don't."

She slowly lowered her arms and turned. He stood in just his jeans, the button undone, his hair mussed, his eyes heavy-lidded. He was a walking, talking sex dream come to life. Damn him.

"Don't what?" She barely managed to get the words out.

"Don't regret it." His voice was low and husky. Hypnotic. He stepped toward her and she meant to step back—she really did—but something in his gaze held her captive. "Don't tell yourself it was a mistake."

Her eyes about popped out of her head. "Are you nuts? Of course it was a mistake."

"Not to me." He reached out and twirled a loose strand of hair around his finger. "Invite me inside, Maddie. Invite me to your bed. I want to touch you again, make you come again."

Catching herself swaying toward him, she stiffened. "No. No," she repeated louder. Firmer.

Oh, but she was tempted. Beyond tempted. She was ready to throw away self-preservation and toss aside her pride just for the chance to be in his arms again. How weak was that? But that's what he did, what he'd always done. Made her forget herself. Made her forget everything but him.

"Look," she said with a sneer, "don't get a big head about—" She waved her hand vaguely. "What just happened. I haven't had sex in a long time, that's all."

"So the only reason you kissed me that way, responded to my touch was…what? Repressed hormones?"

"Pretty much."

One side of his mouth kicked up. "You're lying again. Or maybe you just want me to prove you wrong."

He reached for her and she practically leaped back, afraid it would be oh, so easy for him to do exactly that. To prove she was nothing but a liar. That she still wanted him.

Anger sparked, bright and hot, inside her chest. He had no right to push her this way. To use her own weakness against her. Not when he'd already hurt her so badly.

"Since when has it mattered to you what I want?" she

asked quietly, her pulse drumming in her ears. "I wanted you to love me. To be faithful. When I told you I was pregnant, I wanted you to promise you'd stay with me forever." Her voice grew louder, the words bursting out in a heated rush. "Damn it, you were supposed to stay with me."

Neil went so still, she wasn't sure he was even breathing. "What do you mean, I was supposed to stay with you?"

The secret she'd kept all these years ballooned up inside of her, threatened to explode, to tear her life apart. Worse, to tear her daughter's life apart.

But what had happened between her and Neil tonight proved how important it was for her to break free from him once and for all. They'd been connected too many years, tied together through their shared past, her friendship with his sister and, most of all, through Bree.

If Maddie got close to him again, if she was foolish enough to trust him again even with only her body, she would lose a piece of herself. And this time, she might not be able to get it back.

She couldn't let that happen. Wouldn't.

"I loved you," she whispered, linking her fingers together at her waist. Love had been her driving force, her only motivation. It was a good reason, she assured herself. An honorable one. Understandable even.

But he hadn't wanted her love. Whenever she'd told him how she felt he'd looked overwhelmed, as if her feelings were something to be tolerated. Or worse, endured.

"I thought we were meant to be together forever," she continued. She'd been so young, so hopeful. So sure that what she was doing was right. "I figured after you graduated high school, you'd commute to one of the colleges in Pittsburgh. That you'd play for the Otters for a few more years."

From the time Neil was fifteen, he'd played on the Erie

Otters, a team in the Ontario Hockey League. Though it'd meant a lot of traveling, it'd been a way for him to develop as a player and garner the attention of the NHL.

"You knew my goal was always to play professional hockey," he told her, walking over to swipe up his shirt. He yanked it on, grabbed his wallet and shoved it into his back pocket. "I never kept that from you."

"No, you made it very clear what your dreams were. Believe it or not, I didn't want to keep you from achieving them, I just wanted them…postponed…I guess. I thought if you waited until I graduated to enter the draft, I could go with you when you got picked up." She began to pace, rubbed her hands over her chilled arms. "But then the scouting midterm ratings came out and you were listed as a top-ten draft prospect…and everything changed."

The list had come out in January of Neil's senior year. They'd all known being on it meant there was a better-than-good chance that he'd be drafted that June.

She'd given him her virginity that April. Had been with him as many times as she could from that point on until he'd walked away from her.

She crossed to the edge of the porch, stared out at the dark night. "You were slipping away from me," she admitted. "I knew it was only a matter of time before I lost you for good. I was just a kid. And I was terrified. Desperate…" But none of that excused her behavior. The lies. The manipulation. "It was the only way I knew to hold on to you."

"Maddie," he said from behind her. "Look at me."

She didn't want to but knew avoiding him was the coward's way. And she needed to look into his eyes when she told him.

Hugging her arms around herself she turned. "I lied to

you," she said hoarsely, her throat burning. "Bree wasn't an accident. I got pregnant on purpose."

She held her breath and waited for him to say something, anything. Told herself that no matter how hard it was, she'd accept his anger as her due, would face it head-on.

Only to have her head snap back when he nodded once and said, "I know."

CHAPTER THIRTEEN

"You...YOU KNOW?" Maddie asked, her eyes huge, her face pale in the moonlight. "I...I don't understand."

Neil stabbed his fingers through his hair. "I wasn't positive. When you first told me you were pregnant, I was too stunned to even consider the possibility that you'd done it on purpose."

He'd been too concerned about his dreams slipping away. "But then I started to wonder...and suspect."

He hadn't pushed her to have sex, hadn't wanted to rush into anything because he'd been afraid of being stuck in a relationship, in Shady Grove. He'd been scared of getting too serious. And he hadn't wanted to hurt her. Hadn't wanted to use her.

She'd made the first move, had told him she was ready, that she'd gone on birth control and had wanted to surprise him. She'd told him she loved him, that she wanted to show him how much.

Their initial time had been quick and awkward. He'd hated hurting her but she'd insisted he not stop. With time and practice, they'd gotten better, had found ways to be together as often as possible, usually at Maddie's prodding. He'd been so wrapped up in her—so thrilled to be having sex—he'd bought it. Had eaten every word she said and asked for seconds. He hadn't been able to resist her. And that was why she'd been so dangerous to him.

He thought of how, not ten minutes ago, he'd been making love to her. Her scent clung to him, his fingers tingled to feel the softness of her skin again. Hell, she was still dangerous to him.

"Were you ever on the pill?" he asked, watching her closely.

"No," she said, her voice ragged. "No."

There had been a time when he would have been thrilled to see that guilt in her eyes. To hear the worry in her voice. A time when all he wanted was her confession. And his own vindication.

Until he'd realized he didn't deserve absolution. Not when he'd been equally to blame.

He exhaled, felt as if it was the first time he'd been able to do so since he'd found out she was carrying his child. "Glad the truth is finally out."

He started walking down the stairs.

"Wait." She rushed past him to the bottom of the stairs, held out her hands as if to touch him, but then curled her fingers into her palms. "Where are you going?"

Since he didn't want her running after him down the dark driveway in her bare feet, he stopped. "I'm leaving."

"But…we need to talk about this."

"Why?"

She frowned, looking confused and young with her hair coming out of her braid, her clothes wrinkled. "Because we have to resolve this," she said, sounding more like herself. Bossy. In control. Right. "We'll go inside, I'll make some coffee and—"

"What's the point? It's over. Done." And nothing good ever came of peeling open old wounds. Not when those wounds were still capable of bleeding. Not when he was still struggling to accept what she'd done. "Please remind Bree that I'll pick her up after her soccer practice Monday."

"You're not walking away from me," Maddie growled,

grabbing on to his forearms, her fingers tense, her voice heated. "I need you to listen—"

"And it's always been what you needed," he said softly. "You lied to me, planned this whole thing so you could keep me under your thumb."

Swallowing visibly, she lifted her hands from him. "That's not true. I loved you. I loved you so much. Too much."

"You say you loved me, but you didn't care that I didn't want to be a father at eighteen, that I wasn't sure if I wanted to be a father ever. You took that choice from me. I had plans, dreams that were important to me, and you wanted me to give them up, to give everything up for you."

That's what love did. It was manipulative. Suffocating. It was a trap. Worse, it made you vulnerable. So that when that love was rejected, all that was left was pain.

"I didn't want you to give anything up," she said, her voice steady, but her hand trembled as she brushed a loose strand of hair from her face. "I only wanted to be a part of those plans. I wanted to be the one you dreamed of. But all you talked about was leaving. I thought if we had a baby, our own family, it'd be enough to make you want to stay."

"Stay? What did you think, that we'd get married and live happily ever after?" The look on her face, defiance mixed with remorse, told him that's exactly what she'd thought. "Christ, that's nothing but a fantasy. But then, it must've been so easy for you to believe. After all, you'd spent your entire life in your fancy house, confident that when you were hungry, there'd be food in the cupboard. That when it got cold out, you'd have a new coat to keep you warm. You never went without."

She looked stricken. "No, I never went without. Should I apologize for it? For having parents who loved me and took care of me, a family who was there for me day in and day out? For wanting the same thing for my own child?"

He shoved his hands into his pockets, felt small, mean and hopeless, like when he'd been a kid, trying to protect Fay from their parents' fights, from Annie's depression, Sam's neglect. "All I ever wanted for Bree was security. Stability. But I couldn't give that to her if I stayed." He'd been driven to succeed. Had told himself the only way he'd reach that success was to get far away from Shady Grove. As far from his past as he could. "I envied what you had—your life, your family."

He held her gaze, remembered how broken she'd looked when he'd told her he was still going to Seattle, that he was leaving her. How sure he'd been he was doing the right thing for all of them.

He only wished he was that certain now. "But I never," he continued, "not once, believed I could have it for myself."

MADDIE DID HER best not to let Neil's admission soften her toward him. She had to hold on to her anger, her resentment. Damn it, she had a right to both of them. They'd helped keep her going, helped keep her strong all these years.

If she let them go, she wasn't sure what would be left.

"How can you even say that?" she asked. "You were adopted by the Pettits. You were a part of my life, my family's life, for years. You knew damn well that type of bond was possible. You were a part of it. You just hadn't wanted it."

"No," he said, all calm and cool composure while she felt edgy and undone. "That wasn't what I wanted."

What did you think, that we'd get married and live happily ever after?

Her stomach turned. Yes, that was exactly what she'd thought, what she'd hoped would happen. She'd had it all mapped out. They'd get married and settle down right here in Shady Grove. Oh, sure, maybe he'd continue playing hockey but it would be just for fun. Eventually he'd find a real job, maybe with her father's company. A steady, stable job that allowed him to come home each night by five, so he could spend weekends working on building them a house of their own.

He was right. That was nothing but a fantasy. *Her* fantasy.

One she'd done everything in her power to trap him into.

And he'd known, she thought, humiliation prickling her skin. How many other people had suspected, guessed, what she'd done? How desperate she'd been to hold on to him.

"Why didn't you ever say anything?" she heard herself ask.

He lifted a shoulder. "You didn't get pregnant by yourself. We both had our share of the blame. We both made mistakes."

Did they? It didn't feel that way and she really, really wished it did. All these years she'd blamed him for walking out on her when she needed him most, for not being a better father to Bree. All these years she'd hidden behind her own anger and resentment, blaming him for feeling the same way.

The truth of it made her queasy. Made her ashamed.

"I'm sorry," she whispered. Despite the warm night, her face and cheeks were cold. Numb. "I'm so sorry, Neil."

"Looking for redemption?"

She hadn't been. Had only been hoping to put some much-needed distance between them. "I'm not sure." It was as honest an answer as she could give him. "Maybe.

Or maybe I'm hoping that reminding us both of our past, of those mistakes we made, will stop us from repeating them."

He studied her, all hard-eyed and tempting. "Or maybe," he said, his husky voice rubbing against her sensitized flesh like sandpaper, "we'll learn how to finally overcome that past. To forgive those mistakes."

She couldn't. It was too risky. Because if she forgave him, if she let her guard down around him, she would be right back where she was twelve years ago. Needy. Pathetic. Letting her feelings for him take over her life. Not going to happen.

Not when losing Neil meant she'd ended up finding herself.

"Ow," Bree muttered.

Crouched in front of her, Neil paused in the act of tying the laces of her right skate. "Too tight?"

She sighed and stared over his head. "It's fine."

He raised his eyebrows. It didn't sound fine. It sounded as if she was dying.

Preteen girls should come with some sort of instruction booklet. Maybe then he'd know what the hell was going on with his daughter. When he'd picked her up from soccer practice, she'd slouched in the car while he'd signed autographs for her teammates and a few of their parents. On the way to lunch, she'd given grunts and one-word responses to his questions about how practice had gone. At the restaurant, when he suggested that the grilled chicken salad might be a better choice than the cheeseburger she'd chosen, she'd changed her order then spent the rest of the hour poking at her food rather than eating it.

Finished lacing her left skate, he gave her toes a tap. "How do they feel?"

She shrugged.

"Does that mean they're okay?"

With another of her heavy sighs she stood. "I guess."

"Good. Come on. We only have the ice for an hour."

He'd thought it would be good for them to be here together. A way for them to connect and do something they both enjoyed.

Plus, it would help keep his mind off Maddie. Keep him from reliving what had happened between them the other night, how the taste of her had drugged him. How the feel of her skin under his hands, under his mouth, had turned him inside out. How close he'd come to being pulled back under her spell.

How hard it had been to let her walk away from him.

Maddie had always had the ability to tie him into knots. That hadn't changed. But he was older now. Smarter. It'd just been sex. He shouldn't be getting caught by emotions that couldn't go anywhere, by feelings that were too big for him. That he didn't want.

He swung open the waist-high wooden door and held it for Bree as he stepped onto the ice. She took a hesitant step, her knees wobbling, her arms out for balance. Suspicion, the same one that'd been nothing but a niggling when she'd told him she didn't have her own skates, the one that had grown when she'd been unable to lace the pair Walt had brought out for her, took root. Bloomed when Bree carefully stepped onto the ice. She wobbled, her arms windmilling as her feet shuffled.

Then she fell on her ass.

"You okay?" he asked, offering her his hand.

"Fine," she said somewhat breathlessly as she scrambled onto her hands and knees.

His mouth tight, he lowered his hand, curled his fingers as she used the wall to pull herself up. Only to have her skates slide out from under her again.

He caught her. "You don't know how to skate." He shut his eyes. That had sounded harsh. Accusing. He moved to the side so he could see her face, gentled his tone. "Why didn't you tell me?"

The look she gave him was like a punch to the throat—sharp, unexpected and painful as hell. "You didn't ask."

"Because I thought you could. You used to go skating all the time."

"I only went when you took me. And that was a long time ago."

Did she have to stress the word *long* that way? It'd only been a year, maybe two, since they'd gone skating together. He frowned, had a sinking sensation, as if the ice under his feet was melting. Or had it been three years?

He searched his memory, came up with a vision of Bree wrapped up in a puffy, bright purple coat, her cheeks pink as she beamed at him after making it around the entire rink without falling. Gerry and Carl had been there, too, along with Fay. Who had been pregnant with Elijah.

Which would make it over four years.

He grabbed the back of his head, pulled the hair there. Hard. "Then it really has been a while, huh?" His fault. Again. "I'm sure you'll get the hang of it quickly. You were getting pretty good the last time. Come on," he said, holding out his hands. "We'll do a couple of loops together, like we used to."

When she used to smile at him, instead of scowl. When she used to enjoy being with him. When she trusted him.

Her fingers stayed glued to the wall. "My ankles hurt."

"It takes a little bit of time to get used to the skates." He kept his hands out. "I was your age when I first learned to skate."

"I thought you started when you were a little kid."

What was eleven? A senior citizen? "I'd never been on the ice until Carl and Gerry took me and your aunt Fay skating one day."

It'd been his first official outing with the Pettits. He'd been so excited to see his sister again. After their mother's death and their father's abandonment, he and Fay had been sent to different foster homes, had been separated for eight months. That first day with the Pettits, he'd been terrified he'd do something, say something that would make them not want him. That would keep him away from Fay forever.

"Papa Carl tried to teach me but I kept falling," he continued, remembering how envious he'd been to see Fay gliding gracefully over the ice. "After two hours of falling on my butt, I was wet, freezing and sore. I hated it."

Bree's eyes widened. "You did?"

He nodded and finally lowered his arms. "Carl kept telling me I could do it. I didn't believe him but I kept trying and I managed to skate a few feet without falling. Then a few feet more. By the end of the afternoon, I could make it across the rink."

"You didn't fall anymore?"

"I fall all the time," he told her, wondering if she understood that he wasn't just referring to on the ice but all his missteps with her as well. "Everyone does."

Biting her lower lip, she stared at her skates. "Coach had us run, like, a million miles at practice."

"I promise—" He held up a hand in pledge. "No running. Only skating."

Bree raised her head in time for him to see one of her lengthy eye rolls. "I just mean I already exercised today."

"And you're too tired to skate?"

"No."

He waited but no further explanation was forthcoming.

"Breanne," he said with a huff of exasperation, "what's the problem?"

"Nothing."

"Then let's—"

"Except you only brought me here to make sure I exercised," she said in a low rush. "And I did already."

"That's not why I brought you here." Though he could admit to himself that had been part of the reason. Was that wrong, too? "I thought…" He frowned as he searched for the right words. "Skating helps me clear my head. When I'm on the ice, not practicing or playing a game but just skating, I can lose myself in the movement of my legs, the rush of speed, the sound of blades cutting the ice—"

"Like when I read a good book," she said, as if he didn't sound like an idiot. "I get lost in the story and forget everything else."

"Exactly," he said and damned if she didn't smile shyly at him. He rubbed a hand over the sudden ache in his chest.

She turned, holding on to the wall with only one hand. "So it's, like, your favorite thing to do?"

The memory of making love to Maddie slammed into him with enough force to almost knock him off his feet. All the ways he'd touched her, tasted her, flashed in his mind like a movie.

He cleared his throat and did a mental scrubbing, ridding himself of any and all thoughts of Maddie. "Skating is *one* of my favorite things to do."

Biting her lower lip, Bree slowly reached for him.

He clasped her hands in his. Despite the chill in the air, her fingers were warm, her palms soft and just a bit clammy.

He didn't want to let go.

"We'll start slow. One step at a time." He'd do the same with her, with their relationship, until they were on solid ground once again. "Push off with your right foot, glide on your left. Don't look at your feet," he warned when she almost toppled over. "Just look at me."

She straightened, her expression wary, her legs shaky.

"I've got you," he told her, holding her gaze. Willing her to believe him. "I won't let you fall."

Her brow scrunched up in more concentration than anything less than world peace or nuclear physics warranted, she shoved off.

"Good," Neil said, skating backward. "Now your left foot."

It took them an entire loop of the rink before her grip loosened enough for the circulation to start again in his fingers. Another loop before she took bigger strides. On the third loop she said, "I think I can do it by myself now."

"You sure?" When she nodded, he guided her back to the wall.

But before they could get going again, the door to the boys' locker room opened and Luke skated over to them, carrying his hockey stick and a plastic bucket of pucks.

"Gramps said you were using the ice," he said to Neil before smiling at Bree. "Hey, B. I don't suppose you brought any of those cupcakes with you?"

Blushing so hard Neil was surprised her hair didn't also turn red, Bree shook her head and then sneaked a glance at Luke from under her lashes, a look that struck Neil as way too adult. Flirtatious. "I could make some for you, though."

"Yeah? That'd be great." He turned back to Neil. "You have a few minutes? I'm working on going top shelf with my backhand shot and could use some pointers."

"Bree and I were going to take a couple more laps—"

"It'll only take a few minutes. You don't mind, do you, B?" Luke asked.

"No," she said, her eyes shining in adulation. "I don't mind."

She might not mind but Neil sure as hell didn't like the adoring, infatuated way she looked at Luke. Wasn't she too young for crushes, especially on sixteen-year-old boys?

Luke nudged Bree's arm with his elbow. "Thanks. I'll get the pucks lined up," he told Neil then skated over to the net.

Neil watched Bree as she stared at Luke's back. It was just a crush. Harmless. Innocent. She was only eleven, still such a little kid in her neon-pink sweatpants and the sweatshirt with the sparkly heart on the front, the golden studs in her ears catching the light.

But she wouldn't be eleven forever. In a few years she'd be sixteen herself and if she looked anything like how Maddie had looked at that age, it'd only be a matter of time before boys became interested in her. Before they started sniffing around her like the dogs they were.

Neil remembered what he was like at sixteen. At seventeen and eighteen. Hell, how he was now.

Shit.

Bree needed to know what, exactly, teenage boys wanted from teenage girls. She needed to know how to protect herself so some idiotic, hormonally driven boy didn't sweet-talk her into going further than she was ready to.

Neil wanted to shout at her to stop watching Luke. To stay away from boys like that, boys who were too good-looking, too confident with their charming grins and smooth talking. Wanted her to promise him she'd be smart. Careful. Safe. That she wouldn't give her heart to some boy who didn't deserve it, who didn't know how to care for it. A boy who didn't know how to cherish what he had.

The boy he'd been with Maddie.

All he said was "Keep practicing until I get back."

Without waiting for her to agree, he skated away, the words he really wanted to say stuck in his throat.

Stop growing up so fast.

Luke had half a dozen pucks lined up in front of the net. Neil glanced back at Bree, saw she was, indeed, practicing. Whether that was due to his telling her to or if she was trying to impress Luke, Neil wasn't sure.

Didn't think he wanted to know.

He held his hand out for Luke's stick. It was shorter than what he played with but for demonstration purposes, it'd have to do.

"This is a quick shot," he said, facing the row of pucks, the net to his right. "There are two ways to do it—" He bent his legs, his right hand at the top of the stick, his left a third of the way down. "First one, get low to the ice and just shovel the puck up and in." He scooped up the puck, sending it into the upper net. "Up and in," he said again, repeating the motion for all the pucks. "Got it?"

Luke nodded and took his stick back to line up the pucks once again.

"Good," Neil said when Luke shot the first puck, "but if you want to get the shot off this close to the net, you need to be faster."

As Luke lined them up and shot through them again, Neil checked on Bree. She sat on the first row of bleachers behind him. He lifted a hand, waved for her to join them but she shook her head.

Turning to Luke, Neil taught him another method, this one pulling the puck back a little bit to get some momentum, lifting the puck onto the blade and rifling it up and in with power.

"Good job," Neil said after they'd gone through the drill a dozen or so times. He checked on Bree again. Still sitting. Still watching him in that way that made him feel as if she was sizing him up and found him lacking.

"Thanks for the help," Luke said as the locker room door opened and the members of the high school hockey team skated out. "I'll stay after practice and keep working on it."

One by one the boys approached Neil. He signed sticks, gave advice and had a conversation with the head coach about giving them pointers on their offense, prompting Neil to agree to come back during practice tomorrow. It was ten minutes. Fifteen, tops.

But when the crowd around him finally dispersed and he looked once again for Bree, she was gone.

CHAPTER FOURTEEN

BREE STARED UP at the ice rink from the bottom of the concrete steps. She'd been out there a real long time. Long enough for the sun to have warmed her chilled skin, for sweat to have formed at the small of her back. For her to wish she'd worn something other than sweats.

She'd counted the number of stairs leading to the building and all the cars in the parking lot. And still, the doors remained shut. Her dad hadn't come out, frantic and upset that she'd disappeared.

He probably didn't even know she was gone.

Which was fine with her. She hadn't left so he'd chase after her, so he'd be worried, wondering where she'd gone, if she was all right. She'd been tired and cold. And as much as she liked daydreaming about the day when Luke would fall in love with the older, skinnier, prettier version of herself, watching him flip puck after puck into the net was superboring.

But it wasn't until those other boys had come in and surrounded her dad, all trying to get his attention so they could tell him how cool and great he was, that she'd slipped out. She'd had to. Her chest had been tight and she'd started breathing fast, as if her dad had made her run again. She'd thought for sure she'd puke, right there in front of everyone.

Or worse, start yelling, screaming at them all that they were wrong. That her dad wasn't great.

He was a liar. He'd told her he wanted to take her skating, just the two of them, but as soon as Luke showed up, her dad had ditched her.

She had every right to get away from him.

Besides, it wasn't as if she'd run away or done anything wrong. She was right here, right where he'd easily see her when he finally got done paying attention to everyone else. She'd just explain that she hadn't told him she was leaving because she'd been taught it was rude to interrupt adults when they were busy.

Her dad was always busy. Too busy for her.

But she was awfully hot, what with the sun beating down on her and all. The sunscreen she'd put on before soccer was long gone, which meant she was just begging for a sunburn or worse, skin cancer, by standing on this concrete.

Biting her lip, she scanned the area. There were some trees by the fence near the playground. She'd sit under them and read her book until her dad came out. But when she walked over, she noticed all the pine needles on the ground. If she sat there, they'd poke her. She'd have to find another shady spot to wait.

She glanced at the door again. Still closed.

Moms and babysitters chatted on benches. Little kids chased each other around the playground, their laughter, screams and cries so loud, Bree knew she'd never be able to read if she stayed there. She kept walking but the chlorine smell of the pool made her gag and there were way too many squirrels, with their bushy tails and scary teeth, running around under the pavilion.

At the side entrance to the park, she checked behind her, but the only people following her were two boys around her age on their bikes. Hugging her backpack to her chest, she realized she was far out of sight of the rink. Was that bad? Would her dad be mad?

She wasn't sure she cared.

She could go home. Her house was only a couple of blocks away. But if she did that, her dad might tell her mom and then Bree would really be in trouble. Her dad never punished her—never had, anyway—but her mom didn't have a problem punishing her. The worst was when she forced Bree to go to work with her so she could learn responsibility by hauling lumber, cleaning up after the workers, washing their trucks and sweeping out the workshop where Uncle Eddie built stuff.

Learning how to be responsible sucked.

And if she ever said *sucked* out loud, she'd be in real trouble.

She should go back to the rink. Except…well…she'd gone a long way already, was halfway around the park. It'd be just as fast to keep going. She'd cross the wooden bridge over the creek, then follow the sidewalk back to the rink. Easy peasy.

She glanced back again, but her dad hadn't suddenly appeared. He wasn't calling her name, wasn't chasing after her, wanting her to come back, to spend time with him.

Bree started walking faster, her sneakers scuffing against the sidewalk between the park's large baseball field and tennis courts. A group of teenage boys were playing basketball so she kept her head down as she passed. She felt ugly and dumb in her heavy clothes, her sweat making her hair stick to the back of her neck. She hurried across the bridge. All she had to do was take the walkway to her left and in two minutes—three, tops—she'd be back at the rink.

She didn't move. She was thirsty. Really, really thirsty from skating and all her walking. Uncle Leo said people needed to drink more water when it was hot out so they didn't get dehydrated. As a firefighter, he knew all about being safe and keeping healthy.

There was a water fountain to her right by the T-ball field. With one last look around, she went right. She'd get a drink, a quick one, then be on her way.

The water was lukewarm and tasted as if she'd licked a penny, but she drank it anyway. Kept drinking until she couldn't take in another drop. Straightening, she wiped the back of her hand across her mouth. Still no sign of her dad.

Swinging her backpack from its strap, she walked onto the ball field, crossed to the dugout and sat on the end of the long bench. It was shady and smelled like Uncle James's dog, Zoe, when she got wet. Bree leaned back against the cool stone wall. She had a clear view of the basketball courts as well as the parking lot behind the ice rink. Her dad's rental car was still there so he hadn't left without her.

Maybe she'd wait for him here. It wasn't her fault if he couldn't find her.

He probably wasn't even looking.

She pulled out her book and opened it but the words were blurry and she had a lump in her throat. Sniffing, she blinked rapidly, tried to focus on the story.

"Are you okay?"

She jumped. Her book flew from her hand, landing on the ground in front of the dugout's opening. A man, an old one like Pops, bent and picked it up, brushing the dirt from the cover. He held it out to her.

The lump in her throat grew. Standing, she accepted the book then quickly sat again, sliding farther down the bench. "Thank you."

He nodded but his eyebrows were lowered and he watched her as if he was worried about something. As if he was worried about her. "Do you need help?"

She shook her head, kept her gaze down.

"Do your parents know you're over here by yourself?" he asked.

"My mom's working. I'm with my dad," she added quickly. "He's going to meet me here any minute." She made a show of looking around, as if she really expected her dad to come strolling along any second now.

The old man looked around but not as if he was scared. More like it was a good thing her dad was coming to get her. One of the boys playing basketball made a basket and the old man grinned.

"My grandson," he said, nodding at the boy in the white-and-black-striped shorts. "He loves taking those three-point shots." He tipped his head to the side and read the title of her book.

"*The Giver,* huh? How is it?"

Sneaking a peek at him, she hesitated. She wasn't supposed to talk to strangers, but ignoring him felt wrong, too. As though she was being rude. "It's good," she finally said.

After all, he looked okay. Normal, not like one of those perverts adults always warned kids about. His bald head was shiny, his mustache and beard gray, his eyebrows dark. He had on glasses, khaki pants and a white button-down shirt.

He stepped farther into the dugout and she moved down the bench some more, clutched her bag in case she had to hit him with it or something.

"I'm always on the lookout for books for my grandson," he said. "I spend most of the day reading now that I've retired. Let me tell you, it's a pure blessing not having to sneak a few pages at my desk anymore."

"I got caught reading during math class one time." Her face heated as she remembered how the teacher had yelled at her in front of the class. How humiliated she'd been when her eyes had pricked with tears and one of the boys had sneered and whispered that she was a baby.

"I've been caught more times than I care to admit." He winked. "But it never stopped me."

She smiled. "Me neither."

But she had gotten better, smarter about hiding her books.

"My daughter, Johnny's mama, she's the same way, always has a book with her. But getting Johnny to read is harder than pulling hens' teeth."

"Do hens have teeth?"

He laughed. Not like a crazy person or anything, just like a nice old man. "No, that's what makes it so hard." Sliding his hands into his pockets, he watched the boys again. "He'd rather play ball than do just about anything else, short of eating. But I keep tryin' to get him to expand his mind."

He didn't sound mad, though. More like he was proud of his grandson. Any doubts she'd had disappeared. He was a nice old man. A grandfather who wanted what was best for his grandson, who loved him enough to watch him play ball with his friends, who cared enough about him to know where he was at, what he was doing.

Which was more than she could say about her dad.

"I picked up *The Hunger Games* trilogy for Johnny a few months ago."

"I loved those books," she said, relaxing her grip on her backpack. "Especially *Catching Fire*." Had read all three books in two days then had gone back and read them all again.

"I don't think that boy even cracked the cover of the first one. Said he'd rather watch the movies." The man shook his head sadly.

Johnny must not know the book was always, *always* better than the movie. Boys were so dumb.

The old man sent her a sideways look. "Maybe you could help me out. Give me some titles of books you think a stubborn, sports-crazy thirteen-year-old boy might like?"

Should she? She wasn't sure. Yeah, he seemed harmless and his grandson was there, right there, where they could both see him. And when he sat down, he left plenty of space on the bench between them. Still, he *was* a stranger.

Her dad would probably have a stroke or something if he found out she was chatting with some man she'd never seen before in her life. But he wasn't there. He was never there for her.

So she set her backpack aside and told the old man about her very favorite books.

Bree wasn't in the girls' locker room, the snack room or the hallway. There was no sign of the sneakers she'd worn in or the skates she'd rented.

Where the hell was she?

Neil shoved open the door from the locker room and went into the hallway. He did a slow turn, as if Bree would magically appear out of thin air.

Swinging his bag over his shoulder, he went down the hall but Walt wasn't in his office. Neil turned and went back toward the ice, found the older man sharpening skates behind the rental counter.

"Have you seen my daughter?" he asked over the loud whine of the sharpener.

Walt lifted the skate off the blade. "What's that?"

"My daughter," Neil repeated, impatience giving his voice an edge. "Have you seen her?"

"She returned her skates ten…fifteen minutes ago."

That long ago?

"I…I can't find her," Neil admitted, feeling like a failure. Like the worst father ever.

"Did you check the playground?"

Right. That made sense. The ice rink was located at the park along with a pool, playground, tennis courts, a few baseball and soccer fields. She probably got bored and went outside to play. Or to wait for him in the car. No big deal. No reason to be worried.

He burst through the double doors of the arena, ignored the robins on the grass he'd scared into flight. His pulse pounding in his ears, he jogged over to his car but she wasn't there. Though there was no way she could get inside the car—at least not without jimmying open the lock—he cupped his hands around his eyes and pressed his face to the passenger side window. Just in case.

Empty.

He threw his bag onto the ground. Walking toward the playground, he scanned the area for his daughter's dark hair, a glimpse of her bright pink clothes. Nothing. Nor was she by the fence watching the people in the pool.

He'd just keep looking. He'd find her soon enough.

Unless she had left the park.

His hands curled into fists and he picked up his pace. Damn it. What the hell had she been thinking? She knew better than to take off without telling him where she was going, without getting his permission. He'd never disciplined her before, never had reason to, but so help him, when he found her, he was going to lay into her but good.

After he made sure she really was okay.

What if she's not okay?

Passing the park's side entrance he ground his back teeth together. She was fine. She had to be. She was smart. Resourceful. She walked to the park all the time by herself.…

He slammed to a stop. Of course. She probably just went home.

He pulled out his phone but his hands were unsteady and he bobbled it, almost dropping it before finally pressing the button for Maddie's house phone. While the line rang, he rolled his head from side to side, used techniques he'd learned to calm his breathing, settle his heart rate and gather his focus before taking a penalty shot. He inhaled for the count of five, held it, then exhaled for five more seconds.

The phone rang. And rang. And rang.

When the answering machine picked up, he hung up and started jogging down the sidewalk. He passed the tennis courts, an empty ball field. Stopping on the wooden bridge, he stabbed both hands through his hair. He had to call Maddie. Tell her what had happened. Maybe they could organize some sort of search.... No, he should call the cops first, he realized, taking out his phone again. They could put out one of those APB things—

The sound of laughter had him freezing. Familiar laughter.

His daughter's laughter.

He shut his eyes against the relief that flowed through him, that weakened his knees. His phone clenched in his hand, his thumb still pressing the number 9, he walked to the other side of the bridge, followed the sound to the small baseball field. Spotted Bree in the dugout. Healthy. Safe. Whole.

But not alone.

A man, an older man—sixty-five, maybe seventy—with a slight build, pressed khakis, glasses and a bald head, sat next to her. Too close.

Fury heated Neil's blood, rage built, turned his vision

red and tightened his muscles. He fought it all, refused to let his emotions rule him.

"Breanne." Her name came out as sharp and stinging as the snap of a whip. Guess he wasn't completely in control after all. "What the hell are you doing out here?"

Bree startled then shrank back, her eyes huge in her pale face. She looked scared. Guilty. And so small and vulnerable next to the old man, her only means of escape blocked by him, bile rose in Neil's throat.

"Come out here," Neil told her. When she didn't move fast enough to suit him, he narrowed his eyes. "Now."

Her head down, she got to her feet. The old man did the same, standing in front of the exit. "Is this your father, Bree?"

She nodded.

"No need to get upset," the old guy said with a jovial, we're-all-buddies-here grin. "We were just discussing our favorite books." He laid his hand on Bree's shoulder. "You have a very bright girl here."

Neil stepped forward, linked his fingers through the fence and held the old man's gaze. "If you don't get your hand off my daughter," he warned softly, dangerously, "I'll break your goddamn fingers."

The old man raised his eyebrows and slowly lifted his hand. "Maybe it'd be best if I was on my way." He stepped onto the field, stopping a few feet in front of Neil. "I meant no harm."

Didn't matter whether he had or not, Neil thought as the other man walked toward the basketball courts. Sometimes, even the best intentions had the worst results. He'd tried to be a good father. Had busted his ass to provide for his daughter, to give her a stable life, to ensure her childhood was as different from his own as it could be.

What did he get in return? Bree glaring at him as if she

hadn't scared the hell out of him by disappearing. As if he was the one in the wrong.

He was out of his depth, out of his element and out of patience. How was he supposed to act? What was he supposed to do? He wanted to yell, to let loose the worry and anger inside of him. Wanted to shake her until she realized what she'd done was wrong.

He wanted to grab her and hold her close, just to reassure himself she really was all right, that nothing and no one had touched her. Had hurt her.

He jammed his hands into his pockets, kept his voice even. "Come on."

As soon as she stepped out of the dugout, Neil started walking toward the parking lot. He glanced back. She was, as usual, dragging her feet.

"Either you keep up with me on your own," he snapped, "or I'm going to throw you over my shoulder and carry you out of here."

She ran to catch up to him, kept running to keep his pace. At his car, he tossed his bag into the trunk, only mildly surprised it was still where he'd left it.

"Where are we going?" Bree asked in a small voice from where she was huddled in the passenger seat.

There was only one person who knew what to do with her. How to handle this situation and get Bree to see what she did was wrong. Dangerous.

He started the engine and slammed the car into gear. "I'm taking you to your mother."

"Mommy!" Bree wailed as she burst through Bradford House's front door.

Maddie jumped—which was not a good idea seeing as how she was ten feet up a ladder. Grabbing ahold of the top rung, her heart racing, she glared at Bree. "You'd better be on fire," she warned, only to be smacked with a sharp dose of Mom's Guilt seeing the tears on her daughter's face.

That guilt amped up when James, on a second ladder farther along the hall from her, climbed down and crouched in front of Bree, all concerned and compassionate. "What happened?" he asked. "Are you okay?"

Bree nodded, somehow managing to look brave and sullen despite the wetness on her cheeks.

It was that sullenness—and the anger in Bree's eyes— that had Maddie breathing normally again. She climbed down the ladder, set her hammer and chisel aside— removing one-hundred-and-thirty-year-old plaster molding was a bitch—and tugged off her work gloves. "What's up? Where's your dad?"

"Right here."

Maddie stiffened then forced her shoulders to relax as she turned to find him standing on the porch. It drove her nuts how the mere sound of his voice could make her all tingly. She hated even more how often she'd thought of him in the past two days.

James straightened, his hand on Bree's shoulder, his stance aggressive, his expression dark. "What the hell did you do to her?"

Neil flicked him a glance so cold, she was surprised icicles didn't shoot out his nose. "This doesn't concern you."

But James was in full superhero-protector mode, his hands fisted on his hips, his expression fierce. "You'd damn well better believe it concerns me. If you so much as touched one hair on her head—"

"He didn't." She felt Neil's surprise, but she kept her eyes on James, who looked ready to take a hammer to Neil's head. "Relax, Uncle Avenger. Neil would never hurt Bree. Now, you—" she pointed at Bree "—and you…" She used her thumb to indicate Neil. "Come with me."

James stepped forward. "Maddie—"

"I've got this," she told him, softening the snap in her voice with a hand to his arm. "Really."

She met Bree's eyes and tipped her head toward the door. Sniffing loudly and, if Maddie did say so herself, quite theatrically, Bree passed both Maddie and Neil, her shoulders hunched, her head down.

"Carry on," Maddie said into the living room where Art and Heath had stopped removing the window casings so they could see the action in the hallway. Art turned back to his work so fast, his ponytail whipped around and hit his cheek.

Heath, two years Maddie's junior, grinned. "I had five bucks on James."

"I would've taken that bet," she said. She could always use five bucks.

Stepping onto the porch, she shut the door behind her then gestured for Neil and Bree to follow her into the front yard. No way was she risking any of their lives by standing on the porch with its sagging roof and rotted front corner.

"Okay," Maddie said, wishing she'd thought to bring her sunglasses out. "Who wants to tell me what's going on?"

"Breanne," Neil said, his arms crossed, his mouth pinched. "Tell your mother what happened."

"Uh-oh," Maddie murmured to her daughter. "That doesn't sound good."

"I didn't even do anything wrong," Bree cried, her eyes welling with fresh tears.

Maddie looked heavenward but there was no patience to be found floating in the air. Her kid was fantastic—bright, funny, sweet, eager to please and kindhearted. She was also a drama queen, overly sensitive and a major crier.

Maddie adored her. How could she not? But sometimes,

she was pretty sure if she saw one more tear she'd lose her mind.

"If you didn't do anything," she said, "why are you crying? And why does your dad look like he's ready to pick you bald-headed?"

Bree covered her hair with both hands. "We were at the ice rink and I went outside to wait for him."

And if there wasn't more to *that* story, Maddie would sleep with her nail gun under her pillow. "Did you tell your dad where you'd be?"

"I was going to," Bree said, scratching her eyebrow. "I guess I forgot."

"Forgot, huh? That's not like you."

"It was an accident," she said with such petulance, such defiance, Maddie blinked. Bree shot Neil a sideways glance. "Besides, he was so busy shooting stupid pucks with Luke, I'm surprised he even knew I was gone."

"You're the one who told Luke it was okay if I helped him." Neil ground the words out, his low, controlled voice a complete contrast to the way energy and anger practically crackled around him. "I even tried to get you to join us but you refused."

Bree sent Maddie a pleading look. "I didn't want to skate anymore."

If possible, Neil's scowl grew even darker. "You could've just said that."

No, she couldn't. Or at least, she wouldn't. Bree got her stubbornness naturally—50 percent from Maddie, the other half from Neil—but that didn't mean it wasn't frustrating when you bumped up against that wall. And when she was hurting, she tended to go inside herself and let that pain fester only to come out in passive-aggressive behavior.

Like taking off without telling her dad where she was going.

"Wait by the car while your mother and I discuss your punishment," Neil told Bree.

Maddie raised her eyebrows. They'd never discussed discipline before. Truth be told, Bree didn't often need to be disciplined. And when she did, Maddie handled it alone. What choice did she have? It wasn't as if she was going to call Neil for every mouthy word or broken bedtime, especially when he was never there when the bad behavior occurred.

But he was here now.

Bree stomped off.

"What are you going to do about…that?" Neil asked, stabbing a finger in Bree's direction. "She needs to know this sort of behavior isn't acceptable. She can't go running off anytime she feels like it."

There was no need to go overboard. "She doesn't run off anytime she feels like. She's a kid. She made a mistake. She should have told you she was going outside—"

"No," he snarled, "she shouldn't have told me she was going outside. She should've stayed in the rink until I was done. Instead, she snuck off—"

"I'm sure she didn't sneak—"

"Do you know where I found her?" he asked, his voice rising. "In the baseball field, talking to a man. Goddamn it, Maddie, she was alone with a stranger in the dugout. Who knows what could've happened!"

Maddie's world tilted. "What?" She whirled around, searched out her daughter just to reaffirm that Bree really was all right. Still had a hard time catching her breath even when she saw Bree sitting cross-legged on the grass, her elbows on her knees, her chin in her hand.

"He didn't touch her?" Maddie asked Neil. "Hurt her?"

"No. She said they just talked." His face was drawn and she saw beneath his fury to how worried, how frightened he really was. "But he could have. Christ, Maddie, what if I hadn't found her?"

"But you did."

"I wasn't there." Neil's voice shook, his eyes were haunted. "I wasn't there to protect her."

She grabbed his hand. Squeezed. "Yes, you were. You found her. She's okay. She's safe. I'll talk to her. Explain what she did was wrong."

"She doesn't need a lecture, she needs to be punished," he said, formidable and obstinate. "No TV and an early bedtime for a week."

Maddie pursed her lips. Considering Bree couldn't care less about television, that might not be the best way to go. "Why don't we—"

"And she can forget about that trip to the amusement park this weekend," he added.

"What?" Bree scrambled to her feet. Good to know her hearing was top-notch. "That's not fair," she said, storming up to them. "Mom, tell him that's not fair."

"Well, I—"

"If it was fair," Neil said tightly, "it wouldn't be a punishment."

"You can't tell me what to do," Bree cried, adding a foot stomp for good measure.

Maddie stepped between them. "Let's all just calm down…." And what parallel universe had she stepped into where she was the rational, reasonable one in this mix? "We'll go get a cool drink and—"

"I don't want a drink," Bree said, her face red, the tears back once again. "I don't want to calm down. And I don't want him to be my dad anymore!"

CHAPTER FIFTEEN

HER DAD STEPPED FORWARD, looking mad and sort of scary.

Big deal, Bree thought, angrily wiping away a tear. She wasn't scared of him. She sneaked another glance at his face—all hard and dark, his eyebrows lowered—and swallowed. Okay, so maybe she was a little scared…but he wouldn't hurt her. Not with her mom right there and Uncle James inside.

And she didn't care if he was frowning at her. He was never happy. Not ever. Not even when he saw her after months and months and months. She blinked and another tear fell. When she'd been a little kid, she'd run to him, smiling so big it'd hurt her face. She used to try so hard to make him smile, or better yet laugh, as if it was her job, her mission in life: make Dad happy. Make him love you.

But he didn't love her. And she was done trying to make him happy. He should try to make her happy for once.

"I guess it's too bad you don't get a say in the matter," her dad said in his stupid deep voice. "Isn't it?"

"It is too bad," she heard herself mutter. But then she realized that she was tired of muttering, tired of holding back what she really wanted to say. Why should she? He never cared about saying the right thing to her. "It is too bad," she repeated, her voice loud and snotty, but instead of feeling bad, she liked how she sounded. Strong. Like her mom. "It is too bad. As a matter of fact it…it sucks! *You* suck!"

Her dad looked supermad, his eyes were sort of glowing and his lips were a thin line. But he didn't yell at her. Didn't tell her not to talk to him that way, that he would always be her father. That he would never let her go.

"Whoa, whoa," her mom said, staring at her as if she'd never seen her before, and Bree felt sick to her stomach. Her mom crouched in front of her, beautiful even in jeans, T-shirt, heavy work boots and tool belt. She smoothed Bree's hair back, held her face in her hands. "What's wrong, honey? This isn't like you."

"You always tell me that sometimes people have to stick up for themselves. That I can't be afraid to show some backbone."

"That's true," her mom said slowly. "But I didn't mean—"

"You said it's okay if I get mad." She stepped back and her mom's hands fell away. "If I'm not all happy and sunshiny all the time. Well, I'm mad now. I'm mad at him," she said with a jerk of her head toward her dad.

Her mom straightened. "Yeah. I think you've made that pretty clear. But that does not give you the right to be so disrespectful. Especially not to your father. Apologize. Now."

Though her mom was using her serious voice, the one that meant business, Bree lifted her chin, met her mother's eyes. "No."

"What did you say to me?" her mom asked in a quiet voice.

Bree's lower lip trembled so she bit down on it, tasted her own blood. "I said no. I won't apologize to him. He should apologize to me." She forced her eyes up to meet her dad's. "You should apologize to me for never noticing me. For not ever seeing me on my birthday and for making me eat a stupid salad." She was screaming, her voice hoarse. "I didn't want a salad. I wanted a cheeseburger!"

Now her dad was looking less mad and more confused. As if he couldn't understand why she was so upset. "If I'd known you really wanted a cheeseburger," he said, talking to her as if she was some little kid who needed things explained carefully, "you could've had one."

"You're lying." Tears streamed down her face, her nose ran. She wished she could stop crying. Hated that she was crying over him when she'd promised herself she wouldn't. "You never cared about me. The only reason you've been spending time with me is because you want me to lose weight so I don't embarrass you." She was breathing heavy, sweating. "You think I'm fat."

"I never said that." He looked at her mom. "I never said that."

But he didn't deny it, either.

"You don't have to say it," Bree said, wiping her nose with her sleeve. "You're always telling me to eat this, not that. That I should exercise more."

"I want you to be healthy," he said. "I just want what's best for you."

She almost believed him. Would have believed him a few months ago, but she'd grown up since then and she remembered how he'd ignored her for Luke today, how he never asked her what she liked, what she wanted to do.

"As an athlete," her mom said, "your dad's very into exercise and being fit and eating the right things. It's part of his job and it's something we should all do to be healthy. But, honey, neither your dad nor I want you to worry about this. You're still young. You're going to grow taller and slim down. A lot of girls put on weight at this point in their lives and then lose it when puberty starts. That's what happened to me."

What if it didn't happen to her, though? Her mom didn't

understand what it was like. She wasn't always fat like Bree. And how could her mom take his side? It wasn't fair!

"Pops says blood is thicker than water," Bree said, "which means that family comes first."

But her mom didn't take the bait. Her dad did.

"Family should take care of each other," he said.

"You don't. All you do is send money but you don't take care of anyone else. You missed Grandma Gerry's birthday last year and she cried." His face went white and Bree felt a sense of satisfaction that she had the power to hurt him. "And you never come back for Christmas even though Aunt Fay begs you to every year—"

"You know I'm working."

"That's all you care about. Playing hockey. So I don't think it matters that we're blood. I think Grandma Gerry's right. She says what makes people family is what's in their hearts. And you don't have anything in your heart for me. You never have."

He stepped toward her, blocking the sun. "That's not—"

"You never cared about me. You ignore me and forget all about me and now, all of a sudden, you want to be my dad?" Keeping her eyes on his, she shook her head. "It's too late. But it's okay," she said, her throat tickly. "It's okay that you don't want me, that you've never wanted me. Because I don't want you, either. I don't need you," she told him, wishing she felt better about telling him that. Wishing she didn't want him to tell that he needed her. That he loved her. "Not anymore."

MADDIE WAS STUNNED at her daughter's vehemence. Her kid didn't get angry. It was one of the traits that Maddie had no idea how to handle, wasn't sure it was normal for someone to be so sweet, so passive all the time.

"You might not need him," she said, hoping she was

saying the right thing, praying she handled this the right way for both Bree's and Neil's sakes, "but, honey, he is your father—"

"You don't like him, either," Bree snapped.

Maddie felt Neil's quick, sharp glance. "I never said I didn't like him," she told Bree.

Rolling her eyes, Bree crossed her arms. "You didn't have to. It's obvious. You told me I didn't have to go to Seattle if I didn't want, that you'd tell him I had school. And you never talk about him. You never talk about when you two were together."

"That's because it's all in the past."

Except, she wasn't sure she believed it. Not after her and Neil's little sexcapade the other night. Not when she'd been thinking about him so often. It scared her, especially after she'd spent such a huge chunk of her life mooning over him, wanting him to love her as much as she loved him. Now he was back—in her way, in her face and, despite her best intentions, despite how exhausted she was each night, in her dreams.

"No, it's not," Bree said, a stubborn tilt to her chin. "It's because you're mad at him for leaving us."

Well aware that Neil was an avid audience—and the entire reason for this little familial drama—Maddie let out a long, slow breath. "I was mad at your dad, have been mad at him for a long time. Too long. But I'm not now."

Bree's look was one of pure suspicion. "You're not?"

"You're not?" Neil asked, as if he, too, didn't believe her.

She'd had a right to her anger, hadn't she? Part of her even wished she could hold on to it for a little while longer. It protected her from the pain, from allowing herself to soften toward Neil now. Made it so much easier to keep believing he hadn't changed, that if he got close to her or Bree, he'd hurt them.

Made it that much easier to believe keeping Bree from him was the right thing to do.

"I'm not," Maddie said, only able to hold Neil's gaze for a second before facing Bree. "Look, your father and I both made mistakes—"

"Like me," Bree said, her mouth wobbling. "I was the mistake."

Maddie's own eyes stung. "Oh, baby—"

"You," Neil said, his voice rough, adamant, "were not a mistake."

It was far from a declaration of love, didn't even come close to being an apology. But in that instance, while Bree looked torn between disbelief and hope, as Neil towered over her, all broad shoulders and dark scowl, Maddie knew, in her heart, that he meant it. She also knew that he meant what he couldn't say.

You're important to me. You're special. I love you.

He should be able to tell their daughter what she meant to him, should be able to open up his heart, give Bree the assurances she needed to hear.

Still, Maddie couldn't hold back any longer.

After twelve years, countless tears—hers and Bree's—after all the anger and resentment, the heartbreak and disappointments, she did what she'd never been able to do before.

She forgave him.

She had to. It was the only way she could move forward. It was the only way she was finally able to forgive herself.

Unfortunately, Bree didn't seem so inclined. She was back to glaring at Neil, expecting more from him, unable to see that this might be all she ever got. Maddie rubbed her forehead. She had to take care of this. That was what she did. Took care of her daughter, was used to being solely responsible for everything where her daughter was concerned.

She glanced at Neil. Except that was changing.

It wouldn't be easy for either her or Bree to accept. Guess they'd just have to get used to it.

"Your dad's right," Maddie told Bree. "You weren't a mistake. But what you did today, leaving without telling anyone where you went, talking to a stranger? Those were big old blunders."

"Mo-om," Bree said, drawing the most fabulous word in the world out until it was at least four syllables.

"Breanne. Like how I tied those together? Circled back to what started this conversation?"

"Not really," Bree grumbled.

"Sorry, kiddo. Life's tough that way. Now you will be punished—not only for how you took off at the park, but for talking to your father the way you did."

Bree's mouth dropped open. "That's not—"

"Fair," Maddie said. "Yes, I know. Unfortunately, it's time you learned a very valuable lesson—life is not fair. Now, your dad and I will have a little discussion and once we've agreed on a suitable punishment, we'll let you know. Until then, is there anything you'd like to say to your dad?"

Bree thought it over. That was her kid. She liked to weigh her options and her words carefully.

Just like Neil.

So many of her daughter's traits, big ones and little ones, that Maddie had always tried to brush off as crazy genetics or learned behaviors all linked directly back to Neil.

"No," Bree said, her expression mutinous, "I don't have anything to say to him."

Maddie sighed. "Bree—"

"It's okay," Neil said, watching Bree with patience and

understanding. "I don't want her to say something she doesn't mean."

"Fine." Far be it from her to get in the middle of two of the most quietly stubborn people she'd ever known. "Go inside and wait for me," she told Bree.

"She hates me," Neil murmured when Bree had shut the door behind her.

"Nah. She'd like to hate you, but I don't think she's quite there yet."

"You know this because…?"

He was so grumpy, sounded so confused and put out, she smiled. "Because I'm sort of an expert when it comes to hating you."

MADDIE'S SMILE MADE Neil's mouth dry so he averted his eyes, stared at the front of Bradford House. It was run-down…aw, hell…who was he kidding? It was a dump. It was going to take a lot of work to make it livable. But if anyone could fix it up, make an old, crumbling house shine again, it was Maddie.

She'd always loved tackling new projects, the more challenging the better.

Which, he suspected, was part of the reason she'd been with him.

"So much for not still being pissed at me," he said.

She tugged her T-shirt away from her stomach, waved it a few times as if trying to get some air. "I meant that. I'm just saying that for a long time I did hate you. And I have to admit, wanting to see you skewered and slowly spun over a blazing fire gave me the strength to keep going after you left."

He winced at the image her words provoked—he could only imagine where she would have put that skewer. "It wasn't easy for me, either. Being without you."

"Let's not get into that."

He stepped over to her so that she had to tilt her head to maintain eye contact. "Because you're afraid of a repeat of the other night?"

"Don't let that ego of yours grow," she said, eyes shining with humor. Wasn't she all sorts of amused at his expense? "I'm just finally at the place where I'd like to put the past behind me. For good."

That included him. He could understand that. But for some reason, he didn't like it. "Fair enough. But I'm grateful you let me be a part of that whole thing with Bree."

Though, to be honest, he wasn't sure he wanted to be a part of it. He'd always known being a parent meant being responsible for your child. He'd never shied away from that responsibility, from taking care of his family.

But the fear he'd experienced when he hadn't known where Bree was, the rush of relief when he'd found her safe…those were new.

Maddie gave him a friendly pat on the arm. "Welcome to parenthood." She checked her watch. "Listen, can we finish this later? I have to get back to work."

He nodded but when she turned to walk away, he heard himself say, "I never worried about Bree before. I knew she was well taken care of, that she was safe in Shady Grove. That she was safe with you."

"She is safe," Maddie said gently. "She's fine."

The sun beat down, burning the back of his neck, making him hot and uncomfortable in his jeans. "I've never been so scared in my life," he admitted. His hands still weren't steady so he shoved them into his pockets. "When I couldn't find Bree inside the rink, I went cold all over. I've never felt that level of…"

"Panic?"

"More like terror. Even though I kept telling myself

she was probably fine, that this was Shady Grove and she was at the same park where I'd played as an eleven-year-old, I couldn't stop the feeling that something was wrong. When I saw her in that dugout with that man…" He swallowed but could still taste the panic he'd experienced. "My heart stopped. And I knew that if someone ever hurt her, I'd kill them. That if something ever happened to her… Christ, Maddie, I don't think I'd be able to get through it."

"Being a parent isn't for the weak," Maddie said. "It takes a lot of courage to love someone so much. But the rewards are worth it." She pursed her lips. "Well…usually."

"What if you've been right all these years and I don't deserve those rewards?"

Instead of gloating like she would have a week ago, Maddie looked at him with compassion. "You do."

"She ran off. She ran away from me."

"Sorry, but you don't get to take credit for that. Bree was the one who made the choice to leave. She's always had a mind of her own and once she sets that mind to something, look out. I remember one time…she must've been two…I lost her at the mall. One minute she was pushing her stroller, babbling to herself, charming the other customers, the next…she was gone."

"You're telling me she started practicing her disappearing act early?"

"I'm telling you that you aren't the only one to lose track of our kid."

"What did you do?"

"I freaked. Big-time. I ran around the store yelling her name, shoved aside clothes, dropped to my stomach to look under racks…" She shook her head. "Thankfully, this sweet elderly lady pointed to the window at the front of the store. Sure enough, there was Bree, sitting in the display playing with the mannequin's feet."

He shook his head. "She had a thing for feet at that age."

"She did," Maddie said with a soft laugh. "It was so weird. Anyway," she continued with a wave of her hand, "when I found her it was as if she'd been away for hours. I mean, she was only out of my sight a few minutes, but I swear, it was like my entire life flashed in front of my eyes."

"I'm going to look into getting her some sort of GPS collar," he said, only half kidding. "Like they have for pets."

"You do that. And if you ever want a real scare, ask Fay about the time she was at Shane's sister's house and Elijah wandered off only to be found next to the swimming pool."

His blood chilled and he held up a hand. "I'd rather not know."

She shrugged. "Like I said, parenting isn't for the weak."

"It's not," he agreed gruffly. "But you did it."

"I had a lot of help. My family. Yours."

But not him.

The realization left him reeling. Unsettled. Wondering what he'd missed out on.

She checked her watch once again and he realized he was keeping her from work. That he didn't want to let her go. Not yet.

"I could come over tonight," he said. "So we can discuss Bree's punishment."

She studied him in the way that made him feel too exposed. As if she knew talking about their kid wasn't the only reason he wanted to stop by her place. "We're eating at my parents' tonight. Why don't we talk about it at Bree's soccer game?"

"I don't think I'm going. Bree made it clear she doesn't want me around."

Maddie snorted. "Believe me, there are times she doesn't want *me* around, especially when I'm nagging her about cleaning her room. I don't let it stand in my way."

"I don't want to pressure her into anything."

"So she's ticked off at you. Kids get mad at their parents all the time. Sometimes they don't want us around and sometimes, they even hate us. But you're her father and if you're going to be a part of her life, you'll have to get used to it."

Easy for her to say, he thought as Maddie went back to work and he headed toward his rental car. Then again, no one said being a parent was easy. Today made him realize exactly how thankless, exhausting and all-consuming of a job it really was.

Along with how important.

"WANT ME TO KILL HIM?" Leo asked—as if it was every day someone set up a hit at a preteen soccer game. "I know people."

"You've been asking me that for twelve years," Maddie said to her most annoying bother, "and for twelve years I've given you the same answer. I don't want the man dead."

The man being—of course—Neil, who had arrived at the park in time for the beginning of the game. He kept his distance, though, watching from the sidelines instead of sitting on the bleachers.

The bleachers where both their families sat, taking up the entire center section.

She wondered if he'd mind if she joined him.

Leo tore open a package of cherry licorice. "All I'm saying is that the offer is out there."

"Why don't you ever offer to go play in traffic?" she asked, peeling off a piece of licorice.

"I'd take you up on that," Eddie said from behind them.

He reached over Leo's shoulder and snagged two pieces of candy, handing one to his son, Max.

Max, a stocky eight-year-old with his mom's coloring and nose and Eddie's dark hair and hazel eyes, waved his licorice like a sword before biting it.

Her gaze drifted back to Neil. She hadn't seen him since Monday, he'd kept his distance from Bree, giving their daughter time to cool off, Maddie was sure. Still, she and Neil had talked on the phone Monday night and had settled on Bree's punishment—two weeks of being grounded with no electronics of any sort, an early bedtime every night and Bree's worst nightmare, extra chores.

Now he stood apart from the other parents, his hands in his pockets. As if sensing her watching him, he turned his head, and though he had on dark sunglasses, she instinctively knew he was looking right at her.

She wished she could see his eyes.

"Aunt Maddie," Elijah said, jumping onto her lap and effectively giving her a heart attack, "can I have a dollar for the 'cession stand?"

His bony little knee was digging into her thigh so she slid him to the bleacher between her and Leo. Leo propped his elbow on the kid's head and waved a piece of licorice back and forth. Elijah giggled and snapped up the candy.

"Sure," Maddie said, pulling a crumpled dollar bill from her pocket. "Doesn't your mom have a dollar?"

"I don't know. She's waiting for Daddy to text her and told me to ask someone else for one."

Maddie gave him the money then made her way down the bleachers. She waved at Mitchell, who sat on Carl's lap. Gerry laughed at something Rose said while Frank lifted his fists when one of Bree's teammates stole the ball.

"Hey," Maddie said to Fay, who was reading her phone, "you okay?"

Fay lifted her head as if just realizing Maddie was there. "Huh? Oh…yes. I'm fine."

"I thought Shane was coming."

"He's…uh…running late." Fay shut her phone and smiled but it was a bit shaky around the edges. "He's catching up on yard work. He wants to get it done so he can take Elijah fishing this evening."

"Elijah will love that," Maddie said as Fay's phone buzzed. "If you want to go, too, I can keep—"

But Fay was checking her text message as she walked away.

"Mitchell," Maddie finished. "Or I can just stand here talking to myself."

"What was that?" a familiar voice asked from beside her.

She turned. "Nothing," she told her dad.

She looked back at Fay, who stood under a large maple tree typing on her phone, her brow furrowed. They hadn't spoken in a few days but the last time they'd talked, Fay had been positively giddy over her and Shane's reunion. She and the boys had moved back in with him and he was trying to find work locally instead of reenlisting like he'd wanted.

Frank rocked back on his heels. "I was surprised to see that boy here."

That boy. "Neil is Bree's father."

"Believe me, Madelyn, I realize that. It's just that he hasn't spent much time at her sporting events."

No, he certainly hadn't.

"I can't help but notice that you're having a hard time keeping your eyes off of him," Frank said.

Busted. And by her father. How embarrassing. "He happens to be in my line of vision," she said, her face hot.

"I also can't help but wonder what your feelings are toward him?"

She slid him a sideways glance. "Nonexistent." She prayed that was the truth.

"That's not what you told me the first time I asked you that question."

"That was a long time ago," she said, recalling that conversation vividly. She and Neil had been seeing each other for six months when she'd admitted her feelings for him to her dad.

"He's the father of my child so he'll always be a part of our lives, but that's it."

Frank seemed satisfied with that. "Good to see he's making more of an effort with Bree, at least."

"Yeah, it is. Dad?"

"Hmm?"

"Do you think people can change?"

"Of course. People change every day from good to bad and back again. Do you think your mother and I are the same people we were when we first got married? The same parents with you as we were with your brothers? People learn from their mistakes and try harder. Realize life is short and start living for the important things. Overcome addiction, find God, lose their faith, make amends, seek out forgiveness."

"But what's inside a person?" Maddie asked, wanting to trust the changes in Neil but unsure if she could. "What makes them who they are, doesn't that always stay the same?"

"Maybe," he conceded, "but from what I remember, what was inside of Neil was a decent young man, one focused on improving his life. Seems to me, he's fought hard for the life he has now, and maybe he's realized that money isn't everything. Maybe he wants to focus on other

things, like being there for his daughter and family." Her
father watched her carefully. "Are you trying to tell me
you're the same as that sixteen-year-old girl who told me
you were in love? That you haven't changed?"

"I grew up," she said, feeling as if she was under a mi-
croscope. "I had to."

"You did and you did a good job of it. But along the
way, you got…hard."

She bristled. "Thanks, Dad."

"Merely speaking the truth. It's so important for you
to do everything on your own, to prove your worth to everyone, to prove you're smart and capable and independent when the only person who really needs to believe
all of that is you. We all know you're capable. You had a
baby when you were barely more than a child yourself and
you've done a remarkable job of raising her."

"I didn't do it myself," Maddie pointed out.

"Relying on each other, leaning on those who love you
gives you strength to get through and to be the one they
lean on in return."

She agreed. Her parents had always been supportive.
She'd turned to them—she glanced at her brothers and
Carl and Gerry—to all of them, at one time or the other
when she or Bree needed them.

Unable to resist, Maddie looked back at Neil, not surprised to find him staring at her. She knew who she could
count on. Did she dare add his name to that list?

CHAPTER SIXTEEN

NEIL COULDN'T STOP searching out Maddie. Her hair was pulled back, making her look younger than almost thirty, her shorts showed off the long length of her tanned legs, her tank top accentuated her strong shoulders, the curve of her collarbones. Seeing her in the bleachers reminded him of all the times she'd sat in the stands of his games and even some of his practices.

She'd been a part of his life since her friendship began with Fay in the fourth grade, a constant for eighteen months when they'd been a couple. He'd missed her.

When he'd first walked away, it'd been a persistent ache, a daily longing to see her again. Touch her. Tell her he was wrong, he was sorry and he'd give up anything, everything for her. Then, time had marched on and the ache had eased, the longing had mellowed.

But there were still days even now when he'd think of her, when he wished he could call her just to hear the sound of her voice. Times when he remembered how it'd felt to be with her. How much he'd enjoyed listening to her go on about some project at school. He'd hear something on the nightly news and wonder what she thought of it now, as an adult, was curious as to if and how much she'd changed. After every goal he scored, he still found himself looking for her, hoping to see her cheering him on.

Hell, maybe it was just ego, his desire to have her at his side, devoted to him.

That would be easier to swallow than the other possibility; that he still cared about her. Or his biggest fear; that he always would.

When Bree finally got put into the game a few minutes before the half, he forced his attention to the field. He couldn't believe that was his little girl. She seemed taller, older than even the other day when she'd given him hell. He'd given her time and space, hoped that Maddie was right and Bree would want him here.

She was growing up and he had a flash of everything he'd missed, all the sports games and school activities, all the Christmas mornings, family picnics and game nights.

From the corner of his eye he saw a good-looking man talking to Maddie, flirting with her. She didn't seem very interested, but jealousy still stung Neil. Maddie was a beautiful, smart, interesting woman. How was it that she'd never met someone else, fell in love and got married?

How much longer until she did?

She deserved that. Deserved to have a partner in life, a man who'd be there for her, through the good times and the bad, someone to share her life with, to grow old with. Maybe even to have more children with. To help her raise Bree.

The thought of it killed him. Maddie with another man. Smiling at him each day, making love to him at night. Carrying his child. Bree looking up to some anonymous, faceless stepfather. He'd help her with her homework, play cards with her, drop her off to school and drive her and her friends to the mall, the movies and parties. He'd be there for Bree's first date, prom and high school graduation and on her wedding day, he'd walk her down the aisle.

Some other man who got to watch her grow up, help guide her through the tricky times and love her through it all.

Neil's jaw ached, his hands clenched. Lucky bastard.

A cheer went up from the crowd and he focused on the game in time to see Bree have the ball stolen from her. It took him only a few minutes to realize why the coach had waited to put her in.

She wasn't very good.

She was the slowest girl on the field and had no soccer skills that he could see. By the time the ref blew the whistle indicating the first half of play was over, she'd had the ball stolen from her twice, turned the ball over four times and, on one memorable occasion, kicked it toward the wrong goal.

She was a hindrance to the team.

Worse, she didn't even seem to care. She moved in slow motion, looked sluggish and her expression was one that said that being out there, running around, kicking the ball, playing with a group of girls who could grow to be her good friends, wasn't the joyful experience it should have been. It was torture.

During halftime he spent a few minutes talking with Gerry and Carl, somehow got roped into taking Mitchell with him as he went to the concession stand to grab a hot dog. While there, he had a surprisingly cordial conversation with Maddie's father about the rumors surrounding the Knights' draft choices. At the end of the break, Bree's team walked back toward the field. Toward him.

The athlete in him, the man who'd made his living being a true competitor in every sense of the word, wanted to grab his daughter, demand she do better, to stop wasting everyone's time. But the father in him recognized that wasn't what she needed, wasn't what would get through to her. It would only break her spirit.

"Hi," he said, walking up to her, forcing her to stop.

She looked at the ground as the rest of her team walked by. "Hi."

Okay, not exactly thrilled to have him there, but she hadn't screamed at him again. Hadn't insisted that she meant what she'd said Monday about not wanting him to be her father anymore.

"Good luck," he said. "In the second half."

"Thank you," she said primly. That was his kid, he realized with a rush of love that made him dizzy, this little girl with her round face and guarded eyes. She was polite and sweet and always seemed to be waiting for the other shoe to drop.

He reached into his pocket and pulled out a chain. "Here."

She looked at the necklace. The saint medallion swung back and forth. "What is it?" she asked as suspiciously as her mother.

"It's my lucky necklace."

Now she raised her eyebrows. "You have a lucky necklace?"

Hockey players were notoriously superstitious and it was paining him to even hand it to her because he'd never, not once, let anyone else wear it. He hoped doing so didn't negatively affect it.

But for her, he'd risk a bit of bad luck.

"It's Saint Sebastian," he told her. "The patron saint of athletes. Your mother gave it to me."

Bree finally took it from him. "She did?"

He nodded. "For my eighteenth birthday."

"And it's your lucky necklace? You wear it every day?"

"No, but I wear it for every game. Do you…can I help you put it on?"

He hadn't realized he was holding his breath until she nodded and it exploded from his lungs on a soft whoosh.

She turned around and he hooked the chain around her neck, gave in and ran his hand down the downy softness of her hair.

"There," he said gruffly, "that'll give you a bit of extra luck for the rest of the game."

BREE WRINKLED HER NOSE as she studied the medal. It wasn't very pretty, just a silver circle with words around the outer ring and a picture of a shirtless man tied to a tree and... she squinted...were those arrows sticking out of his body?

Gross.

But it was her dad's necklace. The one he wore to every game. The one her mom gave him. And he was here, even though she'd yelled at him and told him she didn't want him anymore, he'd still come to her soccer game.

He hadn't stayed away.

She glanced at the field but her coach was busy talking to one of the moms. "I'm not very good at soccer," she told her dad, hating how stupid and inadequate she felt admitting that. "I can't run as fast as the other kids."

Because she was fat.

"Sometimes," he said slowly as if searching for the right words, just like she did when she didn't know what to say, "sometimes it's not always about being the best at something. It's about *trying* your best. Whatever that might be." He watched her carefully. "Did you try your best during the first half?"

She hadn't but all she did was shrug. She'd given up trying when she'd realized she'd never be as fast or as good as some of the other players.

Her dad crouched and let his hands dangle between his knees. "You know, I've seen mediocre athletes become stars because they give one hundred percent every time they're on the ice. During every game they do their best, for the entire time, no matter what. And sometimes, even when we give our best, we lose. But knowing we did everything we could to win, to play our hardest, makes losing a lot easier to accept."

Bree wasn't sure she believed him. But when she rejoined her team and the coach told them all to hustle, she ran as fast as she could.

DURING THE SECOND HALF of the game, Bree was on fire on the field. She ran hard, tried to steal the ball and tried her best to get open for passes.

Maddie walked up to Neil. "I'm not sure whether to congratulate you or worry that you put something in her sports drink." When he looked at her she added, "I saw you talking to Bree before the start of the second half. It's like a miracle. Right up there with the U.S.A. beating the Russians in the Olympics."

"Not quite that miraculous—or big of a deal. And it's not me," he said, nodding toward the field when Bree shot at the goal—something she hadn't done before— and missed by a mile, but she at least tried. "It's all Bree."

Maddie loved her daughter but it wasn't exactly a secret that Bree gave up on things that were hard for her. It was nice to see her putting forth some real effort. "I think you both deserve some credit." She gave him a gentle hip nudge. "Good job, Dad."

"You've done the good job," he said, still watching the game. "You raised our daughter on your own and you did a damned good job of it."

His compliment warmed her. "I wouldn't say I did it on my own."

He followed her gaze to their families and nodded. "You did it without me, then."

Yes, she had. Hadn't realized she'd had any other choice

and maybe she hadn't, but she had a choice now. But she knew running her decisions about Bree by him first, letting him have a say in Bree's life, wasn't easy.

It was almost as hard as trying to see his side of things.

But after watching her daughter's face when Neil had talked to her during halftime and seeing her trying so hard now, sharing Bree with him would be worth it.

"She's done a lot to help me, too," Maddie said. "She helped me grow up. Helped me realize that there were other things more important than getting what I wanted and that my original dreams were immature and foolish."

"The dream of being with me, you mean."

He didn't sound upset or angry. Just so matter-of-fact that she answered him as honestly as she could. "The dream of a fairy tale where I'd have a baby and my life would be perfect. I was sixteen. What the hell did I know about life? About love? The kind that would last forever, the kind that was strong enough to survive two different people growing up. I didn't know how to compromise until I had her, didn't know I could have so much patience. And so much love. Real love. The kind that doesn't expect anything in return."

"I took that for granted," he said. "The love she had for me. The love she used to have for me. I figured it'd always be there no matter what I did. Or didn't do. Maybe you were right about the size of my ego."

"She still loves you. She has too big of a heart not to. She's kind and smart, and she amazes me the way she sees the world. Sometimes I look at her and I think…" She laughed softly. "God, I think, how did I get this kid? This sensitive, sweet-natured kid who'd rather read than be outdoors? Who forgives easily, who is slow to smile and who is so careful?" She shrugged. "Then I realized I got her because we made her. She's us, Neil. The very best of us and, at times, the very worst. Mostly, though, she's herself."

"The first time I held her," Neil said, "I wanted to put her down and run away. I didn't want anything to do with her or you. I'd hurt you and I'd turned my back on my own morals, something I'd promised myself I'd never do—I'd acted just like my old man. On top of that, there was this baby and she was so tiny, so delicate and fragile…. She was my responsibility and I had no idea what to do."

"And you thought I did?"

"Yeah," he said slowly, "I did."

"I was a mess, Neil. I was sixteen, a kid myself. I had no idea how I was going to graduate high school, let alone take care of a baby."

"You never let it show," he told her, and she was proud that he, at least, hadn't seen how terrified she'd been. "You were so confident. 'This is what I want,' you'd say, then you'd figure out a way to get it."

He was right. She'd acted as if she had everything under control. When he'd come to the hospital the day after Bree was born, she'd told him how to hold their baby, how much to feed her, when to burp her.

"You didn't need me, Maddie," he said simply, watching the game. "Not like you thought you did."

Their eyes met and something personal and real passed between them. Understanding. Acceptance.

The game ended and they stood side by side waiting for their kid to join them, just like other parents. Like a real family. Even though her team had lost by one goal, Bree was proud, her smile lighting up her face as her teammates congratulated her and each other for a good game.

"The other night, when you admitted what you'd done—" He lowered his voice, ducked his head close to hers. "When you admitted you got pregnant on purpose, you told me you were sorry but that you didn't regret it."

"That's right," she said, unable to ever regret having Bree.

"For the record," he said quietly, "I don't regret it, either."

BREE RAN OFF the field toward her parents. Parents. Wow, that was sort of weird, even thinking of them in that term. Sure, they were her parents but usually they were her mom and her dad. Separate.

But today they'd watched the second half of the game together and there were even a few times when Bree glanced over, that they'd been smiling and laughing. It was sort of…nice.

"Good game," her mom said, wrapping Bree in a hug even though Bree was all hot and supersweaty.

"Thanks," Bree said, stepping back.

"Great job," her dad said, holding his hand up for a high five.

Telling herself she wasn't disappointed, that she didn't want to hug him anyway because she was still mad at him, she slapped his palm. "But I didn't score."

"It's not always about scoring," he said. "You helped your team, were a team player and you gave one hundred percent effort."

She still wished she would have scored. Next game, she decided. The next game she was going to put the ball in the net.

She felt sort of grown up when he talked to her like this, instead of how he usually sort of asked her the same questions that he should already know the answers to. How was school and what did she and her friends do for fun and how did she spend her free time?

She didn't trust him, wasn't sure she wanted him in her life, but he had let her wear his lucky necklace. Remembering it, she scratched the back of her neck, her finger sliding under the heavy weight of the chain. Even though she didn't really want to, she unhooked it and held it out to him. "Thank you for letting me wear it."

Her mom inhaled sharply then seemed to hold her breath when she saw the necklace. Her mom and dad looked at each other and her dad didn't put the necklace back into his pocket, instead he hooked it behind his neck. It made Bree feel sort of warm inside to know he still wore something her mom had given to him. That he'd shared it with Bree.

"You're welcome," he said. "I told you it was lucky."

She frowned. "But we lost."

"Can't win them all."

"Yeah, but no one likes losing."

"True. But it's part of the game. Part of life."

"Right," her mom said. "Besides, it's just for fun."

"I didn't say that," her dad said. "If it was just for fun, they wouldn't bother keeping score."

He smiled at Bree and she knew he didn't smile all that often and it made her so happy that she smiled back before remembering she was mad at him. But maybe…maybe he had reason to be mad at her, too.

One of the other player's moms tapped Bree's mom on the shoulder. While they talked, Bree twisted her fingers together. Forced herself to meet her dad's eyes. "I…I've been thinking and…"

He didn't push her, didn't try to get her to hurry up and spit it out already like other adults. He just waited, didn't seem to mind her silence, that she was trying to figure out what to say.

She rubbed the side of her nose. "I…I guess I'm sorry.

About leaving the ice rink the other day without telling you and for being disrespectful to you."

But not for the things she'd said. She wasn't sure if she was sorry about them or not.

"I appreciate that," he said. "And I'm sorry, too, for leaving you alone for so long. I would've much rather have skated with you than shot pucks with Luke."

She blinked. Blinked again. "You would?"

"Absolutely."

The way he said it reminded her of how he'd sounded when he'd told her she wasn't a mistake. As if she'd better not argue with him or else.

She liked it.

He checked his phone. "It's getting close to dinner. How about I take you out to celebrate having such a good game?"

Bree's mom laughed at something the other lady said and Bree thought of how her parents had looked at each other, how they'd stood next to each other the entire game. She'd never—not once—eaten with both of them at the same time, not even at Grandma Gerry's house last week at the picnic.

"Can my mom come?" she asked.

"Can I come where?" Maddie asked, turning back to them.

Bree crossed her fingers at her side. "Can you come to dinner with me and Dad?"

"I guess it depends on where you're going," she said, as if it was normal for all of them to go out to eat together.

"I thought we'd let Bree pick," her dad said.

They both looked at her. "Can we go to Panoli's?" she asked. They had the best pizza and really good salads with lots of croutons.

"I'm in," her mom said. "Actually, I need to stop by

Bradford House and check that it's locked up so I'll meet you there. And, Bree, you need to say goodbye to your uncles, Aunt Fay and grandparents and thank them for coming."

"Okay." She raced off, gave her uncles and Poppa Frank and Nonna Rose hugs. "I can't find Aunt Fay," she told her dad as she accepted Grandpa Carl's kiss on the cheek.

"She had to leave a little early," Grandma Gerry said, bending to give Bree a hug, her white visor hitting Bree's shoulder. "Something about getting dinner ready for Uncle Shane. And I hear you're eating out tonight?"

"You're welcome to join us," her dad said, but as much as Bree loved her grandparents, she hoped they said no.

"Can't," Grandpa Carl said as he stood. "We're going to the Everetts' tonight. It's Homer's seventy-fifth birthday."

Grandma Gerry gathered the thick bleacher cushions they'd bought during a Shady Grove High School fund-raiser. "Where are you two going?"

"Panoli's," Bree's dad said. "And it's three. Maddie's joining us."

"Oh. Oh." Grandma Gerry sent a raised-eyebrow look at Grandpa Carl, who shrugged. "Well, that's…nice." She smiled at Bree. "But only one slice, right? Pizza is loaded with calories."

"Actually," her dad said, "Bree can have as many slices as she wants. And from now on, none of us are going to tell her what she can or can't eat unless she asks for our opinion."

Bree's head snapped up and she looked at her dad, but he was watching her grandma.

Grandma Gerry didn't seem able to talk, as if her throat had closed, so Grandpa Carl put his hand on her back and nodded at Neil. "Got it."

"Thanks." Then her dad did something Bree had never

seen him do before. He kissed Grandma Gerry's cheek. "You both have a good night."

Walking next to her dad, Bree glanced up at him, her heart so full, she worried it'd burst right out of her chest.

"Let me get that," he said, taking her bag from her shoulder.

Unlike the last time he tried to help her, she let him.

They passed the ball field where he'd found her the other day and she realized how dumb she'd been to run off like that. How stupid to talk to that old man. Keeping her head down, she slid another glance at her dad. His arm brushed hers as they walked, his free hand open. She chewed on her lower lip and slowly reached out—and took hold of his hand.

He stilled then looked down at her as if he was surprised, but in a good way, like when you wake up and school's been canceled for a snow day. He gave her hand a squeeze and held on, all the way to the car.

"THIS IS THE FIRST TIME we've hung out together," Bree said after they'd ordered their drinks at Panoli's. "The three of us."

Maddie frowned, realized Bree was right. "I guess that's true of a lot of kids these days, right? Parents split and they don't often do things together. Like your friend Cailley. Her folks are divorced."

Bree itched her nose. "Yeah, but her dad still comes to her parties and they were married so they used to do stuff together."

"I thought you wanted us to all eat together?" Maddie asked, looking at Neil for help, but he sat next to her expressionless, as if he was taking in what they said, thinking it over.

"I did. I do," Bree said, pulling the paper off a straw when the waitress brought their waters. "It's just…weird."

"That is true," Maddie said because, hey, she'd never lied to her kid before. She wasn't about to start now.

Neil leaned back. People were staring at him. They always stared when he was in town but Maddie doubted the skinny brunette eyeing him up had ever watched a professional hockey game in her life. "How about we all see how we do with this first time?" he asked Bree. "Then we can decide if we want to do it more than once."

"Okay," Bree said, looking relieved.

The waitress came back and took their order.

"Don't you like olives?" Bree asked Neil as she squeezed her lemon into her water. Water, not pop. And neither Maddie nor Neil had said anything about what she should order to drink. They'd ordered two large pizzas—one plain cheese, one loaded, no olives—and three tossed salads.

Maddie stared at the table. She knew why.

"I like them fine," he said. "But your mom doesn't. She can't have them on her pizza at all because she says they ruin it for her."

Bree's eyes widened. "How did you know that?"

"I know quite a bit about her," he said, his voice way too husky and intimate for the situation.

"Like what?" Bree asked.

"Well…" He drew the word out, sipped his water. "She loves pepperoni, which made it tough when she tried to become a vegetarian."

"You gave up meat?" Bree asked her mom.

"It's difficult for me to believe, too," Maddie said. "And I lived through it."

Neil snorted. "For three days."

"Longest three days of my life," she said solemnly.

"What else do you know about her?" Bree asked, thrilled to be getting the dirt on her mom.

"She loves horror movies—the gorier the better—hates country music and her favorite ice cream is mint chocolate chip. I also know that she thought about joining the air force after she graduated, but I knew she'd end up being a carpenter."

"Oh, really?" Maddie asked. "I hadn't realized you were psychic."

"I didn't have to see the future to see how much you loved working with your dad. How much you loved being in Shady Grove."

It was true. She couldn't imagine doing anything else. Her life was all about smelling of sawdust, having calluses and blisters on her hands and wearing jeans, T-shirts and work boots.

Bree stabbed at the ice in her glass with her straw. "Did you have to give up going into the air force because you got pregnant with me?"

"Kiddo, I didn't have to give anything up for you that I wasn't willing to do without. You were worth all of it."

"What was Mom like?" Bree asked Neil. "As a teenager?"

"This should be interesting," Maddie said.

"She was…special," he said slowly. Maddie's throat dried but she didn't dare take a drink, she didn't move, couldn't so much as blink for fear she'd miss what Neil said.

"She was smart and funny," he continued, "and for some reason, she saw something worthy in me that no one else saw. That I didn't even know was there. When I looked at her, I…" He held Maddie's gaze. "When I looked at her, I fell so hard, I didn't think I'd ever get up."

Her skin was tingling and he hadn't even touched her.

He was potent. Dangerous to her sense of self and peace
of mind.

But he'd given their daughter something she'd never
had—a piece of her parents' history. Maddie had been so
careful not to ever bad-mouth Neil in front of Bree, had
never told her to dislike her father or to be angry at him.
But she hadn't been completely honest with her, either.
Had never shared how much she'd loved Neil, how he'd
made her think. Made her laugh. She never talked about
how talented a hockey player he was, how good he was to
his family, how generous with the town and local charities.

She'd kept their past from Bree because it had ended
badly. But by protecting her daughter from what had gone
wrong, she'd forgotten about all that had been right. So
while they ate together for the first time as a family, Maddie let herself remember the good times and finally told
the story of how she fell in love with Neil Pettit.

CHAPTER SEVENTEEN

"Neil," Maddie said, "what are you doing here?"

She sounded surprised, but not disappointed to see him. And she hadn't tried to slam the door on him, which was a good sign.

"I heard Bree's spending the night at Fay's. I thought maybe you'd want to go out, get something to eat."

"Sure. I don't have plans." Leaving the door open for him, she spoke over her shoulder as she crossed to the table where her laptop was open. "I worked for a few hours this afternoon and was going to grab something at a drive-through." She grinned. "But you buying me dinner sounds much better."

He shut the door behind him. "The Wooden Nickel?"

Her favorite restaurant. At least, it had been. He'd taken her there on their one-year anniversary, had saved up for weeks to afford the expensive dinner, but it'd been worth it to see her so happy.

"I'd need a lot of work if we went to the Wooden Nickel," she said, indicating her clothes—jeans so faded they were white in spots and a Black Eyed Peas concert T-shirt.

"Not so much," he said.

She clicked something on the laptop. "Enough that it'd be at least an hour before we even leave here and tack on another thirty minutes for the drive out to the restaurant." She glanced up at him. "I'm too hungry for all that trouble. Want to buy a girl Chinese takeout?"

"Whatever you want."

"Great." She shut the laptop's lid. "I'll grab the menu. I'm feeling lots and lots of pot stickers."

She went to the other side of the kitchen, searched through the drawer while he waited by the table. They'd spent quite a bit of time together—he, Bree and Maddie—over the past two weeks since their dinner at Panoli's. It'd actually become quite the routine—Neil would work out in the mornings, pick Bree up from soccer so they could have lunch together before he did another workout in the afternoon. Evenings were mostly spent at Maddie's house. After dinner they'd go for a long walk or kick a soccer ball around in the yard. A few times he'd stayed and played cards with Bree on the porch.

It was all very...domestic.

And more enjoyable than he'd ever imagined. He loved being with his daughter, getting to know her better, seeing her open up to him again. But it hadn't been easy being around Maddie so much—her smiles and laugh, her smart-ass comments and sarcastic sense of humor all enticed him. Appealed to him in ways they hadn't when he'd been a cocky eighteen-year-old.

They'd had no time alone. Until tonight.

All the things he'd been without since he'd left Shady Grove, everything he'd told himself he didn't want, that he'd never want, rushed over him. Longing for a home, a place filled with warmth and laughter, filled with the people most important to him. Desire for a family, for people who knew him, who would be there for him no matter what, to help him get through the rough times, to celebrate the good times.

A physical ache settled over him and he knew it was because he wanted what he'd left behind. Like the kid he used to be, that poor kid hauling around so much embarrassment and fire inside of him, desire to do better, to be more, the kid who came from nothing, who had nothing—nothing to offer—wanted, once again, something out of his reach.

Except Maddie had been in his reach. She'd been his for over a year, his one weakness, his touchstone. He'd never been able to get enough of her easy, accepting smile and husky laugh. Her soft hands and responsive body.

And he'd given her up.

Like that boy he'd been, he wanted it all again. Wanted to do whatever it took to please her.

Reading the menu, she walked toward him. "I'm thinking the shrimp pad Thai, but I—" She looked up, stopped. Then stepped back. "I'd ask you what you're thinking but I'm afraid I know that look."

He edged toward her, pleased when she didn't move. "What look?"

"That whole let's-get-it-on look. This isn't my first rodeo, baby."

He settled his hands on her hips. "You want to ride the bull?"

She sputtered out a laugh then sighed. "Neil—"

He dipped his head and kissed her. Coaxed a response from her until her hands slid up to his shoulders, her mouth moving under his.

She leaned back, kept her hands linked behind his neck. "Are you trying to seduce me?"

He couldn't stop himself from trailing a finger up her arm. "That depends on whether it'll work or not."

She played with the hair at the nape of his neck, her fingers cool against his heated skin. "I guess that depends on whether you put in one hundred percent effort or not."

"Never let it be said I don't give every job, big or small, my all."

He kissed her again, a warm, lingering kiss, then eased

back. She was beautiful, her eyes wide and trusting, her mouth curved in a sexy, feminine grin. She was everything he wanted.

All he'd ever wanted.

He might not be able to have her forever, but he could have her tonight. He'd make sure that was enough.

NEIL LEANED FORWARD, his breath warm on her neck as he spoke into her ear. "You look good enough to eat," he murmured, trailing a finger down her forearm. "I used to dream of you," he admitted in a husky whisper. "I used to see you and my heart would stop. I wanted…" He lifted his gaze to her surprised one. "I still want. You, Maddie. Always you. And I wonder if that'll ever leave, if it'll ever stop?"

"You don't sound too happy about it. Then again, you were never happy with our relationship, were you?" she asked, realizing that as she spoke the words, they were true. "You were always searching for a way out. For a way to make it less than what it was."

"I was always searching for a way to make my dreams come true. What I felt for you was too big for me to handle. And you were always trying for a way to make it more than what it was. You scared the hell out of me." The look he sent her made her skin hot, her stomach tumble. "You still do."

Then his mouth quirked and her heart warmed. Damn him and that slow, careful smile.

He crushed his mouth down on hers. His kiss swept her away, took her outside of herself. Somehow they made it down the hall and to her bed. If she had second thoughts, a moment's hesitation that by giving in to the inevitable she'd be opening herself to pain, she shoved those doubts aside.

She wanted this. Wanted Neil. She'd forget the past, not

worry about the future and concentrate on now. Right here was what was important.

She wrapped her arms around his strong shoulders and deepened the kiss, reveling in his moan, in how his hands roamed over her. She didn't want to take the time to examine exactly why it was that she was so happy, didn't want to worry or think this could be a huge mistake.

"You are dangerous to me," he told her between quick kisses along her jaw and neck.

She couldn't answer. Her breath had hitched as he lifted the hem of her T-shirt and ran his hand over her stomach.

"So soft. So damn soft," he murmured.

He kept one hand on her waist, caressed the curve of her hip, and the other hand went to her hair, tugging the band off her ponytail. His eyes glittering, he spread her hair across her pillow. Exhaled a shaky breath.

Rising onto her elbows, she captured his mouth, poured herself into their kiss, showing him what she couldn't say. What she couldn't admit to feeling. Breathless, she pulled back and tugged at his shirt, needing to feel his skin against hers.

He pulled the shirt over his head and tossed it aside while she lifted her own off.

"You are beautiful," he told her.

It didn't matter that she wore a sports bra or that she didn't have any makeup on, with Neil's gaze on her, his hands on her, she felt beautiful. He kissed the delicate skin of her breasts before sliding down her body so he could lick one nipple into a peak before sucking it greedily into his mouth.

Maddie gasped, her hands fisting in his hair as her body flushed with pleasure. He ran his hands down her body, a light, feathering touch over her stomach, a firmer caress as he worked the button free of her jeans, slid the zipper down. She lifted her hips so he could tug them off. He shucked his own jeans as she pulled off her bra and panties.

Standing at the edge of her bed, he stared down at her. Instead of feeling vulnerable and exposed, she felt powerful. She lifted her arms and he joined her, his hard body a perfect contrast, complement to her curves.

They made love slowly, gently, their bodies rising together, their breathing quickening until the tension in her grew, coiled in her belly. He held her gaze, linked his fingers with hers as he moved in her. And looking into his eyes, into the eyes of the first boy she'd ever loved, the father of her child, she tumbled over the edge of pleasure, taking him with her.

After, he pulled the sheet over them and enveloped her in his arms. She laid her head on his chest so she could hear his heart, loving his strength and heat, his skin and scent.

Loving him.

Tears clogged her throat. She was an idiot. A fool to fall for him again. And while she couldn't stop what was in her heart any more than she could stop the world from turning, she sure as hell could be smarter this time. Could protect herself and her daughter.

NEIL JERKED OUT of a light doze when his cell phone buzzed. Maddie, curled up next to him, stretched, the movement doing some interesting things to her breasts, the muscles of her thighs.

"You going to answer that?" she asked, all amused and sexy, her voice making him think of a mythical siren. If she was there to lure him to his death, he might just jump in that water willingly.

Clearing his throat, he flipped open his phone. "Yeah? Uh…hello?"

Nothing.

"Hello?" he repeated, sitting up more fully.

"Daddy?"

His blood went cold, everything inside of him stilled at Bree sounding so small and scared. "Bree. What is it? What's wrong?"

Maddie sat up, clutching the sheet over her breasts. "What is it?" she asked, reaching for the phone. "Is she sick?"

He turned so the phone was out of her reach, shook his head. "Breanne," he said, harsher now. "What's going on?"

She sniffed and he could hear the tears in her voice. "I need you, Daddy."

He was already pulling on his jeans, noted Maddie was doing the same. "Okay, baby, it's okay. I'm on my way. We'll be there in a few minutes. Let me talk to Aunt Fay," he said, hoping his sister could shed some light on why his daughter was so upset. He checked the clock, not quite midnight. "Is she still awake?"

"No. I tried. I tried to wake her but…I need you, Daddy," she cried.

He met Maddie's eyes, saw his own panic, his fear mirrored there. "I know you do. I'm coming. But I need you to tell me what's wrong."

"It's Aunt Fay. I can't wake her up."

AN HOUR LATER, Neil had a cup of bad hospital coffee in his hand as he stared blindly out the waiting room window at the dark sky.

"She'll be all right," Gerry said for what had to be the twentieth time since she and Carl arrived at Shady Grove Memorial. In the window's reflection, Neil saw Gerry look to Carl for confirmation. "They got to her in time so she'll be okay."

Neil faced them, saw the worry, the grief in their faces,

how it aged them. Saw how much they loved Fay. And him. "She's not okay," he heard himself say, admitting what he'd feared since he got back to Shady Grove. "She needs help."

Carl came over, laid his hand on Neil's shoulder. "We'll help her through this. If you're worried about what'll happen when you go back to Seattle—"

"That's not it." Or at least, it wasn't just it. He did have to go back to work. Training started in a week and he still had that commercial to shoot, promised his agent he'd do a few promotional opportunities…

"Fay needs more than us watching her kids or telling her to be happier or stronger," Neil said. "She needs professional help. A psychiatrist or a counseling group that deals with attempted suicide—"

"Oh, Neil," Gerry said, her eyes red from crying. "We don't know what happened. Let's wait until Fay wakes up and can explain what happened—"

"She swallowed half a bottle of sleeping pills," Neil said flatly. Gerry flinched, started crying again. He sighed. Set his coffee down and crossed to her, gentled his voice. "There's something wrong with her. It's not her fault. It's not anyone's fault. It just…is. But we can't pretend any longer, can't act like her behavior, the way she reacts to emotional distress, is normal."

His sister was sick. She'd tried to end her own life tonight while her sons slept in their beds and his daughter read. Thank God Bree had gone out to get a glass of water and had found Fay on the couch, the bottle of pills on the floor next to her. She'd called 911 and then him.

His brave little girl.

By the time he and Maddie arrived at Fay's, the EMTs were already there, including Leo, who had Bree and the boys in the kitchen. Maddie had stayed with the kids while Leo gave Neil a ride to the hospital behind the ambulance.

Gerry and Carl had met him there and he'd had to tell them what Fay had done. That she'd been so crushed by her husband leaving her for another woman, she hadn't wanted to live without him.

"Neil's right," Carl said, his chin covered with whiskers, his face drawn. "Fay needs professional help."

Gerry pressed against Carl's side, laid her head on his shoulder. "I…I hate that she was that far gone. That she felt so hopeless."

She started crying softly. Carl turned and they held on to each other for a moment and then Carl held his arm out. Neil hesitated—he'd never needed comfort, had never needed to lean on anyone.

Until now.

He stepped into Carl's embrace, wrapped his arm around Gerry's waist. He wasn't sure how long they stood there, clinging to each other, but at some point, Gerry sniffed and excused herself to freshen up and gather her composure.

Neil and Carl sat next to each other.

"I never thanked you," Neil said, his hands dangling between his knees. "For all you've done for us. Please," he added quietly when Carl started to protest. "Please. Let me say this."

Carl nodded and leaned back.

Neil picked up his coffee and took a long swallow of the cold, bitter brew. "You took us in, you brought us back together. More than that, you gave us so much, little things that most people take for granted—three meals a day and new clothes—but you also gave us so much more. Your time and attention and your love and affection. You gave us security when we'd never had any. You gave me my sister back and for that, I'll always be in your debt."

"That," Carl said, "is a bunch of B.S."

Neil scowled. "What?"

"You think your mother or I want either you or Fay indebted to us?" he asked sharply. "We brought you into our home because we wanted children to love, to take care of. We didn't raise you, discipline you and love you all those years so you'd owe us. You're our children. Our blood may not run through your veins but you're still ours."

Neil was shocked by easygoing Carl's flare of temper. More, he was ashamed by his own thoughts, by how all these years he'd felt as if a debt was owed when all that was owed was his gratitude. And his love.

"You're right," Neil said. "Not about my not owing you because, I'm sorry, but Fay and I do owe you. You gave us a life, a childhood, showed us what a family should be like and I can't help but be grateful. But we are yours." He reached over and grabbed Carl's hand. "Dad."

No SOONER HAD Maddie heard the car pull into the driveway than she opened Fay's front door. It had started to rain a few hours ago, a cooling mist that coated the driveway, sparkled in Neil's headlights before he shut the car off. She watched him get out from behind the wheel and slowly make his way up the walk. It was obvious he was exhausted. Heartsick.

She could relate.

"Tell me," she said as soon as he reached the step.

"She was awake," he said, his eyes bleak.

Maddie shivered in the cool air. Realizing she was blocking him from coming into the house, she moved aside. "Did she say anything?" she asked as she shut the door.

"She said it was an accident."

Maddie shook her head. "How could—"

"Is Aunt Fay dead?"

They both turned. Bree, in her pajamas, her feet bare,

stood in the kitchen doorway, her face tear-streaked, her eyes puffy from crying.

"Why isn't she in bed?" Neil asked Maddie.

Maddie knew he was worried, upset, so she didn't get angry at his harsh tone. She laid a hand on his arm. "She was worried. There was no way she'd get to sleep so I let her wait with me."

He gave an almost imperceptible nod, trailed his fingers over the back of her hand before approaching their daughter. "No, Aunt Fay's not dead. She's alive. Thanks to you."

Bree started crying again, tears leaking silently down her cheeks. "I was so scared...."

Neil scooped her up in his arms. She was too big to be carried, her feet dangling by his knees, but he didn't even pause, just walked into the kitchen, sat on a chair and shifted her onto his lap. "I know you were but you were very brave."

"And very smart," Maddie added, lifting the pot of freshly made coffee in a silent question. When Neil shook his head, she refilled her own mug, added milk from Fay's fridge. "We were able to get the boys settled down about two hours ago," she said, taking the seat opposite Neil. "Elijah was pretty traumatized."

He woke up to the EMTs and firefighters in the house. Luckily, Leo had snatched him up before he'd seen his mother's unconscious body.

"Mom wanted to stay at the hospital for another hour in case Fay woke up again," Neil said. "She wanted me to let you know she'll be here by six or so to relieve you."

Mom? Maddie wondered if he even realized that he'd called Gerry mom but now wasn't the time to ask. "It's no problem. I'm crazy about those boys and I love Fay. You know that."

"I do." He reached out and clutched her hand, their fingers linking. "Thank you."

They sat that way for a moment, she and Neil holding hands, Bree on his lap, her head resting on his shoulder. And for the first time since Bree's frantic call, Maddie's heart rate calmed down.

Bree yawned and rubbed her left eye. "How did they get Aunt Fay to wake up?"

Maddie squeezed Neil's hand then eased back to take a sip of her coffee.

"They had to get the sleeping pills out of Aunt Fay's stomach," he said. "Once they did, they were able to wake her up."

Not as easy as that, Maddie imagined. They would have had to have pumped Fay's stomach—a painful process.

"She was sad about Uncle Shane," Bree said.

"How do you know?" Maddie asked.

"I heard her on the phone with him. She was crying, asking him to come home but then she hung up and told me she was okay. That everything would be all right in the morning."

"We still haven't been able to get ahold of Shane," Neil said. "From what we've gathered and from what little Fay said when she woke up, he took off with that girl from the convenience store. Off to start a new life somewhere."

Maddie hit her fist on the table. "That rat bastard. Oh, God," she breathed. "What if he comes here? What if he wants to take the boys?"

"We won't let that happen," he said, sounding so weary, it broke her heart. "I'll get ahold of an attorney as soon as possible."

In this instance, Maddie could appreciate that he'd take care of it, the way he'd always taken care of his family.

"Why did Aunt Fay take all those pills?" Bree asked. "Didn't she know they'd make her sick?"

"Aunt Fay has been very sad lately," Neil told Bree and began rubbing her back, an almost instinctive, parental gesture that warmed Maddie's heart. "We all get sad sometimes but Aunt Fay's sadness goes beyond feeling bad for a while. Sometimes people feel so sad, they don't think they'll ever be happy again." He breathed deeply. "That's what happened to my real mother."

Bree sat up, her eyes huge. "She died because she killed herself?"

"Aunt Fay and I came home from school one afternoon and found her—just like you found Fay tonight. Except, we were too late to help her."

Maddie knew that he'd only been nine when he'd walked in and discovered his mother dead from an overdose. Six months later, his father abandoned Neil and Fay. It'd been his childhood that'd made him so emotionally closed off, and while she wished he could have opened up to her, she couldn't entirely blame him for protecting himself.

"It's so important that if you're sad, you talk to someone about it," Maddie told Bree, not even wanting to consider the possibility of her baby ever feeling that much pain. Ever feeling as if she had no other choice. "Even if you think nothing will help, you need to reach out to the people who love you. Promise me?"

"I promise." She yawned again.

"Why don't you go lay down on the couch?" Maddie said. "Close your eyes for a little bit?"

Bree slid to her feet. "Will you be here when I wake up?" she asked Neil.

"I have to go back and check on Aunt Fay but I can wake you up before I leave to tell you goodbye."

"Okay." She hugged him and Maddie noted how he held on tight, shut his eyes as if he didn't want to let go.

"We have a very brave daughter," Neil said after Bree had left the room.

Maddie turned her cup. Turned it again. "She held it together while Leo was here. I think she wanted to be brave for her cousins but as soon as she saw me…" Maddie stopped, swallowed as she remembered her daughter's face crumpling when Maddie had walked in the door. "As soon as she saw me, she broke down."

"I'm sorry."

"It's not your fault. But it doesn't feel right blaming Fay, either, does it? It breaks my heart that my best friend was in so much pain she couldn't see another way out. And I feel guilty, God, I feel so damned guilty for telling her to buck up and get a backbone." For expecting her to act like Maddie had when Neil had left. To gather her pride around her and move on, holding on to her resentment as a way to make it through.

"I hate to even admit this," she continued, her gaze on her coffee, "but I'm also pissed. I'm furious that Fay would do this to her children, to our daughter. I want to go to that hospital and shake her until her teeth chatter. I want to grab ahold of her and beg her to never do anything like this again." She raised her head. "Neil, what if…what if she tries again?"

"She might." He shoved his chair back so hard, it banged against the cherry cabinets. "She might and I'm not sure there's anything we can do to stop it. To fix her."

Maddie crossed to him, grasped both of his hands in hers. "We might not be able to fix her, to stop her from wanting or, God forbid, trying to hurt herself again, but we'll be here for her. Always. In any way we can. Maybe that'll be enough."

"I hope so."

So did Maddie. She couldn't imagine her life without Fay, couldn't imagine a world where such a gentle and loving soul as Fay's ceased to exist.

"Maddie, tonight was…"

"Hell."

One corner of his mouth kicked up. "Not all of it," he said, reminding her of how they'd started their evening. "But, yeah, it's been rough. It's also made it clear to me how important it is to let the people you care about know what they mean to you."

Her fingers tightened on his involuntarily. "Neil, now's not—"

"Mostly," he continued, his eyes serious, his shoulders set, "it's made clear to me what I want. What I really want." He leaned down and kissed her, an incredibly sweet and tender kiss. One that scared her to death. "I want you, Maddie. You and Bree. I want us to be a family for real. Forever."

CHAPTER EIGHTEEN

MADDIE WENT WHITE and shrank away from him, but he kept ahold of her hands.

Not exactly the reaction Neil had been hoping for.

"Whoa. Back up, there. Aren't you returning to Seattle?"

"I have to."

"And what are we supposed to do? Throw away our lives here to follow you?"

"You were willing to do that before," he pointed out, scared he was losing something big and important.

She tugged, and he had no recourse but to let go of her hands. "I was sixteen. I was willing to do whatever it took to stay with you."

"Obviously."

She blushed but didn't retreat. "How dare you?" she asked harshly. "You don't say something like that now, tonight of all nights. And what if Bree hears you? What's she supposed to think?"

"She's supposed to think that her parents are getting back together and that they'll be a family now."

"We're not a family. You have your life and career in Seattle and I have mine here. Bree has friends here, her entire family."

"I could ask for a trade," he said, considering it for the first time and realizing it was not only a viable option, but also a good one. "To one of the East Conference teams, maybe even the Pens—they've had interest in me before."

"No. God, I don't want you to do that. I don't want you to rearrange your life for me."

He had to get her to see reason. To forgive him. To give him another chance. "I was wrong. I wasn't the person, the man, you needed me to be back then. Let me prove to you that I'm that man now."

"You're manipulating me and the situation. Look, Bree and I were doing just fine without you, we've done fine all these years without you and we don't need you in our lives. More importantly, we don't want you in our lives."

Neil was crushed but he had to try, one more time. "Maddie, I love you," he told her, finally giving her the words he'd always withheld. The words he'd never been able to say to anyone, not when he hadn't known the true meaning of them. But he knew now. "I've always loved you. Please don't do this. Please give us a second chance."

"I can't," she whispered.

Neil knew what it was. Payback. Maddie's way of getting back at him for what happened before. Her way of showing him she was still in control.

It was Maddie's way or no way.

He'd been such an idiot to fall for her again, to let her under his skin when he needed to focus on what was important. His career. His daughter. Everything else was secondary. Security came first and had to be the most important thing. He knew that but he'd gotten so wrapped up in her, in how he felt when he was with her, how much more he wanted.

Wanting more sucked. It was smarter to only want what he could have, what he could achieve on his own.

"I'll tell Bree I'm leaving," he said, unable to hide the anger and pain in his voice. Hated that it hurt, knowing that Maddie hadn't truly forgiven him, that she couldn't let go of their past.

Not even for their future.

BREE WAITED UNTIL her dad had quietly shut the door behind him, kept still until after his headlights had flashed across Aunt Fay's living room.

He was gone.

He'd given her a kiss, told her he'd call her later and walked away.

Because her mom didn't want him.

Maddie came tiptoeing into the room and Bree sat up.

"God, Bree," her mom said, holding her hand over her heart. "You scared me."

"You made him leave," Bree cried, hating that she sounded like some little kid, that tears clogged her throat and blurred her vision. But she welcomed the anger burning through her. She was mad at her mom. Mad at her aunt Fay. So mad she didn't even care if either of them stopped loving her for it.

"It's not quite as simple as that," her mom said, sounding tired and looking sad. But Bree wasn't going to try to fix things. Not this time. This time, her mom needed to be the one doing the fixing.

She'd heard everything. Hard not to, her parents hadn't exactly been quiet. Her dad wanted to stay, wanted to be with them. And her mom had pushed him away.

"It is simple. He wants us to be a family, his family, but you sent him away. You said you weren't still mad at him but you are. You lied!"

"That has nothing to do with this. Look, this is adult stuff—"

"You always said we were a team."

Her mom nodded slowly. "You're right. We are a team. And I know you're mad at me—"

"I'm not," Bree said, her face hot and her skin itchy.

"You are and that's okay. It's okay to get mad at people sometimes. I'm not going to stop loving you if you get angry with me. And believe me, in a few years, we'll probably be angry at each other quite a bit."

"Why did you do it?" Bree asked, wiping her running nose on her sleeve. "Why did you have to send him away?"

"I had to make a decision about what was best for us—for both of us—where your father is concerned. I have to do what's right for you even when you can't understand that or don't agree with it."

Bree shook her head. "I don't agree with it. I'll never agree."

Her mom sighed. "I have to make the best decisions I know how in order to protect you and help you grow into an independent, capable young woman. Look, I think your dad is trying and that's great. Really," she said, repeating it because that's what her mom did when she was lying but pretending to be telling the truth. "But the fact is that we live here, our lives our here, our families, your friends and school and grandparents and our house and my job. We couldn't just…take off and move to Seattle."

"You could've told him you wanted him to stay here," Bree insisted stubbornly.

"No," her mom said with a short laugh. "I couldn't. Hey, we got along fine without him before, didn't we? It's you and me, babe."

"I guess," Bree said. "Dad's going to go back to Seattle and forget about me again, isn't he?"

"You don't know that," her mom said, smoothing her hair back, and Bree leaned against her side.

"Maybe." But Bree didn't really believe it. Once again it was just going to be her and her mom.

And she wasn't sure that was a good thing.

"I THOUGHT I'D FIND you here."

Bree looked up from the book she was reading. Her dad stood over her, blocking the sun with his wide shoulders.

She hadn't seen or spoken to him in two days but her mom said he was just busy with Aunt Fay. That he wouldn't stay away from Bree just because he was mad at her mom.

"You're still here," she said.

He knelt next to her. "I wouldn't leave without telling you," he said, watching her carefully. "I wouldn't go without saying goodbye."

She wasn't sure if she believed him or not but it was nice that he was there, that he'd found her at her spot under the large elm tree in the backyard. "That's why you're here? To say goodbye?"

Why did that make her feel like crying? She'd never felt that way about him leaving, had always felt sort of relieved, as though she could go back to pretending he didn't exist, like he'd done to her for so long.

He sat next to her. "I have to get back to work."

She stared down at her book. "Oh."

"Listen, I want to apologize to you."

She glanced up at him. "What for?"

"For missing so much of your life. For not realizing what you needed. When I was your age, when I was growing up, my real parents, well, they didn't have much money."

She nodded. "Mom told me you were poor growing up."

"We were poor. We were so poor that some days we didn't have enough to eat and I was always worried about what would happen to me and your aunt Fay. But then

Grandpa Carl and Grandma Gerry adopted us and we had each other. And I forgot that that's what's most important. Having family. I thought that the best way to be your dad was to provide you with things, with money. And…I didn't know how to be a dad. Wasn't sure I was cut out to be a good one or that I even wanted to be one."

"You were mad I was born."

He narrowed his eyes. "Did your mom tell you that?"

"No. But I heard Poppa and Nonna talking once about how you weren't ready to be a father and I figured it out."

"I'm not mad at you. I was never mad at you. I was mad at myself for not being the father you needed. No matter what, none of this was your fault. It was mine." He blew out a heavy breath. "I pretended that I was doing what a good dad would do, making money, but now I know that's not right. I convinced myself that you had everything you needed. You had your grandparents and aunt and uncles. You didn't need me. You probably still don't need me. But I need you."

Her eyes widened. "You do?"

He nodded. "I do. I need you, Bree. I'll do whatever it takes, no matter how long it takes, to prove it to you because I love you. And I'm sorry. I'm sorry I wasn't there for you before. But I will be now—even if I'm in Seattle. And I want to be here for you whenever you need me. Could you give me another chance? Could you do that?"

NEIL'S CHEST HURT while she thought it over, his sweet little girl with her round face, open heart, sensitive nature and thoughtfulness.

This. This was what was most important.

He'd realized when Maddie turned him away that she was giving him what he'd always wanted. Freedom from the responsibility of being a father. Freedom to stop worrying he'd made the right decision to pursue his dreams, to make something of his life at the cost of Maddie and his daughter. Freedom from the guilt that he wasn't doing enough, wasn't good enough to be Bree's father, that he was failing her in some monumental way he could never make up for.

She'd given him a chance at what he used to think he wanted. Now he couldn't even remember being that man. Not when the most precious thing in his life was sitting before him, as beautiful as her mother, as wonderful a gift as he'd ever been given.

"I'll give you another chance," Bree said. Then she smiled at him, a slow smile that lit her entire face. "I love you, too."

Neil had never felt such relief. He was humbled. She had more inside of her, forgiveness and the ability to give second chances, and though he wasn't sure he deserved either, he was grateful and wasn't going to turn them away.

"Thank you," he told her sincerely. He handed her a bag. "I got you something."

She pulled out the latest bestselling paranormal young adult book. "Thank you."

"It's a new release," he said, feeling nervous, more nervous than any other time he'd gotten a female a gift, but this was more important than those times. "The bookstore owner said it just came out today and thought you might like it."

"It looks good," Bree said, already scanning the back cover.

He pulled out a second copy. "I thought I could read it, too. Then we could talk about it. If you want."

She smiled and hugged the book to her chest. "That would be cool."

"I set up an account at the bookstore for you. You have credit so you can buy any book, as many as you want. But that doesn't mean you're to be wasteful. When you're done with a book, give it to the library or donate it to a homeless shelter. And for each book you buy, you can pick out one for the day-care center for the little kids or for your school library."

She threw her arms around him and hugged him and he knew this was home, this was where he wanted to be. No matter what.

The sound of the door shutting broke them apart and they both turned to see Maddie watching them from the porch, her hand shielding her eyes from the sun.

"Do you have to leave?" Bree asked.

"I do," he said. "But first I need to talk to your mom about spending more time with you."

"Okay. 'Bye." As he left, he heard the best thing he'd ever heard. "I love you, Daddy."

MADDIE'S STOMACH CRAMPED as she watched Neil walk toward her. Not from nerves, she assured herself. But because she knew that whatever conversation they had, no matter how quickly it went, would be uncomfortable. It had to be, what with her giving him the boot.

She should feel vindicated. Righteous. Instead she felt as if she was missing something. As if she'd made a mistake.

She shook off the feeling.

"I'm flying out to Seattle tonight," he said in greeting when he reached her. "I want us to rework our custody arrangement."

She frowned. "What? Why?"

"I want joint custody."

Her entire world shifted. She was losing her balance and her hold on reality. "What?"

"I want a formal agreement, a custody arrangement that suits us both and will give Bree and I time together."

"The arrangement we have now is just fine. I've never kept her from you. You did that all on your own."

"You're right. But things are different now and I've changed. And we need to make sure it's legal and binding."

"You don't trust me? That's rich. This is about getting back at me, isn't it?"

"This is about doing what's best for our daughter," he said softly, with no smirk or hint of vindictiveness. "If we can't reach an agreement on our own, I'll be forced to contact my attorney."

"Go ahead," she said, daring him, hoping he was bluffing. But then, Neil didn't bluff, did he? She swallowed back the sick feeling in her throat. "You're not taking my daughter from me."

"I don't want to take her from you. I want to be a part of her life. And, more importantly, I want to prove to her that's what I want."

But all Maddie could think about was that he wanted Bree. He had everything she didn't. Money, fame and powerful friends and acquaintances. She had her pride, her family and her connections in town, but was that enough up against who he'd become?

"Go ahead," she said. "Contact your attorney. But you'll have a fight on your hands."

"I'm sorry it has to be this way."

She almost believed him.

THE PAPERS CAME two weeks later, enough time for her to worry over it every day, to wonder if he'd go through with his threats, his promise. Enough time to keep him in the forefront of her mind.

Oh, who was she kidding? Maddie wondered as she sat at the kitchen table late that night, the words on the pages blurring in front of her. *Custody arrangement, best interests of the minor child, shared custody, agreement for said child to spend time with father.*

She pressed her fists against her temples, shut her eyes. He was doing it. He was trying to take Bree from her.

And still, she missed him. Missed the person he'd become. Had wanted nothing more than to forget about him, to forget about their time together and how she'd almost been such a fool over him again.

"Mom? You okay?"

Maddie lifted her head to see Bree in the doorway, her feet bare, in her pajamas, her hair sticking up on the side. "Hey," Maddie said, trying to smile and shuffling the papers together. "Why are you up?"

"I just finished reading," she said, holding up her latest book. Maddie had to give it to Neil—that credit line at the bookstore had gone over better than anything else he could have done. "I wanted a drink." She looked at the papers. "What's that? A new contract for a job?"

Maddie opened her mouth to tell her that's exactly what it was, to lie to her baby's face, but then she remembered that Bree wasn't a baby anymore. She was a kid, but she was quickly growing up, and hadn't Maddie been the one to tell Bree to always be honest? That they needed to rely on each other to be truthful?

"Sit down," Maddie said. "I need to tell you something."

Bree sat on the edge of the chair. "Is everything okay? Is it Aunt Fay? Did she hurt herself again?"

Fay had started therapy but they all walked on eggshells around her, worried about saying the wrong thing, looking at her the wrong way, fearful of hurting her tender feelings.

"No. Aunt Fay is fine." Maddie inhaled deeply. "These papers are from your dad's attorney." She worked hard not to let any of her resentment or fear leak through into her voice, kept her expression clear. "Your dad wants us to share custody of you."

"Like you do already?"

"More than that. He wants us to legally agree that you can spend more time with him. One weekend a month and anytime you have a school break of at least four days and…two months during the summer when he's not playing hockey."

Bree ran a fingertip across the table. "Oh. He wants that to be like a rule?"

"Sort of. If we agree to it, it'll be put into effect and it'll happen. It won't be him calling when he wants and asking you to come and you having the choice not to go. Right now, I have full custody and he has visitation rights but he wants it to be more. More scheduled. He wants it to be, as you said, a rule so that every month, you'll be with him for that weekend, every other holiday you'd spend it with him."

"He wants me," Bree said, sort of in awe. She raised her head and her eyes were alight, her expression pure joy. "He said he did but I wasn't sure…."

And Maddie realized why Neil had done this. He'd wanted to show their little girl that he meant what he said, that he was going to be there for her no matter what, no matter that he and Maddie weren't together or that he lived across the country. They would be together.

"Of course he wants you," Maddie said. "But only if you want this, too."

"It's okay, Mom," Bree said, sounding so much older than eleven. "I'll always come back to you. We'll still be together."

Maddie choked up. Cleared her throat. "You're right. We'll always be together."

Bree hugged her and went back to bed, and Maddie realized that she didn't want to share Bree. Before, when Neil had kept his distance, it'd been easier for her to hold on to her righteous anger and sense of superiority. Her independence. She could control how things went, how Bree was raised. She could make all the decisions.

Bree was growing up, would be a teenager in two years, then it would be high school and boys and driving and she was already fighting for her independence, just as Maddie had done.

Then Bree would go to college, as Maddie hadn't, but wanted her daughter to.

Maddie's fingers tightened, curling the papers. Yes, she'd accomplished exactly what she'd set out to do. And she'd done so on her own. She was in complete control.

She'd never felt more alone.

NEIL STEPPED OUTSIDE of the Knights' training facility and headed toward the parking lot. The day was overcast and he couldn't help but miss the rolling hills of Shady Grove. He'd talked to Bree last night and she'd assured him it was okay that he wanted rules in place when it came to seeing her. He'd done the right thing.

He looked up and froze to see Maddie walking toward him in that same damn sundress she'd had on at the picnic at his folks' house.

"Maddie." He shook his head. "Is everything okay? Is Bree all right?"

"Bree's fine. Everyone's fine," she said, looking unsure and nervous—both of which were so unusual for Maddie, he couldn't wrap his mind around it. She was here. In Seattle. Her throat worked as she swallowed. "You really pissed me off with that custody arrangement."

"You're here to kill me, then?"

"I thought about it," she said, sounding like her normal self. She tossed her head, her hair picking up in the breeze, dotted with drizzle. "But then I realized you were right. You need to have time with Bree. But I'm not signing it."

His heart sank. He didn't want to drag any of them through some long custody battle but he had to do what was best for Bree. "I'm sorry to hear that. Guess you'll be hearing from my attorney."

He started to walk away, so pissed at her for coming here, in that dress, when he hadn't been able to convince himself he'd lost a few brain cells back in Shady Grove, that what they'd shared those few weeks wasn't some figment of his imagination. He'd wanted to convince himself that he'd made more of their time together than what it was, that she was right to laugh in his face when he said he wanted them to be together, to be a family. That his feelings for her were just remnants of whatever had been between them years ago.

But he'd dreamed of her every night, wanted to talk to her every day.

"Whoa, whoa, whoa," she said, hurrying up to catch him. She grabbed his arm, forcing him to face her. "You don't get to walk away from me. Not after I dropped everything—including the renovations you hired me to do—to buy the airfare to fly out here. Not when I took a red-eye flight, my first airplane trip, across the country to see you."

"What do you want, Maddie?" he asked quietly.

"You," she blurted. She pressed her lips together and met his eyes. "I want you, Neil."

Hope lit inside his chest. He ruthlessly squashed it. "This some sort of trick to get me to back off fighting for shared custody?"

"No. Yes. I mean, I don't want to fight you." The wind blew her hair into her face and she tucked it behind her ear. "And I'm not signing those papers—"

"Goddamn it, Maddie," he burst out, then lowered his voice when one of the assistant coaches walked by. Neil nodded at him, took Maddie by the arm and tugged her aside. "You have no right to keep me from Bree."

"I know that," she said, "but I don't want to share custody of our daughter."

It hurt, more than it should, to have her say it to his face. And he was tired of hurting, so damned tired of pining after her, after something he could never have.

He dropped her arm. "I'm not giving up on Bree. Not ever again. And nothing you say or do will change my mind, so you might as well go home," he said, his words low and flat. His chest felt empty. Cold. "Go back to Shady Grove and leave me the hell alone."

He turned, unable to look at her beautiful face one more second without begging her to take him back. To give him another chance. To finally forgive him.

To love him. As much as he loved her.

Hell, maybe this really was his punishment for being such a fool all those years ago.

"I wish I could leave you alone," she said, her voice

breaking. Strong, confident Maddie Montesano's voice actually broke.

It was all he could do not to take her into his arms but he didn't. He didn't even turn back. But he couldn't walk away, either.

He felt her come up behind him. "For the past two weeks," she continued, "I tried to convince myself I could. That whatever was between us this summer was some crazy fantasy. Or remnants of the past. God, I even thought maybe you were right. Maybe it was all an unconscious need for revenge on my part." Her voice grew softer. "But it was none of those things. It's real. And what I...feel... for you now is nothing like the infatuation I felt twelve years ago."

He swallowed. "What do you feel?" he asked, facing her.

"Scared," she whispered, her eyes glistening with unshed tears. "And hopeful. I was wrong not to trust in you. In us. Wrong not to believe that you've changed when I've changed so much as well." She licked her lips. "The reason I won't sign the custody papers is because I want us to raise Bree together. I want us to be a family. Please, please tell me you still want that, too."

Something inside of him loosened. Warmed. "When we were together before—"

"Neil, it doesn't matt—"

"Just...let me get this out, okay?" She nodded, looked worried, as if he'd turn her away. As if he could. "When we were together before, you gave me your heart. I didn't appreciate what a gift that was until it was too late." He edged closer and clasped her hands. "But I promise, if you give me another chance, if you'll give me your heart again, I'll spend the rest of my life cherishing it. And you.

I love you, Maddie," he said gruffly. "I don't think I've ever stopped."

Her fingers tightened on his. "I love you, too. I can't say that I've never stopped—because I did—so I'll just say that I love you again. I love who you are now."

Somehow that was even better, meant more than her loving the boy he'd been. He bent to kiss her but she leaned back.

"About Bree," she began.

"I wasn't trying to take her away from you," he said quickly. "That's not what it was about."

"I know. It's just—"

"And my agent is in talks with an East Coast team," he continued. He had to make her see that he wasn't trying to hurt her or get back at her. "I wouldn't ask Bree to fly across the country every month. I wouldn't do that to either of you."

"That's all good to know but what I'm trying to say is that we'll go wherever you are." Maddie motioned to the cab idling by the side of the road. "We belong together."

The cab's back door opened and then, there was Bree in her familiar bright sweatpants and baggy T-shirt—Christ, but he'd missed her.

She took her time crossing to them, her eyes going from him to her mom and back again. "Did you two make up?" she asked, as if unable to believe what she saw—her parents holding hands.

"We did," Maddie said.

"Good." Then Bree launched herself at Neil.

After regaining his balance, he held her tight for a moment before shifting her to his side where he could keep one arm wrapped around her. Then he tugged Maddie to him and kissed her.

"Eww," Bree said, one hand covering her eyes. "Are you going to be doing that a lot?"

"I hope so," Neil muttered fervently, then kissed Maddie again to the sound of their daughter's giggle.

He felt Maddie smile against his mouth. After working so hard for so long, he finally was a man who truly had it all.

* * * * *

Be sure to look for the next
IN SHADY GROVE *novel by Beth Andrews!*
Available from Harlequin Superromance
in August 2013.

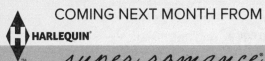
#1848 WHERE IT MAY LEAD by Janice Kay Johnson

Instant attraction? Madison Laclaire never believed in it—until she met John "Troy" Troyer. She's eager for the alumni reunion to end so they can kick this relationship up a notch. But when the college time capsule is opened, secrets spill out that could stop them before they begin.

#1849 A PRIOR ENGAGEMENT by Karina Bliss

Presumed dead, war vet Lee Davis returns home to discover that Jules Browne, who'd rejected his wedding proposal before deployment, has been playing his grieving fiancée. Well, she's not the only one who can act. And he intends to find out how far she'll take this so-called relationship....

#1850 JANE'S GIFT by Abby Gaines

Jane Slater would rather be anywhere other than back in Pinyon Ridge, but she's determined to help her best friend's little girl move on after her mother's death. Thing is, Kyle Everson doesn't want a Slater, especially Jane, anywhere near his daughter. Until Jane reveals a secret that changes everything.

#1851 A FAMILY REUNITED by Dorie Graham

The last thing Alexandra Peterson wants is to return home to Atlanta after her family has been torn apart. But when her brother is diagnosed with cancer, she has no choice. She'll move back—but only until Robert is well. Can Chase Carrolton, her high school sweetheart, convince her to stay?

#1852 APRIL SHOWERS • *A Valley Ridge Wedding*
by Holly Jacobs

Lily Paul is only trying to help pay back the kindness she's found in Valley Ridge. Seb Bennington, former bad boy, insists she's interfering with his family. Both agree the last thing either of them wants is to admit their attraction for each other, and yet...they may have no say in the matter!

#1853 IT'S NEVER TOO LATE• *Shelter Valley Stories*
by Tara Taylor Quinn

Two people come to Shelter Valley, Arizona, and end up as next-door neighbors. One, a rugged small-town man named Mark Heber, is there to accept a scholarship as a mature student. The other, Adrianna Keller, is not who she pretends to be. But Mark doesn't learn that until long after they've fallen in love....

SPECIAL EXCERPT FROM

H HARLEQUIN

super romance

Where It May Lead

By **Janice Kay Johnson**

Being the police liaison for the local college's alumni event should be straightforward for Detective John "Troy" Troyer. That is, until he meets Madison Laclaire! Read on for an exciting excerpt from the upcoming book *WHERE IT MAY LEAD* by Janice Kay Johnson.

"I doubt we'll have any problems this weekend," Troy said, glancing through the schedule. "I think my role is going to be an exciting one. I'll hang around. Maybe even play golf."

Madison tilted her head in interest—and he liked being the object of her interest. "Do you play golf?"

"Poorly," he admitted. "I've got a hell of a slice. But from a security standpoint, having me lurking in the rough probably isn't a bad plan."

Her laugh was contagious...and unintentionally erotic. "I'll look for you there."

"You'll be playing?"

"No. Actually, I'll be frantically arranging the luncheon." She rose gracefully to her feet. "Thank you for coming, Detective Troyer."

"Troy." He stood, too.

A smart man would bide his time, not make any move until after the weekend. He didn't want her to be uncomfortable with him when they had to work together. Troy had always thought of himself as a pretty smart guy.

Turned out he wasn't as smart as he'd thought.

"So. I was wondering." *Slick. Really slick.* "Any chance I could talk you into having dinner with me?"

Madison blinked. "Tonight?"

Tonight, tomorrow night, every night. Startled by the thought, he cleared his throat. "Tonight would be good. Or tomorrow." He hesitated. "Unless you're too busy."

Her expression melted into a sunbeam of a smile. "I would love to have dinner with you tonight, Troy."

Down, boy, he cautioned himself when his enthusiastic response threatened to overflow.

They agreed on a restaurant, then he left before he did something stupid. Like kiss her.

He grinned as he exited her office. She'd said yes. He *felt* young. Half-aroused, too.

He would definitely be kissing her tonight.

The weekend may hold even more surprises for Madison and Troy. Find out what happens in *WHERE IT MAY LEAD* by Janice Kay Johnson, available May 2013 from Harlequin® Superromance®.

REQUEST YOUR FREE BOOKS!
2 FREE NOVELS PLUS 2 FREE GIFTS!

HARLEQUIN®

super romance®

Exciting, emotional, unexpected!

YES! Please send me 2 FREE Harlequin® Superromance® novels and my 2 FREE gifts (gifts are worth about $10). After receiving them, if I don't wish to receive any more books, I can return the shipping statement marked "cancel." If I don't cancel, I will receive 6 brand-new novels every month and be billed just $4.69 per book in the U.S. or $5.24 per book in Canada. That's a savings of at least 15% off the cover price! It's quite a bargain! Shipping and handling is just 50¢ per book in the U.S. and 75¢ per book in Canada.* I understand that accepting the 2 free books and gifts places me under no obligation to buy anything. I can always return a shipment and cancel at any time. Even if I never buy another book, the two free books and gifts are mine to keep forever.

135/336 HDN FVS7

Name _____ (PLEASE PRINT)

Address _____ Apt. #

City _____ State/Prov. _____ Zip/Postal Code

Signature (if under 18, a parent or guardian must sign)

Mail to the Harlequin® Reader Service:
IN U.S.A.: P.O. Box 1867, Buffalo, NY 14240-1867
IN CANADA: P.O. Box 609, Fort Erie, Ontario L2A 5X3

Are you a current subscriber to Harlequin Superromance books and want to receive the larger-print edition?
Call 1-800-873-8635 or visit www.ReaderService.com.

* Terms and prices subject to change without notice. Prices do not include applicable taxes. Sales tax applicable in N.Y. Canadian residents will be charged applicable taxes. Offer not valid in Quebec. This offer is limited to one order per household. Not valid for current subscribers to Harlequin Superromance books. All orders subject to credit approval. Credit or debit balances in a customer's account(s) may be offset by any other outstanding balance owed by or to the customer. Please allow 4 to 6 weeks for delivery. Offer available while quantities last.

Your Privacy—The Harlequin® Reader Service is committed to protecting your privacy. Our Privacy Policy is available online at www.ReaderService.com or upon request from the Harlequin Reader Service.

We make a portion of our mailing list available to reputable third parties that offer products we believe may interest you. If you prefer that we not exchange your name with third parties, or if you wish to clarify or modify your communication preferences, please visit us at www.ReaderService.com/consumerchoice or write to us at Harlequin Reader Service Preference Service, P.O. Box 9062, Buffalo, NY 14269. Include your complete name and address.

HSR13

Love and family found in the most unexpected place

Jane Slater would rather be anywhere other than back in Pinyon Ridge, but she's determined to help her best friend's little girl move on after her mother's death. Thing is, Kyle Everson doesn't want a Slater, especially Jane, anywhere near his daughter. Until Jane reveals a secret that changes everything.

Jane's Gift
by Abby Gaines

AVAILABLE MAY 2013

She holds his future in her hands...

Two people come to Shelter Valley, Arizona, and end up as next-door neighbors. One, a rugged small-town man named Mark Heber, is there to accept a scholarship as a mature student. The other, Adrianna Keller, is not who she pretends to be. But Mark doesn't learn that until long after they've fallen in love....

It's Never Too Late
by Tara Taylor Quinn

AVAILABLE MAY 2013

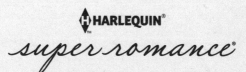

HARLEQUIN®

super romance®

More Story...More Romance

www.Harlequin.com

HSR71853R

It all starts with a kiss

Check out the brand-new series

Fun, flirty and sensual romances.
ON SALE JANUARY 22!

Love the Harlequin book you just read?

Your opinion matters.

Review this book on your favorite book site, review site, blog or your own social media properties and share your opinion with other readers!